SIN AND CIDER

A SWEET SINNERS NOVEL

KIMBERLY REESE

♡ Nicole ♡
Thank you so much
for your support and
for taking a chance on
a new author. ☻
XOXO, Kimberly Reese ♡

Cover Design: Liv's Lovely Designs

Editor: Elevated Edits

Formatter: Elevated Edits

To me,
Whenever you have any doubts about writing, hold this book
and remember that you finally did it.

PROLOGUE

July

Something is wrong with me. Who the hell quits their job on a whim? Their successful job at a leading design firm, no less? Apparently that person is me. I'm MacIntosh—I swear I'm smarter than this—Layne, and I'm not sure I love my life anymore.

Although I have, ugh *had,* a successful career, a healthy social life, and share a gorgeous apartment with my best friend in a trendy downtown neighborhood, the life I've built for myself in the windy city feels lacking.

This glorious epiphany smacked me upside the head while I was at work, and everything derailed from there. My day started like any other day, and everything was fine...until it wasn't. For the rest of my life I'll remember the exact moment my sanity snapped. I was working on a start-up company's branding I had been assigned to revamp when my overbearing manager, Lindsay, stopped by my desk.

Color me surprised when she told me I was late on the assignment I was given two days ago. Turns out the project had originally been assigned to her, and she gave it to me last minute. She wasn't able to give a legitimate reason for doing so, but I know it's because she's a phony. For two years I've worked under her, and she habitually takes credit for other people's work. I thought I could grin and bear it in hopes that she'd promote me or retire, but I belatedly realized that would never happen. She's a vulture who lets others do the work and then proceeds to hover over their success like it's a dead carcass, ready to snatch it and claim it as her own. As she rambled on I stood up, told her to go fuck herself, and announced I was quitting.

Now I'm back home, overindulging in my favorite bottle of red, and contemplating my predicament. When I moved to Chicago six years ago, I was filled with a sense of purpose and felt alive, inspired even. I've lost those feelings and don't know what's missing that's causing me to feel so incomplete. Lord knows I need to figure my life out, I'm just not sure how.

Deciding to take action and not sit around moping, I pour the last dredges of wine into my glass. "I'm going to figure this out," I whisper to myself. My words are soft, a promise. Draining the remaining wine, I say more strongly, "Something *will* change."

1

August

"I can do this," I quietly say to myself as my fingers nervously grip the steering wheel of my rental car. I have no choice. I didn't pack my bags and hop on a plane to Tennessee for nothing. Thinking back to what brought me here, I strengthen my resolve. Although I can feel my nerves buzzing below my skin, ready to pick back up once I start thinking about the many open questions in my life, a small smile steals over my face. I'm back home. I'm beyond ready to rediscover my sense of purpose, and I think going back to my roots will do the trick.

After partaking in too much wine the day I quit my job and spending a considerable chunk of time trying to figure out my next move, I decided to hit the refresh button on my life. I need to slow things down and take a break from city life, which is why I'm entering the city limits of Starwood, Tennessee. Not only is Starwood my hometown, but the apple orchard my parents own will be the perfect place to unplug and find myself again.

As I drive through town I'm bombarded with memories of my childhood: picking apples with my brother, baking pies with my grandma, taking a dip in the creek when the humidity was unbearable, and jumping into a huge pile of colorful leaves with my friends. There are so many wonderful memories here. The closer I get to my family's property, the stronger my feelings of nostalgia and knowing I'm where I need to be are.

Finally, I see the entrance to Shady Layne Orchard. My parents' home sits on fifty acres of lush, green grass and soft, rolling hills. As I follow the gravelly driveway I look at the orchard in the distance. Even though I grew up here, the sight still manages to take my breath away. The trees are tall and stately, dotted with jewel-hued apples and adorned with slender branches reaching up to the sky like dainty lady fingers. Facing the orchard is the old barn we had converted into the cider shop, its white paint chipped and weathered.

I pull up to the side of the house and grab my phone. I promised I'd send Cade, my best friend and roommate, a text so he'd know I made it home safely.

Me: Hey CC, I made it to TN! :)

My phone pings with a response almost immediately. I smile to myself as I think about my protective bestie.

Cade: Good, I was getting worried. You okay?

Me: I will be. Are you sure it's okay for me to be here??

Cade: Don't be silly. Go find yourself. I'll be here if you need me. :)

Me: You're seriously the best.

Cade: Glad you recognize that.

Me: Haha okay, I gotta go. I'll stay in touch. Love ya!

Cade: Love you, too.

Me: P.S.: I left 3 months' worth of rent money in the cookie jar. :P

Cade: It's staying there. I don't need it. Now stop stalling. Go see your family.

Me: Fine, bossy man.

Cade: You know it. ;)

Just texting Cade makes me feel better. Feeling lighter, I tuck my phone away and bound into the house.

"Mama! Papa! Is anyone home?" I shout. I'm greeted with silence, which is unusual. The house is usually buzzing with some sort of activity. I look at the key rack and see a note in my mother's handwriting tacked to it.

Mac, your father and I are working the welcome booth at the farmers' market. We're sorry if we missed you, sweetie. Help yourself to whatever's in the fridge. We aired out your room for you so you can take a nap if you need one. We'll see you soon. We love you!

I hold onto the note for a few seconds, thinking about

what I should do. Should I stay home and take a nap? No, I should take advantage of my renewed energy. Putting the note back down, I turn around and head back outside. Farmers' market it is.

I SEE my parents before they see me. As I amble over to the welcome booth, a fond smile plastered on my face, I take a good look at them. The signs of aging have graced them as gently as newly fallen snow. There are more gray hairs and more wrinkles than I'm used to, but they look like they're doing well. Finally, my mother catches my eye and runs around the booth to me, her warm arms encasing me in a tight hug.

"Oh Mac, baby, I missed you so much!" my mother cries excitedly. "It's so nice to have you back home. You look so beautiful. How long are you stayin' with us?" I can tell by her expression that she's hoping it'll be forever.

"I'm not sure, Mama. I plan on staying for the rest of summer so, at the very least, you have me until the end of September," I say, just as another set of arms hugs me from the side.

"Then two months will have to do, sweetie," my father says from my left. "We're just glad you're back."

I feel my eyes water and stay enveloped in my parents' dual embrace for a few seconds longer. As I pull away, I ask them how much longer they'll be. After hearing they only have another half hour until their shift ends, I decide to walk around and look at the different booths selling local produce or homemade goods.

I used to love coming to these with my family when I was a child. I can still remember the feeling of pride when people bought our apples and cider. Maybe I'll get the chance to do it again since it's almost that time of year. I take my time walking around and make sure to hang back from large groups of people, careful not to draw too much attention to myself. Then, amid the low hum of soft and polite Southern drawls I didn't realize I missed, I hear a distinct masculine laugh. I turn slowly, hoping that I'm wrong in who the owner of the engaging sound is. Unfortunately my suspicions are correct as I spy Lawson Westbrook, my older brother's best friend and the man I idolized growing up. I feel like I've seen a ghost as I discreetly gaze at him. He hales from old money and is the walking definition of a true Southern gentleman. On top of that, his innate charm and rugged good looks make him a catch any single woman in town hopes to end up with.

Thankfully he isn't facing me so I stare a little longer than is polite. Somehow I managed to avoid seeing him on my infrequent visits back home but God, he looks better than he did six years ago. At thirty-one he's seven years my senior, and he's only gotten better looking with age. At well over six feet tall, he stands with the confidence of someone comfortable with his body, his muscular frame clearly at ease. I drink in his short, golden brown hair and trim facial hair that's a smidgen darker. I can't see his eyes, but I know they're an arresting shade of green that puts spring leaves and budding apples to shame. As I stare at him, an old memory surfaces from when I was eighteen.

"MacIntosh Layne, you get your bum down here right now before we're late to your own graduation dinner!" my mother calls.

As I put the last curl in my hair I yell back down, "I'll be right there! I'm just grabbing my shoes!" Spraying on some perfume, I take one last look at my reflection before heading down. My new little black dress fits to the middle of my thighs and showcases a demure sweetheart illusion neckline. I wish it was more form-fitting but I have to work with what I have, which is a distinct lack of curves. The dress, though beautiful, covers my lanky body like a sheet. I pray the person I hope finally notices me won't catch that little detail. My long brown hair looks amazing and bouncy, thanks to my curling iron, and my hazel eyes pop under my long lashes that I enhanced with the help of some mascara. Finally satisfied with my appearance, I grab my shoes and head downstairs.

My family ends up taking me to my favorite Italian restaurant in town for my graduation dinner. I'm a strange mix of anxious and excited because Lawson, my childhood crush, is here. Now that I'm eighteen and a high school graduate, I hope he'll see me as a woman. Specifically, I hope he sees me as a woman he'd like to date.

During dinner, I can't help but glance at him every chance I get. At one point my brother, Smith, catches me gazing at his friend. I feel the blush staining my cheeks and quickly look away when I catch the funny look he gives me. As dinner continues I'm asked by friends of the family what my plans are for college.

"I'll either stay here or go to Chicago," I say. "I haven't been able to decide between the graphic design program at Tennessee State or the one at the University of Illinois. I'll make a decision eventually."

My family expresses their wish that I stay in-state, but I don't tell them what's going through my head. The truth of it is, if there's a chance of anything happening with Lawson I'll be staying in Tennessee.

As dinner is wrapping up, I see my chance to talk to Lawson alone when he gets up to use the restroom. My brother soon follows, but I think the difference in timing will work in my favor.

I wait a moment and excuse myself to the ladies' room. I'm drawing in a breath of courage as I make it to the hallway but stop in my tracks when I hear the low murmur of male voices.

"Law, I'm not kidding. I think Mac has a crush on you," Smith says.

I feel the blood drain from my face in mortification and wait for Lawson's reaction.

"Smith, you're crazy. Even if it were true, why would you tell me?" asks the object of my affection for so many years.

"Because if you think she does you better not hurt her feelings."

"Man, she's like one of the guys. Besides, she's too young for me. I don't date little girls. I prefer women. I do think you're wrong though. She sees me as another older brother. Anyway, it'll never happen. Ever. I can promise you that."

I can't take anymore. I spin around, tears in my eyes, and sit at an empty table far enough away that I won't be seen as I try and regain my composure. I can't even be angry at Smith because I know he was only looking out for me. What guts me is now I know for certain Lawson still sees me as a little girl. I look down and realize my hands are shaking. Knowing I've been gone for too long, I take a fortifying breath and wipe the tears from under my eyes before walking back. So much for a happy graduation day. It looks like I'm moving to Chicago.

"MacIntosh Layne, darlin' is that you?" The feminine voice rips me from my flashback quicker than it takes to fry okra. I respond to the voice and, as I turn, I'm relieved to see Lawson hasn't noticed me yet. Thank heavens for small favors.

Once I notice the person who spoke to me, a genuine smile makes an appearance. Lawson's younger sister, Langley, is a year younger than me but someone I'd consider a friend. Turning so my profile is to her brother, I give her my full attention.

"It is me. How are you doin', Langley? It's been forever!" I haven't seen her in probably three or four years, but she's bloomed beautifully. God help the eligible bachelors. Good looks definitely run in the Westbrook family, and Langley must undoubtedly be the belle of this town. Taller and curvier than I am with her mother's inky black hair, she's a stunner. I can't help but notice that both of the Westbrook children inherited their father's striking green eyes.

"I'm doin' all right. Just trying to sell some pies. How are you? You look great by the way!" she says with a sweet smile.

"Thank you, so do you! I mean it. The men must be chasing you around this town," I say before we both laugh. "I'm okay, but I'm excited to be back in town. Did you make all these?" I take a glance at the pies and assorted baked goods, and everything looks like it was made by a professional. Not only that, it all looks downright delicious. I feel my mouth start to water. Baked goods are my weakness.

"Sure did! I guess all those failed attempts at baking as a kid paid off. Would you like a sample?" She must see the drool collecting because she's already placing a plated sample of what I think is cherry pie in my hand.

I let out an involuntary groan as I take the first bite, the flavors bursting on my tongue. The crust is buttery and flaky, the cherries tart and sweet. "Hell in a handbasket, Langley. This is amazing! I hate to say this, but this is better than my grandma's pie—God rest her soul—and that's saying something."

"Oh, stop it," she blushes. She seems a little uncomfortable with the praise but recovers quickly by grabbing a pie. "It's just a hobby of mine. Here," she hands me the pie, "this is on me since you're in town, and it's been forever since I've seen you. I'm not sure how long you're here for, but we should get together and catch up."

"You are too sweet. I can't take this," I halfheartedly say. Thankfully she's persistent. "I'm here for the summer and would love to meet up."

We make small talk for a couple minutes before I realize the time. My parents should be done with their shift any minute now. As I apologize for my hasty departure we exchange numbers, and I promise her that we'll get together soon. With my new pie in hand I head toward the parking lot. This summer should prove to be very interesting. One thing I know for certain is that while I'll be seeing Langley again, I won't be seeing her brother. This summer I'll be avoiding Lawson Westbrook at all costs.

~

LAWSON

"LAWSON, when are you gonna let me ask your sister out?" Jude asks, his eyes and tone pleading for a chance.

"Never, man. Ever. Even if I gave my blessing, she'd eat you up and spit you out alive. You know how she is. She won't date anyone." I say this in a joking manner, but my coworker knows I'm not kidding. There's no way this guy is getting near my baby sister.

"That's just cause she hasn't gone out with me yet. I'd change her mind."

"The answer is still no," I say a little more seriously.

He relents with a defeated sigh. "Fine, I'll leave it alone. For now. Maybe I'll ask out the pretty thing talking to her. Do you know who she is?"

I turn and try to find my sister's booth. It takes a second

to locate her, and once I do my eyes zero in on the woman in question.

"Not sure, never seen her before. Maybe she's new in town," I murmur as we both stare.

I can't see her face since she's standing with her side to us, but judging solely off of her profile, I really like what I see. A lot. Tall and slender, mystery woman has curves in all the right places. Not overly curvy, but definitely not thin, her body is showcased in a tight t-shirt and jeans. My gaze travels up her body starting at her toes, and I decide this is a body I wouldn't mind getting to know intimately. As I stare, I take in hair that looks long, smooth, and is the color of rich milk chocolate. I wish I could see her face.

Before either of us can say anything else, mystery woman wraps up her conversation with my sister. As she turns and walks in the opposite direction, hair swishing and hips swaying gently with each step, I make a decision. Somehow, I'm going to find out who this woman is and introduce myself.

2

I'm pathetic. Day two back home on my self-discovery hiatus and I can't relax. I wasn't entirely sure what my plan would be once I got here, but I thought I'd start my day extra early with some yoga or meditation. Yeah, not happening. Not only am I more inflexible than I imagined, my attempts at meditation are laughable at best. I guess it'll take some time to drop Chicago's *go-go-go* mentality and adjust to the slower-paced lifestyle I grew up with. My failed relaxation attempts have resulted in me laying in my childhood bedroom, staring up at the Robert Downey Jr. poster above my bed. Don't get me wrong, there's nothing wrong with staring at some eye candy, but right now I have the overwhelming urge to *do* something. At the very least, I should probably eat.

I decide to do something about my restlessness and head downstairs for a bowl of cereal before I see if my parents need help with anything. I figure they'll need some assistance around the orchard. After all, apple season starts at the end of the month, and things will inevitably be hectic around here until just before the holidays.

As I enter the kitchen the scents of homemade French toast, country potatoes, and bacon assaults my senses in the best possible way. This is much better than a bowl of cereal, and the familiar sight warms my heart. I didn't realize how much I missed home until I got here.

Walking around the kitchen island, I plant a kiss on my father's cheek and snag a piece of bacon that's still sizzling on the serving dish. *Mmm*. Easily falling into our old routine, I grab a carton of eggs from the fridge and start prepping them for scrambled eggs.

"How many eggs, Papa? Half a dozen, so we each get two?" I ask.

"No, sweetie. You better do a whole dozen. I called your brother over for breakfast this morning, and you know how he eats," he chuckles.

A smile lights up my face as I laugh along with my father. "Oh, I know how he gets. He's lucky he has the metabolism of a five-year-old, or else I think he'd be the size of the house."

"Don't you know it," he agrees. "Shoot, that boy moved out years ago, and he still comes over almost every night for dinner. We're not complaining because we love seeing you kids, but any day now I'm gonna tell him he needs to start buying the groceries." This sets off a peal of laughter and leads into us reminiscing about my childhood.

We continue to talk as we cook, and just as we finish setting the table, the sound of the screen door opening carries through to us.

"I hope y'all didn't get started without me!" my brother shouts from the hall.

Squealing in delight, I tear out of the kitchen like a whirlwind and launch myself into my brother's arms. "Granny! I've missed you!" I giggle into his shoulder.

"I've missed you too Mac, although I can't say I miss that old nickname," he says as he returns my fierce hug.

I pull away and tilt my head up to get a good look at him. Tall and lanky, he looks every bit the outdoorsman with his sun-kissed skin and light brown hair. The laugh lines around his eyes have grown a little more prominent with age, but the mischievous glint he's had in them since we were children hasn't changed a bit.

"You're lookin' good...for an old man," I tease as I ruffle his hair.

With a laugh he picks me up and swings me around before setting me back down. "At least someone here looks good. You look like you just woke up and are wearing the largest set of pajamas I've ever seen."

"Hey now, don't knock my style. You're still dressin' like one of those hipsters. Where's your book of poetry and your fake pair of glasses?"

"You stop that right now, or I'm gonna go dunk you in the pond. Actually, I'm just gonna go dunk you in the pond," he says as he pretends to pick me up again.

I laugh heartily at his antics. Just as I open my mouth to retort, the screen door opens again. Turning, my laugh dies in my throat as I get a look at who just walked into the house: Lawson Westbrook.

What did I do to deserve this? Of course the man looks incredible, standing there in a worn flannel shirt and faded jeans that showcase his muscular thighs to perfection. He could be a walking ad for a line of lumberjack clothing and here I am, standing in taco-print leggings and an oversized t-shirt that does nothing for my figure. To make matters worse, I'm not wearing a stitch of makeup and my hair is piled on top of my head in a messy bun. I feel like I'm a teenager again. My plan was to avoid seeing him, but now that I have I wish I looked more put together. I discreetly try and tuck any loose strands of hair behind my ears, and after seconds pass that feel like hours, he says something.

"Mornin', Mac. It's been a long time." His words are accompanied by a lazy, lopsided grin. I can feel my cheeks burn as I become a victim of his effortless charm. His gaze travels down my figure so quickly I would've missed it if I hadn't been watching him so closely. I can feel hope spark from his discreet perusal, the tiny flame trying to come to life from the long-forgotten torch I carried for so long.

When his eyes meet mine again he says, "It's like you haven't aged a day. What's it been? Four, five years?"

"Six," I breathe.

"Wow, time sure does fly. You look exactly the same."

"Thanks," I choke out. "You look older. I need to make juice. See ya." My words are awkward and stilted. Doing an about-face, I head back into the kitchen.

I'm sure most people would be elated to hear they look the same as when they were eighteen. Me? Not so much. My little spark of hope effectively dies. It figures the man I was infatuated with for years would think I still look like a kid. I take out my frustration on some oranges I'm juicing, the smell of fresh citrus eventually calming me. I just have to get through breakfast, and then I can deliver on my plan to avoid Lawson for the rest of summer. Ignore him now, and completely avoid him later. This will be easy. I can do this.

Five Minutes Later

I can't do this. So much for easy. Everyone is seated around the table and Lawson is directly across from me, his hotness trying to lure me in like a cowboy with a lasso. In between bites I sneak peeks at him, amazed that he still has the power to affect me. I'm fascinated by his shadowed jawline covered in neat scruff as he chews and the hypnotic way his adam's apple bobs in his strong throat when he speaks. I wonder what other parts of his anatomy would look like bobbing up and down, like his—

"Sweetie, did you hear me?" My mother's gentle voice draws me out of my budding fantasy.

"Sorry, Mama. I sort of spaced out there for a bit. I was thinking about some unfinished business I have in the city," I lie.

"Everything okay, baby?" Her voice is filled with concern.

"Yes, nothing to worry about. What were you saying earlier?"

"We were wonderin' what you were going to be doing during your stay. If you need anything you just let us know and we'll help you any way we can."

"I had planned on relaxing, but I think I'd like to stay busy. I actually miss working on the orchard. I'd love to get involved again, especially since business is about to pick up."

"Baby, we'd love that!" my father says with a huge smile that warms my heart. "We could always use a helpin' hand, and it means we get to spend even more time with you."

"Great! I was also hoping I could help make cider this year. Will you be needing help with that, too?" I ask hopefully.

A silence falls over the table as my parents share a look with one another.

"What's with the weird looks?" I ask.

"Well, sweetie," my father hedges, "we decided to not make cider this year...or possibly any other year."

I'm shocked beyond belief. "What? Why? The cider is a

bestseller leading up to the holidays. Why stop doing something so successful?" I'm genuinely confused.

"Business has slowed down a bit. Not to mention the barn isn't fit for making anything at the moment."

"I just saw the barn. It looks like all it needs is a fresh coat of paint."

"That's what it looks like, but there was a huge storm earlier this year and the roof was damaged. It's just a lot of work when your Mama and I are getting up there in age. We're lucky Lawson agreed to fix the barn, even though he's got a lot of other projects going on this summer."

I look at Lawson and find that he's staring intently at my face. Trying to keep my expression and voice neutral I ask, "You're fixing the barn? By yourself?" I know I sound skeptical, but I don't care.

Not taking his eyes off my face he responds, a small smirk tilting his mouth up higher on one side, "Yep. I run my own construction company. I still have a full list of projects I manage and work on from time to time, but I come here to work on the barn if my team doesn't need me. It's slow work, but it's still progress. The barn should be done by October."

October? That's a whole month later than when we used to start making cider. I'm surprised by how disappointed I feel that I won't get to help this year. It was one of my favorite things to do growing up, and I feel like summer won't be the same without it. Before I can think about this even more, Lawson continues talking.

"If you'd really like to make cider this year, you can put yourself to work and help me with the repairs so we're done by early September. You help me with the clean-up inside the barn and with painting the outside—I'll still take care of the roof—and I'll help ya'll with making cider. Whatever you need help with, I'll do it."

I stare at him.

He stares at me.

My family stares at both of us.

Finally, Smith speaks. Lawson and I don't break eye contact.

"That's a pretty sweet deal, Mac. You want something to do. He needs help. You want to make cider. He'll help you make cider. I say y'all partner up and do this."

He has a point.

"You've got yourself a deal. When do I start?" I ask, determination in my voice.

Lawson's smirk grows into a full-fledged smile. Be still my heart. "How's tomorrow morning sound?"

"Let me check my schedule." With barely any pause I continue, "Tomorrow sounds perfect."

As I say this, Lawson leans forward in his chair and extends his hand to me. I hesitate a moment before reciprocating. It makes sense that we'd shake on this. I watch my hand as I reach out and have to stop a gasp from escaping my lips when our hands touch. I feel his warm grip all the way down to my toes, the callouses rubbing against my palm a reminder that he works hard and with his hands. His large, capable hands. Knowing where my thoughts could lead, I pull my hand back quickly and steer the conversation away from the existing topic.

"So tell me Smith, what are you up to nowadays? Any fun stories from the Starwood Game and Fish Department?" I ask, knowing this is all it takes to set my brother off on a tangent.

My brother, true to form, launches into an entertaining round of storytelling. As he talks, I try to sneak some more glances at Lawson but can see him looking at me out of the corner of my eye. He looks intent like he did earlier, but now his expression is tinged with what I think is confusion. I'm not sure what it means and, from experience, I'm sure I don't want to find out. Although I'm excited to make cider, I'm rather nervous knowing I'll be working in close proximity with Lawson all summer. So much for my plans.

THE REST of breakfast is uneventful, and eventually everyone goes their separate ways for the day: my parents to an appointment, Lawson and Smith to work, and me lounging with a book in a rocking chair on the front porch. As I gently rock and read, I hear my phone ping and excitedly text back when I see who it is.

Langley: Hey girlie! You free Friday night?

Me: Yep, no plans for this girl. What do ya have in mind?

Langley: I'm thinkin' we can go to Smokey's Bar.

Me: That sounds fun. What's it like?

Langley: Good music, good drinks, and good-lookin' guys. ;)

Me: Count me in. What time should we meet?

Langley: I'll pick you up at 8 and we can head over at 9. It'll give us time to catch up.

Me: Sounds like a plan. Thanks for inviting me!

Langley: Perfect! And girl don't thank me, it'll be fun. I'll see you then!

Me: See ya then! :)

Finally, something I can look forward to. My new goal: survive the rest of the week working with Lawson.

3

LAWSON

Using my forearm to wipe the sweat off my brow, I survey my progress on the barn's roof. The process has been slower than I would like since it's a solo project, but I'm still pleased with how things are coming along. I should be done after a few more trips, which is just enough time to meet my internal timeline and help Mac with painting.

Making my way down the ladder, I stretch to my full height once my feet hit solid ground. I raise my arms over my head, the incredible feeling of extending my muscles bringing relief after being hunched over for so long. I grab my canteen and take a long, cool drink of water before dumping the rest over my head. *Damn, that feels good.* I shake the excess off and start to gather my tools, ready to go home for the day. It's still fairly early, just past six o'clock, and the sinking sun sets the fields and trees around me ablaze in fiery oranges and warm golds.

I'm drinking in the scenery when I hear a soft grunt off

to my right. Turning, I see Mac is carrying an armful of debris to the dumpster. Judging by the small pile that's left over, it looks like she's almost done for the day, too. We've worked together three days this week, and I'm impressed by her work ethic. On days when I'm not able to make it, I can tell she's been hard at work because the areas in and around the barn, which have been sadly neglected for months, are looking better each time I see them.

I head over to the small pile of leftover rubbish and hoist it into my arms, following in Mac's wake. As I walk I think about our interactions since Sunday. When I first saw her I was awestruck by her face; it is really the only part of her that looks like it has aged. I remember I had walked up to the house per usual and was caught by surprise when I heard the sweet, feminine voice drifting out onto the porch. Smith had mentioned that Mac was in town, but I hadn't expected her voice to be a little deeper and a whole lot sexy. I headed up the porch steps slowly and silently watched her reunion with Smith through the screen door before I was overcome with the urge to move closer.

She was so at ease with her brother, and her happiness was so obvious it was like staring at the sun. Her breath-taking smile momentarily stunned me. When I couldn't stand waiting outside any longer and entered the house, her shock at having another visitor was almost comical. Her brown hair was in a messy pile on top of her head, and even though it was obvious she had just woken up, all I could see were wide, hazel eyes and full, pink lips. Free of all the crap women put on their faces, her skin looked soft and the flush on her cheeks made my cock twitch in my jeans. I gave her a quick once-over and was disappointed to see that she was as skinny as she was when she was a teenager. No matter how beautiful the face, I prefer to only touch women who have some curves. I'm a big man and don't like the feeling that I could potentially break someone in bed if I'm not careful.

I look ahead to Mac as she tosses the armful of trash away. Every day I see her she looks the same: hair up in a ponytail, dark blue coveralls that look like they could drown her thin frame, and sturdy work books. As she turns around her eyes find mine, her long lashes sweeping down as she visibly takes a breath before looking back up.

"I brought the last of it," I say as I throw away my small armful.

She seems a little awkward as she shuffles her weight from foot to foot, her hands shoved deep into the pockets of her coveralls. "Thanks, but you didn't have to."

"I know, but I'm done for the day. It's no biggie," I explain.

"Oh. Okay. Well then I guess I'm done, too. Thanks, Lawson. See ya," she replies as she heads off toward the house.

"See ya!" I call out after her. I don't try to engage her in further discussion and instead head back to my truck. The few attempts I've made at small talk have been unsuccessful. She keeps our interactions all business and doesn't stay in my company for too long. Not that I'm complaining. Mac's cool, but I have better things to do than force conversation with my best friend's kid sister.

The ride home is quick and uneventful. I hop in the shower as soon as I get in and relish the feeling of hot water washing away the dirt of the work day. As the steam envelopes my body, I think about the mystery woman at the farmers' market. I can't recall the last time a woman intrigued me to the point where I think about her the next day, let alone a faceless mystery woman I haven't met or even bedded. Being the son from a prominent family in a small town has its benefits, but being able to get a good fuck in without the gossips running their mouths is not one of them. If the women of this town so much as thought I was interested in more than one night, I'd never get any rest.

It's still been too long since I've found release with a woman, and mystery woman's body is definitely memorable. That's all I really need to think about to get hard. I take myself in hand and pump slowly up and down my length, the hot water and body wash making things extra slick. Groaning, I think about the things I'd make her feel if given the chance. I think about her grabbable curves—tits that are at least a handful or more and an ass that looks like the perfect cradle for my cock as I pound into her welcoming pussy. I think about her long hair—soft and fistable, I'd love to see it wrapped around my hand as I pull it and breathe in the scent of her neck. I work myself faster until I feel the impending orgasm tingling at the base of my spine. My release is swift and unsatisfying. As I clean up and get out of the shower, I realize it's been too long since I've gotten laid. I either need to find mystery woman or find a willing woman to warm my bed for a night.

About an hour passes, and my doorbell rings as I'm making dinner. I go to answer and smile when I see it's my little sister.

"Hey Langley, I'm just makin' dinner. Do you want to stay over?" I ask.

"I can't, I have plans tonight. Thanks though, you're too sweet," she teases as she makes herself at home and sets this week's delivery on my kitchen island. Every Friday, like clockwork, she brings by baked goods that she wants me to sample and provide feedback on. I love it but know I'd be in serious trouble if I didn't work off all the extra calories at work .

"All right, maybe next week," I reply. She nods her assent and looks like she's ready to head out. "Actually, before you leave I have a quick question for you."

"Yeah, what's up?" she asks.

"This last weekend at the farmers' market you were talking to someone." I pause as I try to figure out how to continue.

"Lawson, silly, it's a farmers' market. I talked to a lot of people," Langley laughs.

"Stop it, you brat," I chuckle. "It was a woman." I can feel my cheeks redden slightly. I shouldn't feel uncomfortable, but I never ask my sister about women and I never show overt interest in anyone. I'm hoping she doesn't rib me for it.

"Oh? What's her name?" She looks curious.

"That's just it. I'm not sure." Ignoring her dubious look, I continue. "It was almost closing time. She's shorter than you, long brown hair. I didn't see her face since I only saw her from the side, but I think she might be new in town."

Her brow slightly furrows as she thinks, and I can tell she's quickly reliving the day in her mind. Her eyes widen slightly and she asks, "Did she buy anything from me?"

I think back to their interaction and am pleased when I can confidently respond. "Yes, she walked away with what looked like a pie."

My sister's confused expression turns sly as a shit-eating grin spreads across her face. "Oh, *that* woman!" she declares. "She's a friend of mine." She looks pleased as punch. I wait for her to continue but she just stands there, staring and smiling at me.

"And? What's her name? Details, woman!" I laugh.

"Uh uh uh," she tsks. "I'm not telling you anything about her."

My laughter dies and my tone turns serious. "Why the hell not?"

"Calm down, killer. I'm just saying I won't tell you anything because you can ask her yourself."

"Wait, I'm confused."

"Of course you are, Lawson. You're a man. It comes with the territory," she says as she rounds the island and sympathetically pats my chest. With a kiss to my cheek she walks to the front door and opens it. I'm about ready to call out to her for more information when she turns back toward me and continues, "Smokey's. Nine o'clock. If you wanna see her she'll be there with me tonight." With a final wink and smile my way she shouts "Good luck!" as she clicks the door shut behind her.

I smile to myself as I absorb this information. Well now, things just got interesting. There's no chance I'm passing up the opportunity to meet my mystery woman tonight. I feel the anticipation of finally seeing her face and knowing her name rise up within me. She doesn't know it yet, but tonight I intend to invade her thoughts and senses to the point she won't want to see or spend time with any man but me. If she isn't interested, I'll turn up the charm and change her mind. This'll be fun. I sure do love a good chase.

4

I'm beyond ready for a girl's night out. Working all week has helped take my mind off things, but being near Lawson is a lesson in suffering. Even though we only worked together three days this week, seeing him in his element has been torture to my sanity; I'm turning into a Neanderthal. Whenever I get a glimpse of him wielding tools and dripping in sweat, his taut muscles under his shirt exposed every time he stretches, I'm not sure if the feeling in my stomach is my ovaries exploding or my nerves telling me to get the hell away. Just earlier today when he started pouring water over his body, the droplets creating their own little paths down his strong neck and under his shirt over what I know must be a cut body, I realized I had taken an involuntary step toward him. Thankfully I came to my senses before I could embarrass myself and headed off in the opposite direction.

Now, a few short hours later, I'm in my room putting the finishing touches on my outfit for tonight. A feeling of excitement wells up in me at the prospect of hanging out with Langley and forgetting life's problems for a little while. Looking at my reflection, I take in the worn jeans and flowy, floral blouse I chose for tonight. Satisfied with my cute and comfortable choice, I toss my hair up in a ponytail and turn away from my mirror as I hear the doorbell ring.

"Mac, sweetie, Langley is here!" my mother shouts from the entryway.

I hear her say she can head on up, and a moment later Langley is stepping into my room. I turn to give her a greeting and stop myself once I see her outfit. I am severely underdressed. She looks incredible dressed in a short, off the shoulder red dress the color of garnets and wine. The dress hugs her curvy figure, and the bottom flares out just a touch so that each time she moves it flirts with the eye. Thankfully, her outfit falls back into the realm of casual with the black cowboy boots she's paired it with. Her hair is in long, loose waves and is the perfect topper to her innocent seductress look. Before I can even tell her how great she looks, she speaks first.

"Oh honey, I'm glad I showed up early. You are not wearing that tonight," she exclaims, looking my body up and down as she speaks.

"Well, I certainly don't have anything like *that*," I gesture up and down with my hand in her direction.

"You didn't pack any cute dresses?"

"Um, no. I packed some jeans and tops and fully intended on doing a lot of laundry."

She's looking at me as she chews her bottom lip, a contemplative expression on her face. Looking around my room, her face lights up as she spots my closet. She makes her way over and starts looking through all my options.

"Darlin', while I look for something you can wear I need you to take your hair outta that ponytail right now. Keep it straight or curl it, I don't care, but you have beautiful hair and you need to show it off in all its glory."

I listen to the expert and remove the elastic from my hair while she mutters about my clothing selection. The hangers scraping against the closet rod fill the silence, and the fact that she's hasn't said anything has me worried.

"Mac, you look cute in jeans, but I need you to *wow* tonight."

"And why is that?"

Turning from her task, she has a mischievous smile. "Why? Well, if you look amazing then all the men will wanna talk to you, which means they'll bring a friend along to play wing man. I so do love to play." She turns back to my closet with a wink and continues looking for something I can wear. Almost a full minute passes before I hear her exclaim.

"Ooh girl, I found something!" she squeals with glee, her excitement obvious. "I'm not sure why you buried it back here, but I love this dress!"

I know confusion is written all over my face, but as she turns around it dawns on me what dress she must be referring to.

"No, I'm not wearing it."

"Oh yes, you are!"

"Nope, not happening."

"MacIntosh Layne, you will wear this dress!" she insists, brandishing the dress toward me like it's a sword. I look at the dress and look at her, a defiant expression on my face. She must see that I'm not kidding, because she pushes forward instead of backing down. "You either wear this dress or we are not going out. Ever. I'll also tell the town gossips that you think you're too good to go to country bars now that you've lived in the big city."

"You would not!" I gasp. "There's no way anyone would buy that!"

"You wanna try me? I've lived in this town my whole life and have not set one toe outta line. I'll ruin your summer before it's really started." She must see the shock on my face because her tone softens. "Sweetie, I'm doin' this for you. It's just a dress, and I know you'll rock it. Come on," she coaxes as she holds the dress out to me.

I wait a beat before I reluctantly reach out and grab the dress out of her hands. It's been six years since I've worn it, and it's still as beautiful as I remember. Without saying a word, I whirl around and head toward my bathroom to change. I quickly strip and don the dress with my back to the mirror, the soft material caressing my skin like an old lover—both familiar and bittersweet. Before I lose courage, I fling the bathroom door open and step out for Langley's inspection and opinion. Instead I'm met with silence.

Langley is staring at me with a huge smile plastered on her face and a gleam in her eye. "Girl, you are gonna cause every man to rip out his heart and want to walk across hot coals just to talk to you. I knew you were gonna look good but damn! Did you see yourself?"

I shake my head before she gestures for me to turn around. I follow her direction and have to remember to breathe when I finally see my reflection in the mirror. Where the dress used to hang off me like a tent, I fill it out now in all the places that count. I'm not especially curvy like Langley, but this dress enhances what I have to the best advantage. The sweetheart illusion neckline is no longer sweet but, dare I say it, sexy. The cut deepens the shadow of my cleavage and makes it look amazing, while the illusion neckline teases in a tasteful way. I'm the same height, but the dress is higher on my thighs because of the added curves on my body. My long hair frames my breasts, and I have the perfect pair of red boots that will keep things casual. I look great and, I realize sadly, exactly how I wished I looked in this dress six years ago. I'm hoping I can finally turn the memory of this dress into a positive one so, with a smile, I tell Langley I'm ready to go.

SMOKEY'S IS a huge bar with a modern club feel. I've been to clubs in the city, but this place is a mix of upscale and country, which is definitely more my style. I take in the country decor and gleaming hardwood floors as Langley and I make our way toward a bar that's almost the length of the building. Out of the corner of my eye, I spy a large dance floor filled with close-knit bodies dancing to today's hits as cute servers flit around like shot fairies in their short skirts.

Langley must work some sort of witchcraft because we quickly move through the crowd waiting for drinks and get seats that are prime real estate right up at the bar. Leaning over, she catches the eye of one of the bartenders and turns to me as he makes his way over.

"What's your poison, Mac?"

Feeling like I should order something other than wine, I place my fate in her hands. "I'll have what you're having."

"You got it," she nods.

The bartender reaches us and looks us both over before his bright blue eyes zero in on Langley like a homing device. He's good-looking and with his tall, lean build and shaggy blond hair, he looks like he'd be right at home on a beach or surfing.

"What can I get you pretty ladies?"

"We'll take two yellowhammer slammers, please," Langley says sweetly as she places a twenty on the bar.

"You got it, sugar. This round's on me. Just make sure you come back and ask for Bo if you need anything else tonight," he murmurs as he slides the money back to her with a wink.

"Why thank you, Bo. We sure do appreciate it!"

As he readies our drinks, Langley turns to me with a smile. It's only a matter of seconds before we have our drinks in hand and Bo is off helping another customer.

I take a sip of the drink Langley ordered for us both and am relieved when the citrusy taste of pineapple and orange juice dances across my tongue. I was worried she'd order something crazy but am pleased to find that I can barely taste the alcohol.

As we drink and catch up with one another, I notice she periodically looks over my shoulder toward the entrance of the bar. After what must be the third or fourth time, I decide to ask her about it.

"Who're you looking for?"

"Huh? What makes you think I'm looking for someone?"

"You keep looking at the bar's entrance," I point out.

"Oh, just seein' if I know anyone," she answers quickly. "I'm also on the lookout for any eye candy. Lord knows this town needs some. Tell me all about those city men. Actually, did you leave anyone back home?"

"Me? Leave anyone back home?" The idea is laughable. "To answer your first question, there aren't a lot of men in Chicago who have caught my eye, at least not for anything long-term. Of course there are attractive men, but I feel like they were either suits or hipsters. I'm not sure if it's because I'm from the country, but I like a man who is hands-on with what he does and doesn't spend all day behind a desk or recycled coffee cups."

This elicits another laugh from Langley, who begins to fan herself with one hand. "I know what you mean, but I sure do love a man in a nice suit. I just bet some of those suits are closet freaks who get down and dirty after business hours."

"I haven't met any that have. And to answer your second question, I haven't left anyone at home besides Cade."

"Oh, who's Cade?" She looks curious and has an expression that I can't pinpoint. She looks almost worried, but I don't know what she'd be worried about.

"He's my best friend. He's a suit," I laugh, "but he's one of the few I've met who's a complete man's man."

"Nice! Did things ever cross the line with this best friend?" Langley asks as she leans in closer to hear me.

"Never! I mean, he's one of the best-looking men I've ever seen. It's ridiculous actually, but we've never felt a vibe other than friendship with one another. It's nice. He's seriously like a brother to me. One hundred percent platonic there," I insist. "Why do you ask?"

"Oh, no reason. I just wanted to see if anything is tethering you to the city now that you've left your job."

A moment of silence passes as I think about her statement. Besides Cade, I can't think of anything that's keeping me in the city. Now that I'm back home I realize how much I missed it, which certainly makes things more confusing for me. Thankfully, I have plenty of time to figure out what I want. Not ready to make a decision since I'm still here to get my life figured out, I opt to respond after I take another sip of my drink.

"My life is still there, but I definitely have a lot to think about."

I know my answer is vague, but Langley seems satisfied. We chat for a few more minutes before she looks over my shoulder again. Unlike the previous times, her expression lights up and a smile crosses her face.

"Who do you see?" I start to turn so I can follow her line of sight. Before I can rotate my neck forty-five degrees, she places a hand on my arm to stop me.

"One moment, Mac. You'll see in just a moment." I'm confused and know the expression must be showing on my face because she continues. "Just trust me. I see a catch comin' this way, and I'm being a good wingwoman."

Relief floods in now that I know what she's up to. "Langley, he's probably coming to talk to you."

"Nope. Please just trust me."

"Okay," I say, certain that I'm right in this instance. Unsure of what to do, I grab my drink and go in for another sip. As I'm swallowing the fruity liquid, Langley speaks to someone right over my shoulder.

"Hey there, fancy seeing you here." I can hear the teasing note in her voice clear as day. "I want you to meet my friend." I start to turn, and she continues before I make a full rotation. "Well, you already know her, but it's been a long time. You remember Mac, right?"

I finish my rotation and feel a blush rise to my cheeks. My eyes drop to the floor. It's Lawson. Lawson's in the same bar as me. Oh God, why? Mustering up my courage, I trail my gaze from his dress shoes up his dark jeans, over the forest green button-down that's rolled up at the sleeves, up past his throat and sexy scruff, up past those lips I dreamt about for years, and up into those eyes that freeze me in place and light me up all at once. I've seen him sweaty and dirty, but sweet Lord above he cleans up well.

We look at one another, and it's like everyone else in the

bar disappears. No one else exists in this moment, and all I hear are his shallow breaths. He looks shocked to see me and stares me in the eyes for endless moments. Just when I'm about to say hi, his eyes drink me up like I did just a moment ago to him. His eyes drop to my feet and travel up my legs, up my chest where his gaze lingers, up my neck, up to my lips where his gaze lingers even longer, and back to my eyes. This time I have to stop myself from gasping because he finally has the look on his face I always dreamed of seeing: desire. There's no mistaking it as his eyes sear me because this look is electrifying. Holy shit. I must be dreaming.

5

LAWSON

Holy shit. I must be dreaming. Mac is my mystery woman from the farmers' market. *MAC*. I did not see this coming. I repeat: holy shit. She's my best friend's little sister, and we are working together this summer. This cannot happen.

When I came into Smokey's, it was easy enough to spot my sister and the back of the person sitting next to her at the bar. There is no mistaking it is the mysterious woman who caught my eye last week. Her long brown hair is hanging straight down her back, the curve of which is doing a great job of enticing me. I quickly make my way over and try to keep the eager expression off my face. As I walk up to Langley, I notice the shit-eating grin she had on her face at my place has multiplied tenfold. Once I am behind mystery woman, I stare at my sister with a raised eyebrow, waiting for my introduction. To my utter surprise, she introduces me to someone I have already met.

I admit shock is the first emotion that registers. There's

no way mystery woman and Mac are the same person. I stare at Mac's face and am momentarily distracted from my shock because she looks gorgeous. A once-over of her body is all the confirmation I need to prove she is mystery woman. Long, lean legs stretch out forever from the excuse of a dress she is wearing, and her tits are teasing me from behind some see-through fabric shit. Whatever the hell it is, it makes her look sexy and sweet, and it makes my mouth water. She has definitely filled out in all the right places, and those damn coveralls were hiding all of it.

Shaking myself out of my stupor, I find myself looking her in the eyes again. She looks just as shocked as I do. Her blush deepens as I stare at her, and it's in this moment I decide that it doesn't matter that she's Smith's sister or that we're working together or that I'm surprised as fuck. The fact that the woman who intrigued me last week has been under my nose all this time and seems just as affected by me as I do her has my cock twitching in anticipation. I didn't think it was possible, but I'm even more intrigued than before. I know she's only in town for the summer, and I decide to pursue her since I'm not looking for anything serious. I feel the smile start to form on my face as I stare at her. This is happening.

THIS IS *NOT* HAPPENING. Lawson's looking at me with his signature sexy smirk. "Surreal," I mutter under my breath. I am not used to being on the receiving end of his interest and attention. Needless to say, it is downright unnerving.

Seconds tick by as we stare at one another; he looks cool and unruffled, while I am freaking out inside and am fighting my blush. Before either of us can say anything,

Langley speaks up. I am so engrossed in this surprise run-in with Lawson I forgot she was here.

"Lawson, I asked you a question. You remember Mac, right?" She is looking back and forth between us, interest clear on her face.

A beat passes before he responds. "Yes, we've been working together this week. I almost didn't recognize you without your baggy coveralls." He takes this as another opportunity to give my body a once-over that leaves goose-bumps in its wake.

"She looks nice though, right? I'd say more than nice. The men haven't been able to leave her alone tonight."

At this I turn to her and give her my *what the fuck?* face but not before I see the slight lift of Lawson's eyebrow. I don't know why she's lying to him because no one has approached me tonight. I widen my eyes in hopes she'll give me an answer, but all I get is a smile in return. Before I can think on this further, Lawson draws my attention back to him.

"Definitely more than nice," he drawls. My goosebumps from earlier are on the verge of morphing into a full-blown shiver at the sound of his low, gravelly voice.

"Thank you, Lawson. You clean up well, too." Under-statement of the century. There's never been a time when I've seen him looking anything less than delectable, but of course I won't tell him that.

"Speaking of cleaning, I just remembered that I have to clean my kitchen!" Langley's announcement comes out of nowhere. "I've got to go!"

"You have to clean it right this minute?" I ask, my confu-sion reaching its max.

"Yep, cleanliness is next to godliness. Besides, my kitchen is where I make the magic happen. I need it immaculate," she spouts at us as she gets up and throws her tip down for Bo.

"Okay, I'll come with," I say as I start to stand up as well. Before my butt can lift two inches, Langley is pushing me down by my shoulders.

"Oh, no you don't! You need this time to unwind, Mac."

"But how will I get home? You were my ride. I can take a taxi, but I don't mind leaving with you now."

"You will not have to take a taxi. I'll ask Bo to take you home," she says as she raises her arm to catch his attention.

Lawson interjects before I can protest. "I'll take her home."

I can't even respond or insist I'll take a taxi before Langley speaks for me. "No, she can go with Bo. He said earlier he'd take care of whatever she needs tonight."

That's not exactly how that conversation went earlier, but Lawson responds before I can correct Langley. "No, she'll go with me. End of story, Langley." Turning to me, he leans in closer and speaks close to my ear. "I'll take you home. I don't trust anyone here to take care of you like I can."

"Perfect, it's settled then! Lawson will take you home, Mac! What a gentleman," she says quickly.

Before I can even process what is happening, she's up and hugging us both and leaving the bar in a whirlwind . Now I'm left alone with the one man who always managed to turn my insides to jelly, and he's looking at me like I'm the last Klondike bar in the world.

"I can take care of myself, you know," I say with a little more sass than he's heard from me before.

"Oh, I'm sure you can." He steps even closer to me, the woodsy scent that clings to him like a jealous lover clouding my senses. His knees brush mine and the contact gives me a jolt, causing me to shift on the bar stool. My knees separate slightly from the movement, and he takes the opportunity to move closer between my legs. If I cross my legs I'll have to ask him to move, and I refuse to do that. I do not want him to know how he affects me.

"Then why insist on taking me home?" I manage to breathe out.

"Because," he leans down a bit so his face is closer to mine. "I think," he leans in now so his lips are next to my ear. "Actually, *I know* that I can take care of you tonight. No one else will have that pleasure. Not you, and sure as hell not some other guy." His warm breath feathers across my ear as his lips barely brush my earlobe. I'm not entirely sure we're talking about a ride home anymore.

"I'm not your responsibility." My voice comes out as a throaty whisper.

"What if I want you to be?" His voice has lowered to a whisper as well, and I have to check myself to stop from shivering at the proximity of his body to mine. I tamp down the hope and excitement because there's no way he can mean that.

I lean back in my seat and lift my eyes up to his. "Not happening."

He looks surprised, but before he can retort I see Bo out of the corner of my eye and jump on the opportunity to break the hold he has on me.

"Excuse me, Bo?" I call out.

He stops and saunters up to me from behind the bar. "Hey, beautiful. Another slammer?" His eyes shift briefly to where Langley was sitting and to where Lawson is standing, which is still a little too close.

I reach into my clutch and start pulling out some bills. "Yes, please."

Bo stops me before I can pull my money out. "This one's on me. I wouldn't feel right charging the prettiest girl in the bar."

Oh he's charming, this one. I snort with laughter because while I appreciate his words, I know he only has eyes for Langley. "Why thank you, but I insist."

"No, I insist," Lawson surprises me by cutting in. "This is your livelihood, and you're taking care of a lot of people. I'll buy the lady's drink."

Lawson's demeanor hasn't changed and, ever the gentleman, he is being polite and thoughtful. Normally I wouldn't think twice about him doing something like this, but right now there's a sharper edge about him. He's stepped closer to me, all the while maintaining his eye contact with Bo, and I can feel the authority and heat radiating off of him. He hands over a twenty, and I can't say I'm shocked when Bo accepts. With a smile and a nod Bo readies my drink and gets back to work, leaving me with Lawson again.

"Thank you. I appreciate the kind gesture, but I don't think that was necessary."

"Oh? I disagree, darlin'."

"And why is that?" I'm curious, and although he's still standing close to me, he isn't speaking in my ear like before. Thank God for that.

"One, I told you I'd take care of you and not anyone else. That's just me sticking to my promise. Two, if you accepted he would've gotten the wrong idea."

Before I can stop myself I blurt out, "Who says it would've been the wrong idea?"

Lawson's eyebrows rise up, and his jaw tenses for a moment before he recovers from his surprise quickly. "Are you saying you're interested in the bartender?"

"In Bo?" I take a moment to look down the bar and am

obvious in my assessment of the blond bartender. "I could do a lot worse." I look at Lawson again and smile brightly.

"True," he concedes. "But you could do a lot better."

"Can I? I don't see better." I feign looking around the bar, and when I turn back to look at him I see he's inched closer.

"That's 'cause you're not lookin' in front of you, darlin'." His voice and his message cause excitement to rush through my veins.

"Oh, you mean you?" I toss back at him. I try to sound sassy but can hear the quiver of need in my voice.

"Yes," he leans closer to me again. Reaching out, he grabs a lock of my hair and runs it through his fingers before responding. "I mean me. I told you, I want the pleasure of taking care of you. In any way you need."

"In any way?" I feel my panties dampen and try to discreetly rub my thighs together to ease the ache he's creating in my center.

"God, yes. In any way," he practically groans. The look he's giving me is intense and makes me feel both powerless to resist and powerful. "Just tell me how."

I feel like I'm dreaming. After all the years of pining for this man, he's finally showing me some attention. I quickly scan my memory to try and figure out what changed and realize with chagrin that he must finally be attracted to me physically. While I feel triumphant, I can't help the brief feeling of disappointment that flashes through me. It would've been nice if he saw me as a person instead of another potential lay. Besides, he and I are working together, and I'm leaving again in a few months. I need to nip this in the bud but decide to have my fun first.

"Well," I breathe as I toy with the buttons on his shirt, "you can start by taking me home." The look he gives me is an intoxicating mix of surprise, excitement, and pure hunger. "But no touching. A little wait never hurt anyone."

"Deal," he concedes with a groan. "Let's go, Mac." He leans in close and whispers against my lips. "Tonight you're mine."

In a matter of minutes we are out of Smokey's, and he's pulling open the door of his pickup for me. The ride home is short and seems to pass more quickly because of the sexual tension that fills the car like a humid summer day— hot and stifling. I'm aware of his glances in my direction and can't help but sneak peeks at his strong profile when I can. He really is gorgeous.

Before I know what's happened, we are in front of my parents' house. Lawson is looking at me with heat in his eyes, and I see his hand moving toward his seat belt buckle. I act before he can get it undone and unsnap my own seat belt while reaching for the handle. Ever the gentleman, he starts to insist he'll get the door for me before I cut him off.

"I've got it, Lawson. Like I told you earlier, I can take care of myself. In any way I need." Recognition dawns on his face as I exit his vehicle and lean down to speak to him. "Thanks for the ride, though. It'll be the only time I'll need one from you. Good night!" With glee I smile, shut the door, and catch his shock morph into an answering smile before I turn on my heel and saunter inside the house. I hate to admit it, but that was fun.

6

The weekend comes and goes, and by some miracle I just barely manage to avoid Lawson. I found out that he stopped by the house yesterday morning while I was out grabbing some groceries. My father had expressed his confusion over his stopping by on a Sunday because Smith wasn't at the house, and he had already provided an update on the barn's renovations. I know in my gut he wasn't looking for my brother. Like the rich combination of apples and spices, our attraction is wickedly delightful. Eager for a bite of the forbidden fruit, I know he'll find me eventually. I'm still not entirely ready to deal with that, but it's the start of the work week and I'm fairly certain I'll see him today. What have I gotten myself into? At least I don't look appealing in my work gear so maybe that'll cool his ardor from Saturday night.

Or not. I can't find my coveralls for work. What the hell? I remember washing them and putting them in their normal spot on my desk. I just finished tearing my room apart in my hunt and have come up with nothing. I hear my mother moving down the hall and decide to ask her if she knows where they are.

"Mama?"

Her footsteps come closer to my doorway. "Yes, baby?"

"Have you seen my coveralls? I usually set them on my desk but can't seem to find them."

My mother is now in my room and is looking at me, confusion painted on her face. "Oh Mac, you must've forgotten."

Okay, now I'm the one confused. "Forgotten what, Mama?"

"Langley stopped by on Saturday night shortly after y'all left to go out. She said somethin' about needing to clean her kitchen and that you said she could use your coveralls."

That definitely did not happen, but I'm not going to call Langley out in front of my mother.

"Oh, silly me! Thanks for the reminder, Mama!" I give her a kiss on the cheek as she heads back out of my room and reach for my phone. I've got to get this cleared up.

Me: Langley!!!!! Is there something you forgot to tell me, missy?

The little snake's response comes quickly. She's lucky because she does not want me yelling at her over the phone.

Langley: Uh oh! The jig is up. I was waiting for your call or text.

Me: Why'd you take my coveralls? I want them back. Now, please! I have to get to work and need them.

Langley: I told you at Smokey's, sugar. I needed to

clean my kitchen and didn't want to ruin my clothes. I didn't think you'd mind. Thanks, btw!

Me: I wouldn't mind if you returned them to me ASAP, please. I gotta get to work.

Langley: Don't be mad, BUT I ruined them. I washed them and don't know what happened, but they were completely destroyed by my washing machine. Like, torn in shreds, completely unrepairable, never to be worn again destroyed.

Me: ....

Langley: Before you freak out, I bought you a replacement set! They're in your bottom drawer.

I run to check and see a little bundle wrapped in ribbon with a note. I must've missed it because I was looking for my old coveralls.

Sugar, thanks for letting me borrow your coveralls. Sorry about not telling you but I'm sorry about their destruction. Kind of. No wonder Lawson said he didn't recognize you. I bought you a pair that should be more comfortable for you in this heat. ;) You can thank me later. xoxo, Langley

Oh no. Just as I go to unwrap the bundle I get another text from Langley. Her timing is impeccable.

Langley: Don't freak out. Just try them on. Also, I called all the local stores and no one is to sell you a pair that doesn't fit you properly. It's part of the Westbrook magic. ;)

With shaking fingers I unfold Langley's gift. Based off of her messages I know this pair will fit better, but I don't expect the lack of fabric. I'm holding a tiny pair of dark blue "coveralls" that resemble a jumper. Instead of covering my legs, the coveralls have short bottoms and a pair of knee-high socks falls out of the bundle. The sleeves are non-existent and resemble a tank top, and the deep vee of the neckline looks like it might be a bit too low. Where on God's green earth did she buy these? A strip club? A sex store? Before I text her I do as she says and try them on.

I look at myself in the mirror and immediately feel my face redden. The outfit is very formfitting and, although short, I have to grudgingly admit they're more comfortable. My old pair made me feel like I was in a pressure cooker once I started to get sweaty. Although these are much cooler, I can't help but feel exposed. I'm wearing a white tank top underneath, but the neckline still seems really low and the shorts a little too short. When paired with the knee-high socks, I look like I'm going to deliver a naughty telegram. I snap a pic for Langley and tell her so.

Langley: Hot damn, Mac! You look good! The women at the sex store told me it was perfect for some extracurricular activities outdoors, but I didn't think you'd look so classy. I know you're showing more skin, but that's got to help in the heat. Besides, it's not like you're doing anything too crazy out there.

Me: I'm going to ignore the sex store comment in

hopes that you're joking. You're insane. And yes, they're more comfortable. I just feel naked.

Langley: You're a big girl. Own it, Mac. I'm helping you. I gotta go, but I can't wait to hear how much you love these by the end of the day. I'm sure Lawson will appreciate them, too. Like I said, you can thank me later. ;)

Me: I hate you, you snake.

Langley: Hissssssssssssss. :P

I take another look at myself in the mirror as I throw my phone back on my bed. I have nothing else to wear and need to get started before it gets too hot. I'm going to kill Langley.

TODAY I'M FOCUSING on uprooting a bunch of the weeds that have sprouted up around the barn. I could mow them down, but I don't want them to sprout up like a case of bad acne once it rains. When I stepped outside to work Lawson was nowhere in sight, thank goodness. To be safe, I start at the back of the barn and away from the road so no one can see me. Time passes quickly and, although I'll probably regret it later, I savor the burn in my muscles from the exertion. Eventually the burn starts to get to me, and I decide to take a break. Walking over to the faucet on the side of the barn, I look forward to cooling down a little and bend down for a drink of water.

The cool water is a relief to my dry throat, so much so that I extend the relief to my neck by splashing some of the water on my skin. As I rub the water on my throat and moan at the cooling sensation I hear a crash behind me, followed by a curse. I turn slowly as dread fills me and douses my relief; of course, Lawson is here now. My heart rate picks up as I see him standing there, his tool box laying forgotten at his feet, staring at me. Seconds pass as he stares and then he starts to move toward me, the intense look in his eyes putting the look he gave me on Friday night to shame. The closer he gets the hotter I feel and, before I can blink or draw in a breath he's standing in front of me, looking at me like I'm the last drink of water that will give him life. Lord, help me.

Lawson

SHE'S TRYING to kill me. I was hoping I'd run into Mac and had even tried to stop by over the weekend, but luck wasn't on my side. I got caught up on another job this morning and raced over to the orchard, hoping I'd see her and continue our conversation from Friday. As soon as I pulled up I kept an eye out for her but didn't see her anywhere inside the barn. I decided to check around the barn and was not prepared to be struck speechless as soon as I rounded the corner because *hot damn.*

I'm not sure if I'm hallucinating and my imagination is going into overdrive, or if today is finally my lucky day. Mac is bent over by the faucet in a sorry excuse for clothing. I don't know where her baggy coveralls went, but I know I never want to see them again. The dark navy color empha-sizes the gold tone of her skin, the short bottoms teasing me as her ass cheeks play peekaboo. I'm hypnotized by her lips as they try to capture the pouring water and by the long line of her legs. Her hair is up in a messy bun instead of her usual ponytail, and I'm jealous of the wet, wispy tendrils of hair that have escaped and are kissing her neck. She stands and the slow stretch showcases the sleek curve of her back.

I was hard the instant I saw her, my lengthening cock uncomfortably smothered by my jeans. I reach down and adjust myself and wince at the pleasure-pain. Mac doesn't help my situation at all because she cups some water with her hands and starts patting her body with it. Her slender hands are rubbing it onto the back of her neck and into her throat. The low moan she lets free runs through my body like lightening, and I groan at the erotic sound. I don't even realize I've dropped my tool box until her body stiffens slightly. Slowly, she turns to look at me and the rose-colored flush on her cheeks is what I imagine would be there when she's coming. *Fuck.* I stare at her and she stays still, the only movement from the bite she gives her plump lower lip and the bead of water or sweat that rolls down, down, down into the deep vee of her outfit.

I can hear her suck in a breath as she stares at me, and it spurs me to move. I ignore my fallen tools and stalk over to her, determination and an overriding need to touch her adding purpose to my strides. Her eyes widen slightly as I get close and the spark, the heat—whatever the fuck is between us—consumes me. I walk right up to her and stop right before our bodies brush, both of us silent for a moment. As much as her body tempts me, the combination of that with her gorgeous face makes it impossible to stay away. I have to have this woman.

As if she's trying to speak, Mac swallows a couple times. I can see arousal and apprehension in her eyes, which prompts me to pick her up just as her lips part. Her parting comments from Friday night come to mind; I can't let her think this won't be a good time or that she can take care of herself. Her gasp of surprise runs straight through my body and makes me walk faster. I head for my pickup truck, which is parked on the other side of the barn under some trees, as I maneuver her legs so they're wrapped around my waist. She doesn't know yet but I'm about to show her a glimpse of just how well I can take care of her needs.

I make it to my truck, and I hold her body up with one arm while the other releases the catch for the bed of my truck. I set her down on the tailgate and stay between her spread thighs, my big body keeping them spread apart. As I move closer I can see a fleeting hint of pain or discomfort cross her face.

"Are you hurt?" I ask, leaning down a little bit so we're eye to eye.

"What? Why do you think I'm hurt?" Her look of confusion is adorable, but I know what I saw.

"When I do this," I move a little closer between her legs and she winces, "you do that. What's wrong?"

Her skin flushes a darker shade of rose. "My thighs burn from pulling weeds outside the barn all morning. It was a lot of squatting and bending that I'm not used to."

Her tight ass and toned thighs could've fooled me. I look at her and feel a smirk creep up on my face as an awesome idea comes to me. I take both hands off the tailgate and bring them to her thighs. She jolts and slides backward slightly, but I hold her in place.

"What are you—?" Her sentence cuts off and a strangled moan escapes her throat as I start to massage her thighs. Before she can overthink what's happening or say anything, I move forward with my plan.

"I told you I'd take care of you, Mac." Her eyes must've

closed with my ministrations because her eyes fly open at my words, a mix of panic and arousal swirling in their hazel depths. "Now," I say, leaning in closer to her ear as I continue to massage her thighs, "tell me what happened on Friday night."

OH GOD, he's rubbing my thighs and it feels incredible. Lawson Westbrook is massaging my thighs. Have I died and gone to heaven? His big hands make my thighs feel small, and the callouses on his palms and fingers add a slight scratch to his movements. I feel myself getting wet with each pass of his thumb and each squeeze of my skin. I can barely think, and now he's asking me questions.

"I'm sorry, what?" It's so difficult to get the words out and, judging by his sexy smirk, he knows what he's doing to me.

"You told me on Friday night you can take care of yourself, in any way you need. Well," he arches a brow, "how is that working out for you? Cause from where I'm standing, I'm the one doing that."

My thoughts are sluggish, but I fight to put them together in a way that makes sense. "I hardly think that giving my legs a massage constitutes as taking care of me."

He smiles and that, combined with his hypnotic hands, sets my body on fire. His voice is raspy as he responds. "I beg to differ. I think, from these sexy as fuck blushes and your shallow breaths, that you're a little turned on, darlin'."

I can't even lie because it's the truth. Damn him. His smirk widens as I sit here.

"And since that's the case, I think we both know your response to my touch is a clear signal I'm the only one that'll give you any type of relief." As he says this his hands move higher up my legs, the seductive swipe of his thumbs adding more pressure to the inside of my thighs. He's getting dangerously close to my center, and all I can think about is how I don't want him to stop.

"We c-can't, Lawson," I stutter.

"And why is that? Seems like we're both attracted to one another, right Mac?" *Swipe, squeeze, swipe.*

"Yes, but we work together." I'm desperately trying to keep it together and hold my ground, but it's so hard. So, so hard.

"Not really. I'm not your boss, and I'm just helping your family out. We've known each other for years, Mac. What else do you got?"

"I'm only here for the summer."

"Well, that's not a bad thing. I'm not looking for anything serious. Are you?" His voice is deep, slightly raspy, and is lulling me further into his clutches.

With the little resistance I have left, I lean back a bit to get some air. "No, I plan to go back to Chicago. I'm not that kind of girl, Lawson. I won't be your hit it and quit it girl. I came here to focus on me."

"Mac, darlin', I respect you enough to tell you now what my intentions are. I'm not lookin' for anything serious at all, and I think we could have some fun this summer. You can still focus on you. Just," he pauses, leans back into my space, and runs his nose along the length of my neck, "let me focus on you, too."

Oh God, how can I say no to that? I don't even want to risk getting my heart broken in pieces because surely that's what will happen if I give in to him. For years I harbored feelings for this man, and even if my heart as a woman wouldn't break upon leaving him, I know the heart of the insecure teenage girl I used to be would.

As my mind freaks out, he slowly runs the tip of his nose from my neck across my jawline and to the corner of my mouth. Oh God, is he going to kiss me? He continues to nuzzle me and traces the shape of my lips before he stops, resting his forehead against mine.

"Lawson?" I question, my breath once again getting caught in my chest.

"Hmm?" He leans in closer so his mouth is almost touching mine. Our breaths mingle, and I can see the rise and fall of his broad chest.

I'm sure once he realizes I'm not that easy and won't be giving in, he'll give up and ignore me like he used to. I'm not sure how I manage it, but I speak and force myself to sound sure. "I can't, Lawson. I'm sorry. Let's just stick to being friends."

He doesn't sigh or express his displeasure in any way, which I grudgingly admit is disappointing. Instead, he steps back from me and slides his hands back down my thighs, his fingertips catching on my knees. He looks serious and with one last look at my lips he says, "Okay."

I should leave it at that and get on with my day, but I can't stop the word vomit that erupts from my mouth. "Were you about to kiss me?" I sound breathy and, dammit, excited.

My words cause his smirk to reappear. He doesn't touch me, but he leans in a bit closer and lowers his voice. "Trust me, you'll know when I'm going to kiss you because my lips will already be on yours. There will be no waiting or wondering. Besides," he leans out of my space and takes another step back, "you're not ready for my kiss. Not really.

When you are you'll beg me for it or I'll just take it, which-ever comes first."

Then, with a wink, he steps away from me and swaggers back to his forgotten tool box. As he walks away I can feel my resolve start to chip away faster than the barn's faded paint. I am way in over my head with this man.

7

I gave myself a pep talk in an effort to steel my resolve and convince myself to not be a hussy after the thigh-rubbing incident on Monday. On Tuesday I woke up ready to say no and didn't have to turn Lawson down, not once. I still haven't bought a new "complete" set of coveralls and decided to stick with the more comfortable, showy version Langley got me. I thought for sure Lawson would try to seduce me into giving in, but he's stayed a complete gentleman. I'll even shamefully admit that I've bent over at the waist a little more than is necessary when pulling weeds and still get no response. If we happen to cross paths he keeps his distance and gives me a polite nod before getting back to work.

Now it's Thursday, and he hasn't so much as made an inappropriate comment or stepped within five feet of me. I know I told him I didn't want anything outside of friendship, but the lack of attention when he had been so into me just days ago is driving me absolutely crazy. What makes it worse is he's upped his sex appeal, the bastard. I thought I had it bad last week when he was pouring water over himself, but it's infinitely worse now. Whenever he's here he's working shirtless and good God, seeing those muscles glistening in sweat are tempting enough to make a devout nun lift up her skirt and pray for an orgasm. I knew Lawson had a cut body but I think seeing him in his element, wielding tools and fixing things, leaves my mouth dry and my panties wet every single time. Right now I'm ogling him because he's lifting spare slats of wood out of the bed of his truck, his biceps flexing with each movement. He's really too gorgeous for my sanity.

Shaking the lust from my mind, I decide to turn my focus to the inside of the barn now that I've finished the thankless task of clearing out weeds. I had pulled out some of the rubbish inside already but still have a lot of work to do. I pull one of the doors to the side, the gentle creaking sound washing over me in a wave of nostalgia. I make my way inside and step over dried leaves and debris, each step kicking up a layer of dust. I look ahead and broken slats of wood are on the ground; those must be part of the original roof that was destroyed. I survey the space and take in the old tanks where we used to make cider and the empty jugs, some whole and some broken, lining the walls on shelves covered in cobwebs. When I was a kid this barn was spotless and welcoming, the perfect place to make cider and greet visitors. Now it looks like an old photograph and not the treasured memory it really is. I take a deep breath and the smells of dust and mold fill my nose instead of crisp apples and warm spices. It's in this moment I make a promise to myself: I'm going to restore this barn to its former glory.

I pick my way across the worn and dirty hardwood and undo the latch on one of the windows. As soon as it swings open the sweet smell of flowers permeates the air and rays of sunshine filter in, the shafts of light instantly brightening up the room. I open the window on the other side and feel excited about the task at hand. This barn is a dirty penny and just needs to shine again.

I'M in the middle of clearing out the barn of everything so I can dust when I catch another glimpse of Lawson through the window. He's right in my line of sight and is adjusting his tool belt. The belt hangs low on his hips and is only surpassed in indecency by the even lower rise of his faded blue jeans. He can't see me drooling like an open faucet because his head is lowered, focusing on the task at hand. His torso twists as he modifies the fit of the belt, all the sinew and lean muscles of his abs bunching slightly whenever his body shifts. My gaze keeps drifting between the deep vee of his hips and the light happy trail that starts after the last set of abs and leads straight into his pants. His body is perfect, and the muscles I'm so openly devouring are made through the hard work he puts in each day and honed further in the gym. He finally seems satisfied with how the belt sits on his hips and glances up at me. His eyes capture mine and I quickly look away, a heated blush suffusing my cheeks. How embarrassing. A few seconds later I chance a glance back at him and am relieved to see he's turned his back to me. I lick my lips as I realize the view from the back is almost as enticing as the view from the front. He's all broad shoulders, hard muscles, and his tight ass looks good enough to squeeze.

"Get a grip, Mac," I mutter to myself. "Stay strong."

With renewed fervor I finish clearing out the barn, which is now wonderfully empty since everything is outside in organized piles. I twist my hair up further from the pony-tail I haphazardly made this morning and put it in a messy bun, thankful to have the hair off my neck. Placing my hands on my hips, I survey the space and am pleased with the progress. Now I just need to do a deep clean, organize, and decorate. I smile to myself and feel beads of sweat drip from my forehead and into my shirt. Now that I'm standing still I realize just how warm my body is and decide to take a break. I wipe my brow and fan my face with my hands in an effort to cool down.

Before I have the chance to turn and head outside a heated presence appears at my back, searing me from the inside out. The heat intensifies as Lawson leans down to speak in my ear in his low, raspy voice. *Sweet Jesus.*

"Here darlin'," he whispers. "You look hot."

My body jerks in surprise as he brings a wet washcloth to my skin. He starts at my throat, his arm around my body, and the only contact between us is where the cool cloth caresses my overheated skin. The contrast in sensations and his proximity causes me to shudder and release shallow gasps.

"Doesn't that feel better, Mac?" he asks, dragging the wash cloth briefly over the part of my breasts exposed by my coveralls and moving to each arm. My only response is a hitched breath as up and down, up and down he runs the cloth along my arms, simultaneously cooling my skin yet creating an inferno in my panties.

Finally he moves to the back of my neck, the cooling sensation mingling with his warm breath. After one last swipe I feel the hot press of his lips against me. It's the first physical contact we've had since Monday, and I feel like my skin is on fire. His lips linger on my neck and, just when I think he's going to pull his lips away, he lifts them and gifts me with another kiss. His arms are down at his side now, and I'm tempted to grasp his hands and put them all over me. Instead I stand here like a deer who caught sight of a hunter, unable to move or process what's happening.

He continues to pepper light kisses against my neck before he speaks. "Mac?"

"Yes?" My voice is faint and weak.

"Does this feel better?" He's moved to the side of my neck now.

"Mmm?"

I'm momentarily startled out of my lust-induced fog when he nips my neck with his teeth. Before my brain can fully process the slight sting, his tongue swipes out to soothe the little bite.

"I asked you a question," he says. "Does this," he kisses my neck and gives a little suction against the tendon there, "feel better?" Again, he follows this with a nip and a swift lick.

"Y-yes," I manage to get out.

"Good girl."

My eyes flutter closed at his words. Lawson Westbrook was a consistent fantasy growing up, and part of my brain is unable to process that this is actually happening right now. Warm puffs of breath replace his kisses as he starts to gently graze my arms with his fingertips, a multitude of goose-bumps left in the wake of his featherlight touch. Before things can progress further, I step away from his touch and feel the immediate loss of contact when I turn around to look at him.

"Lawson, I told you I can't."

"Bullshit, Mac," he grounds out.

"Excuse me?" I say forcefully, my voice rising an octave.

"I said," he takes a step toward me and I reflexively take a step back in response, "I call bullshit!" He stalks toward me slowly and my pulse starts to quicken again. He isn't angry, but he's much more forceful that I'm used to, his gentlemanly exterior rougher and unbridled.

"And what's bullshit about how I feel, Lawson? Huh? Enlighten me, please."

"Oh, I'll tell you, darlin'." He's still walking in my direction, and I realize belatedly that we are heading further away from the barn's entrance and are almost to the back wall. I'm running out of places to go. "What's bullshit is that you're lying. You've been eye-fucking me for days now. I don't even have to look at you to know it's happening. Just admit it. You want me just as much as I want you. The last few minutes alone have proved it. What's so hard to admit about that?"

I swallow, not entirely sure what to say. Yes, I'm attracted to him. I won't even bother trying to deny it. I may as well be honest.

"Yes, Lawson, I want you! Happy now? But," I pause, "I won't be some fuck buddy you call when you can't get laid by one of your other regulars."

He stops in his tracks and looks surprised. "Is that what you think of me?"

"I honestly don't know what to think."

"I told you I'm not looking for anything serious, not that I have a call list of women to fuck. True, I don't have trouble getting laid when I feel so inclined. I just don't fuck the same woman twice because I don't want things to get complicated."

"This isn't helping your case," I tell him as I cock an eyebrow.

"Let me finish," he growls. "We're both attracted to each other, and the past few days have been pure hell because we haven't been doing anything about it. Like I said, I don't usually fuck the same woman twice because I don't like that they expect more than I'm willing to give. You know my family, and you know me. I'm willing to try something new and make an exception for you."

"I'm honored," I deadpan.

"All I'm saying is I'm willing to step out of my comfort zone and give you what you need this summer," he says. His steps have slowed but he still makes his way to me. "I told you I'd take care of you, and I know you're not a one-time girl. Honestly, I'm not even sure I'd be satisfied after just one night. I'm not looking for anything serious, and I'm telling you now so there are no surprises or false expectations. What's holding you back?"

I finally reach the end of the line and feel my shoulder blades press into the back wall of the barn. I lean back, trying to figure out what to say. I can't tell him that I'm terrified of taking things to the next level because I'm not sure I can separate lust and feelings. Instead, I look up at him and try to figure out what to say. He's standing before me, our toes almost touching, and he looks so earnest and sexy that I feel my resolve fade away bit by bit. It's in this moment I decide to come clean.

"What's holding me back," I say slowly, "is that I haven't done this before. What if I become like those other girls and start to think about hearts and flowers?"

He stares at me for seconds that feel like eons, his eyes intent on mine. I have no clue what's going through his mind, but he hasn't stepped away. If anything, he leans further into my personal space.

"Can you be honest with me?" he asks.

"Yes."

"If you start to feel that way, the moment it starts, let me know. Okay?"

I can't believe I'm even entertaining this. "Okay..."

"And," he continues, "are you still going back to Chicago after the summer?"

"That's the plan."

"Are you looking for anything serious?"

"No, I'm not. I told you the other day I just want to focus on myself."

He surprises me by smirking and places one of his palms behind me on the wall. "I already told you..." he says. He brings his other hand up to my face, tucks a flyaway strand of hair behind my ear, and lightly caresses my jawline before he continues. "You focus on you and I'll focus on you, too. What do you say?"

I can't breathe and my mind is foggy. "Say?" I utter. I'm so disoriented that I'm reduced to one-word responses.

He chuckles and God, that sound will never fail to get to me. The sound rolls over me and hits me in all my aching spots. "What do you say to trying a temporary arrangement? We'll give in to this attraction we both feel, only for the summer, and will stop if things get weird. Ball's in your court, darlin'."

At this point he's pulled his hand back from my face, but I'm still caged in by his strong arm to my left. I stand here and think about his proposition, grateful that he's not rushing me or pressuring me. I know in my gut that if I turn him down it'll be the end of the discussion; Lawson is walking, talking lust, but at his core he's a gentleman. I know this is a terrible idea and that I risk getting addicted to the man I crushed on for years, but looking at him now I realize I don't have it in me to say no. This is what Eve must have felt like when faced with the temptation of biting into the forbidden apple, drawn in like the tide and unable to resist no matter what was racing through her mind. I take a deep breath and decide to let whatever happens this summer play out. I came here to find myself, break away from the unexciting norm that is my life, and take risks. This will have to be one of them. I fidget and can't bring myself to look at his eyes, so instead I stare at his full lips.

"Yes." My answer comes out quiet, so quiet he doesn't hear me.

"What was that?"

Clearing my throat, I answer more loudly, "Yes. I said y—"

My words are cut off as Lawson leans in and presses his lips against mine in a scorching kiss that's better than anything I've ever imagined. It starts off soft and slow so I'm able to savor the contrast between his lush lips and scratchy stubble. Within moments the gentleness recedes as we are both consumed by the lust that has been brewing between us since our reunion. He groans, and I feel the vibration from his chest all the way to the tips of my toes. His hand is still against the wall but he places his other hand behind my head, simultaneously steadying me and holding me in place as he controls our kiss.

I place my hands against his chest, turned on by the hard wall of muscle beneath my palms. His tongue darts out and gently presses at the seam of my mouth, seeking entrance. As soon as I part them and grant him access he licks into me and massages his tongue against mine, the sensation hardening my nipples to painful points. The feelings he stirs in me are a mix of pain and pleasure, bitter and sweet. He continues to taste my mouth, and as he consumes me I think to myself that he tastes like the most decadent whiskey—dark, strong, and sinful. I surrender to him as he masters me with his lips and his touch.

I don't know how long we kiss for, but I feel like I've indulged in every guilty pleasure known to man. Eventually his lips gentle and he slowly removes them from mine. I'm in a daze and stare at him in wonder as he removes his hands and steps back, giving us both space. His eyes are heavy-lidded with desire, and his lips are twisting up into his trademark sexy smirk. He gives me a heated once-over before he takes a few more steps backward.

I'm overwhelmed and stunned by him. I've never had anyone kiss me with such skill and passion, as if they were overcome and could barely restrain themselves. I gradually feel my mental faculties return as more distance is created between our bodies. "Wait, where are you going?"

He smiles as he continues to move away from me. "I've got to get back to work."

"That's all I get?" I ask, a smile lifting my swollen mouth up at the corners.

"No," his smile fades immediately, and the inferno of lust he unleashed moments ago is briefly visible in his eyes. "That's definitely not all. Be ready for dinner tomorrow at six."

"Dinner? Tomorrow?" I ask incredulously.

His smile returns and dazzles me for a moment. Damn this man. "Yep. Like you told me last week, Mac," his smile widens mischievously, "a little wait never hurt anyone."

My mouth drops open in shock and he laughs, the sound full-bodied and sexy, as he finally turns away from me and heads out of the barn.

I stand here, stunned, unsure what to think. I bring my fingers up to my heated cheeks and am still smiling when he turns back and yells "Six o'clock!" over his shoulder, his stride not slowing down. I don't move as I watch him walk away, a warm feeling buzzing in my chest. *This man.* With a final smile I push off the wall and get back to work, entertained by thoughts of what might happen tomorrow.

8

Time passes slower than sticky molasses on a hot summer day, and I think it's because I'm nervous and excited for my dinner date with Lawson. To make matters worse I haven't seen him since he left me in the barn yesterday, confused and filled with lust. It's finally the end of the work day, and I'm standing in my room trying to figure out what to wear. I really wish I had seen him so I could get an idea of where we're going or what the dress code is.

I look at the limited selection I brought with me from Chicago and almost settle on jeans and a t-shirt. As I reach out to grab the shirt I pause, my hand lingering above the cloth. Langley's visit last week when we went to Smokey's comes to the forefront of my mind, and I reconsider my outfit choice. I don't want to change my personal style but certainly I can sex things up a bit, especially if we're going to be sleeping together. A burst of inspiration hits me so I move over to my dresser and look through the clothes I wore in high school. I know it sounds ridiculous, but if my dress was such a hit last week then maybe I should do the same today.

I sort through the piles of neatly folded denim and come across an adorable pair of black high-waisted shorts with lace pockets buried at the bottom of my dresser. I loved this pair of shorts as a teen, but they were always a little too baggy and dressy for everyday wear. I shimmy into them and am glad to find they fit better than they used to. A lot better. I look at my legs in the mirror and am pleased to note that while I'm showing a lot of skin, the length of the shorts is still respectable. Not only that, the fabric and cut make it so that I can easily dress these up with heels if needed. I look through my tops and find a cute white tank top that has a deep v-neck that's both comfortable and straddles the line of casual and dressy. I try the top on, and my lace bralette adds the cleavage coverage I need so I don't look like a hooch. Now, depending on where we go for dinner, I can opt for heels or cowboy boots and will fit right in.

I check the time on my phone and note that Lawson will be here any minute now. I give myself a once-over in the mirror and am happy with the final outcome. My fishtail braid looks amazing, and my minimal makeup enhances my features without being overdone. With one last swipe of lip balm I head downstairs and wait in the foyer for my date to arrive.

Not even a minute passes before I hear a soft knock. My parents are out running errands so I walk barefoot to the door and open it to reveal the sexy bachelor behind it. I feel my mouth drop open slightly as I look up at him because he looks mouthwateringly good. The porch light isn't on so he's backlit by the setting sun, his broad shoulders and good looks only enhanced by the shadows. He's wearing dark blue jeans and a turquoise henley. He must know how to dress to enhance his eyes because they're striking against his shirt's bright pop of color.

A blush steals across my face as I realize I'm staring at him. I seriously need to stop doing this, or he's going to think I don't have a brain. I part my lips to speak but stop, my cheeks reddening further as I realize he's staring at me as well. His eyes do a slow perusal up my body and keep switching focus between my legs and eyes.

"You look beautiful, Mac," he finally says as he hands me a small bouquet of irises.

His sweet compliment and gesture catch me by surprise. I bring the riot of purple, blue, and white blooms to my nose and enjoy their soft, sweet fragrance. I can't even remember the last time a man gave me flowers, let alone my favorite kind. It's nice.

"Thank you. How'd you know these are my favorite?" I ask as I continue to enjoy the flowers.

"I remember always seeing bunches of them in vases here at the house. I didn't even realize they weren't a regular occurrence anymore until breakfast last week. It was the first time I'd seen them here in years and figured they were your doing." He looks sheepish, which is an endearing look for him. "It was a lucky guess," he throws out as if it doesn't matter. He may think it doesn't, but to me it's the little things that mean the most.

Sensing his slight discomfort, I take the lead with the conversation. "Your guess was spot-on. Thanks again," I smile. "I'll just place these in some water and we can get going. You can come in."

He steps over the threshold into the house and his presence fills up the small entryway, immediately hitting me with a surge of lust. Why does he have to be so big and insanely good-looking? I quickly turn and head back inside before I toss the irises away and launch myself into his arms. Instead, I head toward the kitchen and place the flowers on the counter while I look for a vase under the sink. I'm rummaging around in the cabinet and finally find one that will work. Before I can straighten I hear an almost inaudible groan. With a discreet look behind me I see Lawson standing in the doorway to the kitchen, his broad frame almost filling it entirely.

I straighten and don't turn back to him as I fill the vase with water. Once I'm sure my cheeks have cooled I turn, place the flowers in the vase, and try to arrange them. As my fingers maneuver the soft petals I glance up at him and see that he's watching me intently.

"So," I start awkwardly, "where is it we're going tonight? I wasn't sure what to wear. If I need to change let me know."

He swallows deeply before he replies. "You look perfect, although I do recommend wearing comfortable shoes. As to where we're going, that's a surprise."

I'm not going to lie, I'm intrigued. "Well let's go then, handsome. I'm curious to see what you have in store," I say as I head toward him.

He doesn't move from the doorway as he responds. "I'll just bet you are," he says on a low murmur. "Guess you'll just have to wait and find out."

"I guess so," I breathlessly say. I'm in the doorway with him now, our bodies so close together that the slightest movement will have us plastered against each other. We drink each other in for a few seconds before he clears his throat.

For the second time tonight, he surprises me when he leans back and gestures out the doorway. "After you."

A small part of me was expecting him to pounce on me as soon as he had the chance, but for reasons unknown to me he's behaving himself. I follow his lead and head back toward the front of the house with him close on my heels.

I slip on my cowboy boots and we head out of the house, the gravel crunching beneath our feet as we head to his pickup. He opens the door and I climb in, the feel of his palm on my lower back heating me up from the inside out. I buckle in and have to keep a knowing smile from gracing my face when I catch his eyes on my legs again. He makes sure I'm all set before he comes around to the driver's side and hops in.

Buckling up, he looks at me and says, "Let's get goin, darlin'. The night is ours."

~

LAWSON

FOR THE FIRST time in years I find that I'm nervous about a date. Why the fuck am I nervous? I'm used to wining and dining my one-night encounters, but I'm not sure if it's the fact that I've agreed to more than one night, our plan for the evening, or the woman seated beside me that has me on edge. I have a sinking feeling that it's a combination of all three.

We make brief small talk about the barn's progress on the short drive, and I have to remind myself to keep my eyes on the road and not on Mac's long, tan legs. We pass her family's property line and continue for about a mile before I turn onto the unkempt path on the neighboring land. It's at this point her curiosity is visibly piqued, her slender form leaning closer to the window to try and see where we're going.

"So...is there something you're not telling me?" She sounds suspicious.

"Nope. If there's one thing you can count on with me, it's that I'm unfailingly honest."

"No, I think you're going to kill me and hide my body somewhere on this land."

I hear the teasing note in her voice come through and can't help but smile. I can't blame her for cracking a joke because the land has been vacant for years and is in desperate need of some TLC.

"Mac, darlin', I have plenty of plans for your body and harming it and burying it are nowhere on that list," I drawl.

A sexy blush tinges her cheeks and I smile, reveling in her reaction to my words. To save her from embarrassment I continue speaking. "Our dinner is actually somewhere on this property."

She looks grateful for the quick subject change. "It is? Are we having a picnic?"

"You can call it that, except we won't be sitting on a blanket among the weeds. You'll see. We're almost there."

Silence fills the cab of the truck as I slowly drive over rock and shale toward our destination. The trees arching overhead provide relief from the brightness of the setting sun and mute the blazing oranges and reds to vivid golds and pinks. A few minutes pass quietly until we reach a clearing, and I hear Mac's indrawn breath when she spots where we're having dinner.

In the middle of the clearing is the construction site for a new build. The large home isn't complete but the shell has been erected so it's technically safe to go inside. Once it's finished the home will be beautiful, and I can tell by the expression on Mac's face that she agrees. A moment later she confirms my thoughts.

"I know it isn't done yet, but it's lovely," she says, a trace of awe in her voice.

You're lovely, I think. Instead I say, "Thank you. It's my most recent build and is hands down my favorite."

Mac swivels in her seat and looks at me in surprise. "You're building this?"

The pride is evident in my voice as I respond. "Yes. I wanted to show it to someone." She looks at me for a moment, and I realize that may have sounded a little too intimate. Shit. I stop myself from saying anything else because then it'll just seem like I'm trying to cover it up.

"Thank you," she murmurs.

I nod in response, and once I pull up to the house I hop out and open up the door for her. As she gets out of the cab the faint smell of her perfume or whatever the fuck she wears wafts up to my nose. I feel a smile tug at my lips as I realize that she smells like apples, tart and sweet, just like her personality. I reach over into the bed of the truck, pull out the cooler that holds our food, and guide her to the large wraparound porch. The electricians haven't been out yet so I set it up so we can have our picnic outside.

As we climb the steps Mac squeals in delight. "This is awesome!" She bounds up the rest of the way and goes to sit on the swinging bench. It's the only piece of furniture on this piece of land and is the perfect place to relax and watch the sunset. Seeing her swinging merrily in the chair makes me break out in an answering smile.

Chuckling as I join her on the bench, I say, "I know. I only ever do awesome things."

"Oh, you're so modest." She lightly punches my arm and giggles. "What are you gonna feed me?"

"Only the best." I open up the cooler and start removing

the contents. "I hope you weren't craving sandwiches or something that wasn't messy."

"As if," she scoffs. "I worked up an appetite today."

"Good. Cause I brought hot chicken, macaroni and cheese, fried green tomatoes, and chocolate chip whiskeys."

"You're trying to kill me," she momentarily groans as if she's in pain. "And what are chocolate chip whiskeys?"

"The best things ever. Chocolate chip cookies with whiskey mixed in. The little extra kick from the liquor makes all the difference."

"Well what are you waitin' for, Lawson? Plate me up, please! I'm famished."

I laugh and prepare her plate for her. We sit in companionable silence as we look out at the horizon and devour our food. I'm relieved and admire that she isn't trying to hide the fact that she eats like a regular human being, unlike some other women I've gone out with. Mac is real, and that's part of her appeal. After we stuff our faces full of food we both lean back and relax, the bench rocking gently.

"Wow, I didn't realize how much I missed homemade Southern food until I came back. That was the real deal. Did you make all that?" Mac looks content and is patting her flat stomach.

"Ha, no. I can cook, but my cooking will never be as good as that. Langley helped me out and cooked."

"Langley cooked? I know she is an incredible baker but wow, that meal was something else."

"She makes magic happen in a kitchen. I have to restrain myself from overeating sometimes or I'll lose my girlish figure." I waggle my eyebrows and Mac laughs, a sweet tinkling sound that carries on the breeze as we sit and sway.

"I don't play for the other team, but I may need to ask your sister to marry me." She glances at me out of the corner of her eye, and we both burst out laughing again. We sit and watch the sunset for a few more minutes, the fading rays of sunshine making everything glow before she breaks the silence.

"Lawson?"

"Yeah, darlin'?" I turn my head to look at her and her eyes are already on me, her expression sweet and innocent.

"This is nice. Thank you."

Her words are simple, but the sincerity rocks me to my core. I've been out with a lot of women and none have been genuinely content to spend time with me when things weren't getting physical. Mac, however, just seems happy to sit here with me and do nothing, all physical stuff aside. We revert back to silence, and it's then I realize that I'm comfortable and enjoying the non-physical stuff as well. *Shit*. I'm in trouble with this girl. I'm so glad this is only temporary.

I REALLY WISH this wasn't temporary, I inwardly sigh. Wait, what? No, I can't afford to think like this. No matter how amazing this date has been so far, I can't fall victim to Lawson's infamous charm. It would help if he was an asshole or something, but he's not one at all. I'm getting too comfortable hanging out with him like this. Between his body heat warming up my insides and the dying rays of the sun warming my skin, I decide to disturb the peaceful silence. Shaking my head at my inner musings, I angle myself toward him just a bit.

"So tell me about this project. From what I can see it's incredible."

His chest seems to puff up a little bit in what I assume is pride. "You'd think that since I own a construction business

I'd have built a lot of homes by now, but that's not the case. A lot of the jobs I'm contracted for are for repairs or additions. This is my first build from scratch."

"Who designed it?"

He smirks as he asks, "Are we playing twenty questions?"

"Just answer the question," I say, lightly shoving him with my hand. Even that brief contact causes a zing of awareness to race up my arm. I'm pathetic.

"I worked closely with the landowner and besides a list of basic requirements he was looking for, I was given free reign. I feel like a kid at their first fair, but it's been a lot of fun. Sometimes I can't believe I'm making something on this grand of a scale from nothing."

"I can't even imagine building something like this from nothing but my imagination."

"Well, what is it you do in Chicago?" He's angled himself toward me as well so our knees are now touching.

"Ugh, you mean what I *did* in Chicago?"

"What you did? As in past tense?"

"Your twenty questions started one question ago," I tell him, my voice serious.

His deep chuckle rolls through me when he answers, that slight rasp rubbing across my senses. "Fine. What did you do in Chicago?"

"I worked as a graphic designer. Before you ask what happened, I'll give you a freebie. I quit. I'd been working there for a few years, and it was a long time coming. I can't tell you how frustrated and fed up I was with the lack of recognition and opportunity from management. For months I felt like something was missing, and when my witch of an ex-boss pissed me off I up and quit."

"Wow, that's brave of you."

I can't help but laugh at his positive assessment. "Or

stupid, depending on how you look at it. Now I'm here, trying to find myself. Goodness, that sounds so cliché."

"I don't think so. If you needed to get away from things for a bit, what better place than where you grew up?" His voice is serious, and his expression is clear of judgement.

"You've got a good point. I'm still trying to figure out what I want in life. I wish I was like you, so sure of what you want or don't want. Not to mention the fact you build homes out of thin air," I say in an effort to lighten the weight of my words. Lawson, however, still looks serious.

"You're not very different, Mac. I'm sure you have to create branding or images out of an idea in your head or your client's head. It's the same concept really, we just use different mediums."

I'm impressed by his insight and openness to discussing this with me. "Hmm, I haven't thought about it that way."

We continue to go back and forth with questions, the conversation flowing easily between us. I am shocked to find out he's never been to Chicago and have to bite my tongue to stop myself from inviting him to visit me sometime. I'm not sure if that would cross a line or not, so I hold off on issuing an invitation. We're both nearing the end of our twenty question limit before he surprises me for the umpteenth time tonight.

"Tell me something I don't know."

"Um, that's not a question."

"Fine, what's something I don't know about you?"

I contemplate my answer and don't know if it's the food coma I'm about to become victim to or the intoxicating feeling of being in his presence for so long. Mustering up my courage, I decide to throw caution to the wind and tell him about my long-standing teenage infatuation. He asked for it.

"I had the *biggest* crush on you when I was a teenager. You're actually the reason I chose to go to college in Chicago."

My words come out in a rush, but I know he understands my words because his body stiffens slightly. I don't even want to see his expression so I force out a laugh and look down at my lap.

"Ha, just kidding." Wow, I suck. That didn't even sound convincing.

"Mac." His voice is firm, but I can't bring my eyes to his. I keep my gaze trained on my shorts and pick at non-existent lint.

"Mac," he repeats. "Look at me."

I can't avoid the command in his voice a second time, so I slowly look up and stare into his eyes. "Now," he continues, "say that again, please. And what do you mean I'm the reason you moved to Chicago?"

"It's, uh, it's..." I stumble and clear my throat. "It's silly and doesn't amount to a hill of beans."

For a moment I have trouble catching my breath because he doesn't even crack a smile at the old Southern phrase. Instead, all his focus is unflinchingly on me as he responds. "No, it's not. Not to me."

Heavens to Betsy, why couldn't I keep my mouth shut? I stare at him and he continues to wait for my answer, looking at me expectantly. What have I gotten myself into?

9

LAWSON

I stare at Mac as she sits next to me, her face blushing furiously. She looks uncomfortable, but she can't just throw that shit out there and then try and take it back. Her eyes dance with mine, her lashes fluttering like delicate butterflies as she tries to deal with her nerves. I don't break my stare because whether she likes it or not, I'm getting an answer. She takes a deep breath, casts one last glance my way, and pointedly looks out at the landscape when she finally starts to answer my question.

"So, uh, yeah," she falters and visibly centers herself before continuing. "I had this mega crush on you as a teenager. This is so embarrassing," she says as she blushes an even deeper shade of red. "You had to have known. I must've been so obvious."

"Honestly, I had no idea. I'm a guy, Mac. We're pretty clueless," I smile gently, hoping that she'll be less nervous.

With an answering smile she responds. "Yeah, that's

true. Anyway, do you remember the night of my graduation dinner?"

I scrub a hand over the back of my neck as I try and remember. I have to think far back and vaguely recall going, but details are fuzzy. "Um, I remember going. That's about it." I can't help the embarrassed chuckle that comes out.

"That's fine, I don't expect you to remember. It's probably only vivid in my mind because I was mortified." She notices the apologetic look on my face and brushes off the apology with a wave of her hand before I can vocalize it. "It's not your fault. That night I kept getting asked about my plans for college and if I'd ultimately end up pursuing my graphic design degree here or in Chicago. Well," she pauses, "I had my answer that night after I overheard you talking to Smith."

"What happened?"

She glances at me, and her expression is serious. "I have to preface this with the fact that I was young and stupid. I can promise you that I'm not an inexperienced eighteen-year-old girl anymore, so you won't have to worry about this happening."

"O-kay?" I say, the word drawn out slowly and sounding more like a question than a statement. I'm curious to hear where this is going.

"I was hoping you would see me differently and that I'd have a shot with you. Crazy, I know." A short, self-deprecating laugh leaves her lips. "I went to go talk to you after you left the table and heard my brother telling you he thought I had a thing for you. You didn't believe him but, needless to say, you made it very clear that I wasn't womanly and that you'd never see me that way. And of course, me being a dramatic teenage girl, that sealed the deal for me moving out of state for school."

God, I'm an asshole. A grade-A asshole. "Mac—"

She cuts me off before I can attempt what would be my second apology tonight. "Lawson, it's really okay. We were both young. I was stupid. Obviously you're attracted to me now." Her mood seems to lift and her eyes have a sparkle to them when she throws out her next words. "I mean how could you not be? I'm freakin' amazing."

She's trying to make light of the situation by laughing about it, but I can tell she's trying to move on from this topic. Before I let that happen I have to clear the air.

"That you are, Mac. That you are." I flash her a smile. "I'd still like to apologize. You're right, we were both young and I was a stupid guy in my mid-twenties. I won't lie and say I ever thought about you in anything but a brotherly fashion before now, but I want you to know that I'm sorry for what I said. I didn't mean to hurt you."

She looks touched and embarrassed by my apology. Before she can say anything I continue. "Now, though, I can honestly tell you that everything *but* brotherly thoughts are racing through my mind. You're a beautiful woman, Mac. I mean that. I'd like to make it up to you."

I reach over and grab the end of her long braid, savoring the silky texture as I rub the strands at the end between my fingers. The air is charged with our mutual attraction and I can hear her breathing get shallower, her chest starting to rise more rapidly.

"You'd like to make it up to me?"

"Mmhmm, just tell me how."

"Okay, I've got it. I know how you can make it up to me."

"And how's that?" Man, I really hope she says I can make it up to her with my fingers or my mouth or, better yet, my cock.

"Tell me about your most embarrassing moment."

I stare at her for a moment, not sure if I heard her correctly. Her expression is playful but I know she's serious. I groan because this is not a story I want to tell. "My most embarrassing moment?"

"Yep! If you do this I'll accept your apology and call us even."

She looks excited now, and even though it isn't the kind of excitement I was hoping for, I can't find it in me to take it away.

"You have yourself a deal." I release her hair and lay my arm behind her on the bench. "It's bad that I don't even have to think about it, but my most embarrassing moment happened when I was twenty."

"I'm listening."

Oh, she's listening all right. Her look of anticipation is so obvious. If I gave her a bucket of popcorn she'd look like she was sitting in a movie theater.

"This never leaves you. Ever," I clarify.

"My lips are sealed," she says as she runs her fingers over those lips I've been obsessed with, the same lips I had mine on yesterday.

Forcing my mind away from the dirty path it wants to go down, I relive the details of a day I'd rather forget. "I blame myself, and I definitely blame Langley. We used to play pranks on each other all the time, and this was one of those times when a prank goes wrong. We've always been really close. At the time she was only twelve, and even at that age she was always in the kitchen, trying to make things. It was my turn to get her back, and I thought I was so smart because I was going to put laxative in one of her baking experiments."

"Oh, this is gonna be good," Mac says, leaning forward slightly so she can hang on to my every word.

"Probably not the word I'd use," I say. "I had it all planned out. She was making crème brûlée that day, and I put laxative in her batch. At the time she was her main taste tester because no one really believed she'd get very good. We all thought it was just a passing hobby. Anyhow, I had a date that night and planned on getting ready after my run. I remember coming into the kitchen, and Langley handed me my protein shake like usual. To this day I still don't know how she managed it, but it turns out the little witch was on to me. She found the laxative drops I had stashed away, dumped the batter I ruined, and added the drops to my shake."

"No!" Mac gasps. "She didn't! What happened next?"

Her shock makes me laugh. "Oh, she sure did, darlin'. Langley is a clever little sneak. Let's just say I was having issues the entire night, and they kicked in shortly after I left for my date. For most of the night I was having to rush off to use the bathroom."

At this point Mac is trying to stifle her giggles by covering her mouth with her hand. "That's terrible!"

"It gets worse." Fuck, why am I continuing this story? I realize it's because I like hearing her laughter. "I think my date was willing to overlook my need to use the bathroom because she leaned over to kiss me when I dropped her off at home at the end of the night. Before we could even kiss, my stomach made itself known and...uh...*Iendedupsharting*," I rush out.

"Huh? You what?"

At this point I'm running both hands over my face in embarrassment, my face heating. "I ended up sharting. Needless to say, I never saw that girl again. She actually ended up moving."

Of course she bypasses my last two sentences and goes

in straight for the kill. "You mean shit-farting? You sharted? That's actually a thing?!"

"Yep. It sounded and smelled awful. Worst. Moment. Ever."

I'm still hiding behind my hands, but when I don't hear her respond I lower them to check on her. She's gone from sitting straight to almost laying down next to me, silent tears streaming down her face. She's clutching her stomach, and her face is redder than the apple she's named after.

"Mac, you okay?"

All I get in response is a sound that resembles a wheeze. Seeing her lose control soon has me joining in on the laughter. I'm not sure how much time passes, but we both sit here and laugh uncontrollably. Eventually Mac tries to pull herself together and is practically hiccuping with the effort to stay calm. Wiping the tears from her eyes and cheeks she looks at me and, for the first time ever, I'm glad I told someone that story.

"That was priceless." Some giggles escape, but she does a nice job of not losing it again. "Your secret is safe with me, but *wow*. That story trumps my embarrassing story and that of everyone else I've ever met."

"Gee, thanks." My sarcasm is heavy but I can't fight the grin that's stuck on my face.

"Langley is officially my hero. I'll need to ask her how she knew."

"Yeah, well, if you find out let me know. She's refused to tell me over the years, and I figure I'll only find out the truth on my deathbed."

This sets Mac off on a smaller round of laughter, the happy sound making me feel warm inside. "If I find out I promise I'll let you know."

"Thanks, I appreciate it."

"Mmhmm," she sounds out, her eyes sparkling from the tears of laughter she shed. She looks so happy, her mouth turned up in a smile and her cheeks a warm peach color from her giggles.

Seeing her so carefree and unburdened of her self-doubt leaves me unable to resist her sweetness any longer. Before she can process my next move, I lean in and capture her smiling lips with mine. I swallow the tiny laugh that turns into a gasp and savor her honeyed taste. Our kiss is just as explosive as it was yesterday, and before I know it she's halfway on my lap.

Every place our bodies touch causes the current of desire underneath my skin to rise like the tide. I fist one hand in her hair and place the other at her waist as I groan, deepening the kiss between us even more. I lick into her mouth, and her tongue tastes like sweet milk chocolate and smooth whiskey. She moans into our joined lips as she runs her hands up and down my torso. The feel of her small hands roaming across my body almost snaps my control. I force myself to reign it back in before I strip her bare and fuck her on the porch with nothing but the twilight sky and trees to serve as witnesses.

I slow my kisses and press my forehead against hers, our labored breaths mingling together as we try and compose ourselves once again.

"Sorry, I couldn't help myself," I say, even though the tone of my voice shows I'm anything but sorry.

"Mmm," she lightly moans. "No need to ever apologize for that."

Both of her hands have moved around my neck, and I'm enjoying the feeling of having her close. "How about we take this back to my place, darlin'? We can continue there."

I keep my eyes on her lips as I wait for her response.

Seconds pass, and I'm worried I may have pushed her. I know we're both on the same page about the nature of our relationship, but I was raised a gentleman. If she wants to wait, then we'll wait. I think she'll tell me just that when her lush lips finally part to give me her answer.

"What was it you said the other night?" she asks before her lips lift in a smile. "Tonight I'm yours. Let's go, Lawson."

Thank fuck.

10

The ride back to Lawson's place isn't short enough. If I thought the ride home from Smokey's was filled with sexual tension, it's nothing compared to the atmosphere filling the truck's cab like a heady aphrodisiac. We don't speak the entire ride, the only communication between us heated glances that linger like a lover's kiss. I feel like years of quietly admiring and wanting this man are finally culminating in a night I could have only experienced in my wildest dreams.

The desire that's been bubbling below the surface has me feeling ready to combust when we finally arrive at Lawson's place. I have a hunch he feels the same because as soon as we pull into his parking spot he cuts the engine, hops out, and is at my door in the blink of an eye. I unbuckle and gasp in surprise when he grabs me and throws me over his shoulder.

"I can walk, you know," I say to his back, my braid swishing with each step he takes.

"I know darlin', but I don't want to give you the chance to escape me like last time." His words are matter-of-fact, honest, and turn me the hell on. Just the idea of being at his mercy causes my panties to dampen.

He swiftly carries me up the stairs, and I can't help but be impressed at his strength. I mean I see the man carrying around piles of wood all day, but experiencing his strength firsthand makes me impossibly hotter. I try to discreetly rub my thighs together to relieve the ache in my center when he smacks my ass cheek with one hand and grips my thighs with the second. "I told you I'd take care of you, Mac. Don't be doing that."

I quietly groan in frustration and renewed lust. Oh Lord, is this happening? I send up a silent prayer that I won't wake up and discover that this is some cruel, ultra-realistic fantasy. I feel my excitement ratchet up further when I hear the jingle of keys and the opening of his door. As soon as we enter he kicks the door shut with his foot, and my world spins as he sets me on my feet.

We stand here and stare at one another for drawn out seconds before he steps close to me and presses my back against the wall. He raises his hand, and I'm disappointed when he reaches past me to lock the door instead of touch me. He must be able to read my expression because his answering smirk is devilish.

"You sure about this, Mac?" His words drip with want, his voice deeper and his drawl more pronounced.

"Yes," I breathe out eagerly.

"Good." He moves closer. "I hope you don't mind that I'm putting out on the first date."

His words and the accompanying wink he gives momentarily alleviate the lust hanging in the air. "I hope you don't mind that I'm doing the same."

He moves closer and presses his body against mine so

I'm trapped between him and the door. "I'll show you just how much I don't mind," he growls.

In the next moment his mouth slants over mine, and I'm lost to the sensation of our kiss. It's as if we picked up right where we left off back on the bench, our lips moving frantically and with uninhibited passion. As our tongues duel I circle my arms around Lawson's neck and play with the hair at the base of his head. He groans into my mouth and I arch into him, wanting to get as close as possible. With a shift of his hands from my lower back to my hips, I'm lifted up into his arms and pinned against the wall. He guides my legs to wrap around his waist, and his hands start to roam over my fiery skin. Even if I wanted to I couldn't escape, and I rejoice in that fact.

We kiss and learn each other's lips for what feels like hours before his mouth starts a burning path to my neck. I tilt my head back and press further into the door to give him as much access as possible. He lays open-mouthed kisses to my neck and continues on to my collarbone. I gasp in surprise as he sucks on the tender spot at the base of my throat and moves to lift up my shirt at the same time.

"Off. Now." His voice is guttural and spurs me to quickly yank my tank top over my head. Lawson immediately leans in and resumes his kissing across my breasts.

"Yours, too," I pant. The words are barely out of my mouth before he reaches for the fabric at the back of his neck and pulls it over his head, the only things keeping me in place his hips and growing hardness. Seeing him shirtless is like looking at a golden statue come to life; he's all hard angles and warm, lean muscle.

I run my hands over his chest and abs, the muscles shifting and tightening under my touch. I think he's going to remove my bralette, but he surprises me yet again when he trails his kisses down my cleavage and over my exposed stomach. He is close to my belly button when he startles me by swiftly unbuttoning my shorts and pulling them down my thighs along with my panties, all while I have my legs wrapped around his waist and am pinned against his front door. I don't even have time to blush at being exposed in front of him because he grabs each of my legs and efficiently unhooks them from behind his back. He gets down on both knees and simultaneously places my thighs over his shoulders with the grace of a dancer and steadiness of a surgeon, fitting his head between my pussy and my shorts. He does this, and the entire time my feet never touch the ground and our bodies never lose contact. The man has talent.

He looks up at me before leaning in and placing a gentle bite on each of my inner thighs. A small jolt runs through me at the contact, and his eyes lower to my center, which is spread open and weeping with desire. He stares at my pussy for long moments, and I start to feel nerves creep in because my past experiences with receiving oral have been lackluster. I open my mouth to tell him we can move on to other things.

"Lawson, you don't have to. We can skip this."

His eyes slowly travel up my body, and when they meet my gaze he quirks an eyebrow. He holds me captive with his eyes as he leans in closer to my pussy and gives it a long, slow lick from bottom to top. I bow my body out from the wall at the sensation and he chuckles.

"Darlin', trust me, I want to. We are not skipping this."

I try one last time to convince him, but he interrupts my efforts. "Shh, Mac. A true gentleman knows a lady always comes first." His cool breaths puffing against my lower lips creates the sweetest ache as they contrast with the heat radiating from my body. "Just sit here and enjoy it cause I sure as hell will. Enjoy *me*," he grounds out as he leans back in, doing everything *but* gentlemanly things to my body as he devours me.

I'm going wild from sensory overload as he licks me and almost jump out of my skin when I feel his focus shift from my folds to my clit. His tongue alternates between flicking it with the tip and circling it with the wide, flat part, each and every movement driving me insane. His hot, wet tongue and the soft and scratchy feeling of his facial hair causes goose-bumps to erupt all over my body. I squirm against his mouth, and it seems to turn him on further because his grip on my thighs tightens as his hands spread me wider for his oral assault.

"Your pussy is so fuckin' sweet, darlin'," he says against me, the vibrations and the words themselves driving me closer to the brink.

He leans back in, and his licks are unhurried as he tastes me. I lose track of time as he licks along my slit and shifts his focus between each part of me. My eyes are squeezed shut, and I have a hand fisted in his hair that I use to keep him close. I feel one hand move from my thigh, and my eyes fly open once I feel him penetrate me with his fingers.

"Mmm, Mac, you're so tight," he moans. The combination of him pressing his long, capable fingers inside of me as he continues to flick his tongue against me is awe-inspiring and has me at the edge of an impending orgasm.

I press more of my weight against the wall as I sit on his shoulders and enjoy the onslaught of sensation as he takes his time with me. I dance along the edge of release until he pulls away for a second and says, "Come for me, darlin'."

"Law—*awww*!" His name is both a curse and a prayer because in the next second his fingers press a spot inside of me that has never been touched before. The feeling is devastatingly intense, but I'm pushed over the edge into an orgasm when he brings his lips to my clit and sucks as if his life depends on it.

Holy fuck. I cry out as I come against his face, the shudders racking through me for endless moments as I see stars. He gentles his ministrations as I finally start to come down from my high and, with one final kiss, he leans back and smiles at me. My breathing is labored and my legs are relaxed as I sit here. I'm still recovering when he stands back up, my legs still around his neck, and maneuvers me like we're swing dancing. My feet still don't touch the ground as he carries me through his darkened condo to a comfortable-looking couch.

He lays me down, and I languidly watch him with eyes heavy from my release as he starts to strip. He removes his jeans, and I briefly admire his strong thighs before my attention is drawn elsewhere. In the next instant my eyes widen because he drops his boxer briefs to reveal his cock. *Holy shit.* I'm no virgin and have had a few sexual partners over the years, but I've never seen Lawson's equal. I fear I might be ruined after tonight. He's long and thick and so hard for me, a tiny hint of precum leaking out of the tip. I sit up, eager for a taste and ready to return the favor, when he stops me.

"I need you now," he says, his voice throaty.

I'm disappointed and decide to let him know it. "Fine, but just know I want your cock in my mouth at some point." I'm utterly serious.

He looks happy to hear my words, and his trademark smirk comes back for a moment. "Deal. You ready for me, Mac?" he asks as he fists his long length.

I'm hypnotized by it and nod, my affirmation barely audible. He chuckles, grabs my thighs, and drags my body to the edge of the couch so my butt is hanging slightly off of it. He's still standing, and I watch as he removes a condom from his back pocket and slides it on. He grabs one leg and throws it over the crook of his elbow as he grabs his length and brings it to my entrance.

"I need you to say it, darlin'. Are you ready? Do you want this?" There's no way in hell I'm changing my mind, but I appreciate the fact he's still checking with me.

"Yes and yes," I say, loud and clear. I lean up and press a quick kiss to his lips before laying back down on the couch. "I'm yours tonight, Lawson. Do what you will," I smile cheekily.

My words cause a low groan to escape his taut throat, and I feel the tip of his cock finally press against me.

I've never been with someone of his size so I am thankful that he takes his time entering me. With each inch that enters he gives me time to adjust, slowly penetrating and withdrawing until he knows I'm ready for more. I don't know how long it takes, but once he's fully buried inside I feel fuller than I've ever been before. Having him inside of me and above me is overwhelming in the best possible way. He gives me a few more moments to adjust to his cock inside of me as peppers kisses on my lips and over my cheeks before he starts to move.

And oh, does that change things. The heavy drag of his cock as it leaves my body has me whimpering for more, only to gasp in pleasure when he starts to press back into me. I writhe against the couch as he picks up his pace and as his thrusts become more intense. His stamina is unmatched as he continues to drive into my body. At some point my bralette is removed and he uses the roughened pads of his fingers to play with my nipples before leaning in and capturing them with his hot mouth one at a time.

I'm delirious and, shockingly, feel another orgasm start to build at the base of my toes and travel to all of the painfully aroused parts of my body. "Oh my God," I moan, my voice keening. "I'm so close. *Soclosesoclosesoclose.*"

"Fuck yes, darlin'. Give it to me," he pants as he looks at my body hungrily.

"I don't know if I can," I breathe, not sure what it'll take to get me there.

He seems to know what I need because all he says is "You can" before his thrusts pick up and he starts to slam into me. It feels incredible, but I'm rendered speechless when his cock starts to hit the spot inside me that his fingers found earlier. He couples this sensation with his fingers as he reaches down and starts to circle and then pinch my clit.

My vision blacks out as I come for the second time, my inner muscles pulsing and squeezing him as he continues to drive into me. He chases his orgasm relentlessly while I come apart underneath him and, with a hoarse cry moments later, he joins me as well. I feel his cock twitch inside me as he is overtaken by his orgasm, and my muscles continue to squeeze him tightly. I can't help but admire his body, fascinated by his flexed muscles and blissful expression as he finishes coming.

When we both recover somewhat from our release he pulls out and efficiently removes his condom. I close my eyes as he steps away to toss it in the trash and am touched when he returns and wipes me in between my legs with a warm cloth. I smile; he really is a gentleman. Once he finishes taking care of me, he lifts my body and spins so that he's laying on the couch with me on top. We lay there for God knows how long, basking in the aftermath of our shared pleasure. I was expecting it to be good, but I wasn't expecting it to be so passionate.

I decide to finally break the silence. "I didn't think it'd be that good when you said you'd take care of me," I say jokingly, although I think we both know I'm completely serious.

"Oh Mac," he chuckles, "You haven't seen anything yet. Just you wait. I have a lot more taking care of you to do."

Lord, help me. I may just die from pleasure.

SUNSHINE KISSES MY EYELIDS, the gentle warmth lulling me out of the most satisfying sleep I've had in ages. I stretch my limbs and find that I'm deliciously sore and feel my face break out in a smile as I open my eyes. As I look around and down at my body beneath the blanket, I realize I'm still naked and am still on Lawson's couch. The sex really must've been as mind-blowing as I thought if I was able to sleep so well on a couch. I realize belatedly that I'm alone on the couch and sit up, looking around the condo for the man responsible for my body's feeling of euphoria.

I run my hand through my tangled mess of hair that fell out of its braid at some point last night and see a small rectangular card on the coffee table next to me. I grab the small note and rub my thumb over the heavy, textured card stock as I read.

Hey darlin', I had a few errands to run and couldn't bring myself to wake you. Something must've tuckered you out last night. ;) It might be a little late for this but my cell number is on the back. Call or text whenever you want a repeat of last night, which was amazing. You were amazing. You ARE amazing.
—Lawson

I turn the card over in my hands and see it's one of his business cards, his cell number scrawled neatly at the bottom under the embossing. I feel my smile widen as I clasp the card and pull it close to my chest. He can sure be sweet for someone who says he only wants something temporary. I wonder if he's like this all the time or if, like every girl hopes at some point, this is different. I know what I signed up for, but a tiny part of me really wants this to be different. Old feelings really do die hard with this man.

11

LAWSON

I panicked and, like a spineless wuss, I left. I didn't even realize that Mac and I had fallen asleep in my living room. One minute we were laying down on the couch as we came down from our memorable fuck, and the next the soft scent of apples was teasing me awake. Once I woke up and realized why I wasn't asleep in my bed, I took a good look at the woman draped across my chest. I'm not in the habit of having sleepovers with the women I fuck, even accidental ones, so I was surprised I even put myself in this position in the first place.

Who knew that someone who looks like such an angel would be such a hot fuck? I expected our sex to be explosive, but I didn't expect this feeling of closeness with her. It's probably because I've known her for so long. That's gotta be it. What's more surprising is that I didn't feel panic or the immediate need to wake her up and send her on her way. I couldn't shake the feeling of how right it felt having her in my arms. Even in sleep she's stunning, and I had to force myself to stop gazing at her. Her long hair curled around her body and her soft breaths feathered across my skin, creating a deep feeling of contentment in my chest.

I couldn't resist touching her and ran my hands gently up and down her back. My touch caused her to stretch and purr like a kitten, a sweet sigh of satisfaction finally leaving her lips before she nuzzled closer to my body. I stayed there listening to her sleep, and although I could easily wake her up for another round, I decided that I couldn't bring myself to wake her. I could, however, remove myself from the equation and get back on familiar ground by leaving. I scrawled a note on the back of a business card for her and had to shake my head in disgust at my sweet message. What the fuck am I doing?

A few hours have passed, and I've finished running the errands that could have waited until another day. I'm headed home from the gym and decide at the last minute to stop by the grocery store so I can get my meal prepping out of the way today. I may as well continue my productive streak. I pull into Starwood Grocer's parking lot and head inside. I don't even make it ten steps into the store with my cart before someone calls my name.

"Lawson? Lawson Westbrook? Is that you?" I groan internally at the saccharine, high-pitched voice. I force a smile on my face as I turn toward the voice and wave.

"Yes, Mrs. Du Bois. The one and only. I hope you're having a great day," I say. I fully intend to keep walking but see that she starts to make her way over to me.

"Oh goodness, you get handsomer every time I see you," she titters. "How's your family doing?"

"My family is great, thank you. How's your family doing?" I already know where this is leading in three, two, one...

"Oh, Della is doin' great, thank you. I'll tell her you asked about her," she beams.

I didn't ask about her but okay, you do that lady. I stand here for what must be five minutes as she prattles on and on about her daughter. This just reinforces my decision to not date, let alone anyone in this town, because I can't go anywhere without some overzealous mama trying to pair me up with their daughter. This town is a nightmare for any eligible bachelor. My patience finally reaches its limit so I jump on the chance to speak when she takes a breath between sentences.

"Okay, well I've gotta get goin', Mrs. Du Bois. It was nice talkin' to you. You have a good day now, okay?"

"Alright, dear. You take care. I know you live on your own, what with you bein' a bachelor and all, so if you need a home-cooked meal you let me know. My Della is the best cook in town and we'd love to have you over."

Yeah, not happening. She seems to have forgotten that no one can outcook my sister and that I can easily visit my family at their estate. Sometimes I really hate being part of such a prominent family.

"I'll keep that in mind," I say as I start to step away. "Thanks for the offer. Good day now," I tip my head and take long strides away from her. Sweet freedom.

I manage to do most of my shopping without interruption. I go through my mental checklist and realize I just need to grab a gallon of milk before I get out of here and head to my place. I'm on my way to the dairy section when I hear a familiar humming noise down the ice cream aisle. I turn in the direction of the sound and see Mac grabbing a small tub of the good stuff. Before I decide if I want to keep walking or at least say hi, she lifts her head and her eyes are right on me.

I thought that some of my desire for her would burn out after we fucked and that we'd continue our fling in a casual, comfortable way. Yeah, no way in hell there's anything casual about how my cock twitches like a metal detector that found a pot of gold when she looks at me. If anything, I want her more than before because I know what she tastes like and what she sounds like when she comes apart underneath me. I grip my shopping cart and try to get my thoughts under control because a beautiful smile spreads across her face as she heads toward me.

"Hey you," she says.

"Hey yourself," I reply.

Neither of us say anything as we look at each other. She gives a slight shiver, and I'm not sure if it's from the charged feeling growing between us or from the cool air in the aisle. Either way, I'm tempted to push her against one of the freezer doors and heat her up with everything I've got. Before I can say anything she reaches to the right of me, grabs something off of the endcap, and places it in her basket. The need for sex that is overriding my brain is momentarily distracted as I take a look at what she grabbed.

"What is that?" I ask.

"It's syrup?" Her statement comes out as a question, and she's looking at me like I'm crazy.

"Everyone knows the best stuff is Hershey's. Everything else is just a knockoff." I cross my arms over my chest and lean down slightly, trying to impress upon her the importance of my words.

"You and everyone else are wrong," she retorts, a sparkle in her eye. "You've been missing out. You've never had Coco Shell syrup?"

"Um, no."

She looks shocked and amused. "It's the best thing ever!"

Excitement fills her expression and tone as she talks about how the syrup hardens over the ice cream and creates a chocolate shell. She really is adorable, and I can feel myself hardening as I watch her animatedly describe fucking syrup. I'd really like her this animated over something else I could show her that can harden.

I don't even realize I've taken a step closer to her until she stops speaking.

"Sorry, darlin'. I got distracted." I can't even lie. I stare at her lips, and she licks them nervously before she speaks.

"It's okay. I was sayin' you could try it some time. You should stop by the house." Her voice has lowered and is breathy with desire.

I don't have the chance to respond and tell her I'd like that very much before a familiar voice grates along my senses. Jesus. I was so caught up in Mac that I forgot where I am.

"Why would you be going to the Layne household, Lawson?"

I grit my teeth, take a few steps away from Mac, and turn toward Mrs. Du Bois. This woman is really trying my patience today, and it's really none of her damn business what I do.

"Oh hi, Mrs. Du Bois. It's great to see you. How are you?" Mac asks politely.

The old biddy's attention shifts to Mac for a moment while she responds. "Just fine, dear. Now Lawson," her eyes shift back to where I stand, "why on earth would you be goin' to the Layne household?" This woman's nosiness knows no bounds.

"I was just telling him that he should come over and try —" Mac manages to get out before I smoothly interject.

"She was just telling me I should come over and try the

new wood cutter her father bought. The only reason I go over there nowadays is because I'm working on renovating the old barn, ma'am."

"Oh, that's all? I thought somethin' else was going on." Mrs. Du Bois laughs as if the thought is absurd. What a rude woman.

Out of the corner of my eye I see Mac bristle. She looks like she's about to say something so I continue explaining. "Smith Layne is my best friend, ma'am. I've been a friend of the Layne family for a long time. Everyone knows that, especially Mac. We're friends, too."

"Yes, ma'am," she says, her voice slightly strained. "Just friends. Lawson's just a great friend of the family. He's doing us all a favor by helping us out."

I can see her smiling and feel relief wash over me. I'm so glad she gets it. The last thing I want is this town gossiping about us and thinking that I'm starting to date. That'd be awful, and the endless parade of available daughters would increase in voracity.

"Well, good. I need to get goin', but don't forget what I said earlier, Lawson dear. It'd be so nice to have you over for dinner. I know Della would love to see you again," she smiles. With those parting words Mrs. Du Bois scuttles away and leaves us alone in the aisle again.

I turn to Mac, and she speaks once it's obvious Mrs. Du Bois isn't coming back. "Well, I need to get going. It was good seeing you."

"Yeah, you too. I'll see you later." She starts to scoot around me, and before she's out of my sight I call out to her. "Hey, Mac?"

She stops and turns, her expression curious. "Yes, Lawson?"

"You've got my number now. Let me know when you'd

like to pick up where we left off," I say with a wink. I'd really like to get her out of her clothes again.

An unreadable expression flashes across her face, but it's gone faster than a hummingbird's wings and is replaced with a mischievous smile. "You got it. See ya, Lawson."

I watch her ass as she walks away and can feel the anticipation to have her start to build again. I hope she calls soon, or I may have to take matters into my own hands.

I TRY to control my breathing as I walk away from Lawson and head aimlessly in the opposite direction. I don't know why I'm so bothered by what just happened. I've known from the beginning what he wants from me but didn't think he'd fail to even acknowledge any type of intimate relationship with me in public. Even though it was awkward and sucked, I'm glad I know now so I can keep myself in check. I decide to head to the self-checkout aisle and quickly ring my items up. Our conversation comes to mind as I bag the ice cream and chocolate syrup, and I have to stop the smile from forming on my face.

I can't have feelings for this man, and things can't get weird. Ever. Why does he have to be so damn sexy? His scruff looked extra delicious under the added shadow of his baseball hat, and his muscles were shown off to perfection in his gym clothes. I need to keep things physical. That is, after all, all he wants from me.

So much for being different, a small, sad voice in my head says.

12

It's Wednesday, and I've managed to keep my pants on and my sanity in check. I'd like to attribute this to the fact that I'm staying strong, but it's helped that Lawson hasn't come to work at the orchard the last two days. Between finally sleeping together and the incident at the grocery store on Saturday, I've jumped at the opportunity to use this time to think. Am I equipped to have a no-strings attached relationship? Am I overreacting? Do I secretly hope for something to blossom between us outside of sex? Am I sexed up so well that I can't think straight? After having time to think, I've finally been able to answer these questions.

Can I keep it casual? Yes. I haven't done casual before so this is a good opportunity for me to work on any hang-ups. Who knows, I may want to try this again in Chicago.

Me, overreacting? Maybe. I don't like feeling like someone's dirty secret, even though we did get down and dirty. I can't get too angry though because it's not like I can casually tell everyone in town that I'm jonesing on Lawson's dick and am having newfound orgasm withdrawals.

Do I want more than sex? My inner teenager does. Grown ass woman Mac? Hell no. I just need to separate the two and I'll be good.

Scrambled sex brain? Yes, yes, so much *yes*. Lawson literally fucked the memory of every other guy out of my brain and to think, he is just getting started.

A shiver runs through my body at the thought of how he makes my body feel. That man is dangerous. As much as I want to have a repeat or two or three of our steamy encounter, I'm torn on how to move forward. On one hand, I don't want to seem desperate for the way he makes my body come alive. On the other hand, maybe I should just reach out and show him I can handle this. Why does this have to be so hard?

Thankfully I'm able to work through some of my frustration, both mental and sexual, on the inside of the barn. The past few days have been dedicated to giving it the deep clean it sorely needed. I survey the interior and feel a deep sense of genuine satisfaction, which is something I haven't felt in a very long time. Planting my hands on my hips, I turn in a slow circle so I can get a good look at what I've been able to accomplish. Every surface of this place has been wiped, scrubbed, and wiped again. The once dusty, neglected barn is now glistening and welcoming. I draw in a deep breath and enjoy the clean scents of fresh summer air and lemon cleaning solution. Now I'll be able to fill it with supplies for making cider and can reconfigure the layout so guests won't be able to resist the invitation to come inside. I feel my excitement amp up as I think about all I need to do.

"I'm going to be busy," I happily say out loud.

"Hopefully not too busy for me," a deep voice says behind me.

A decidedly unladylike shriek leaves my throat as I whirl

around, one hand clutching the fabric over my heart and the other reaching for the closest thing as a weapon. Unfortunately for me, said weapon is a spray bottle full of cleaner but hey, maybe I can momentarily blind whoever snuck up on me so I can make a quick getaway.

I make my full rotation, and for a moment my mind doesn't truly register what's in front of me. Instead of some strange man, I see Lawson in all his lumbersexual glory. He's standing in front of me, looking ridiculously handsome with an expression on his face that's a cross between surprise and an urge to hold in uncontrollable laughter. We stand and stare at each other for a few moments, the spray bottle still outstretched between us, and the laughter wins with Lawson. He throws his head back and laughs, the sound deep and uninhibited, and I have to check my jaw for drool as I watch him.

I put the bottle down and cross my arms over my chest as I wait for him to quit laughing. While I wait I admire his strong form encased in dark jeans and a blue shirt, the sleeves rolled up at the elbows showcasing his insanely sexy forearms. Leave it up to the bastard to show up at the end of the day looking sexier than hell when I'm sweaty and dusty.

It takes a solid minute before he can calm down enough to stop laughing, which is enough time for me to pull my gaze away from his arms. A couple rogue chuckles slip out, but he does an admirable job trying to compose himself, his mossy eyes filled with mirth as he looks at me. His gaze drifts over my body and his eyes darken, his expression becoming more serious when his gaze catches on the cleavage created by my folded arms. I shake my head. Men are so predictable.

"Why'd you sneak up on me?" I ask. "You should know that's rude!"

"I'm not exactly a small guy, Mac," he retorts. "I didn't even try to sneak up on you. I figured you would've heard me."

"Well, I obviously didn't. Don't do it again," I say, brandishing a fist toward him as I give him my best *or else* look.

"Or what, Mac? You gonna spray me with cleaner? I'm a dirty man but that's not going to stop me." His eyes are twinkling as he looks at me with a damned crooked smile curving his lips.

"Shut up. It was all I had," I huff indignantly.

At this I can see that he's trying to compose himself again. He places his large hand over his mouth and scrubs at the facial hair on his jaw in an attempt to stay calm.

"Why were you talking to yourself, anyway? Who does that?"

I give him my best blank stare. "It's perfectly normal to talk to yourself."

"Oh, is it now?" he asks.

"Yep. Oh, and what do you mean by you hope I'm not too busy for you?" I glare at him suspiciously.

"I haven't heard from you and decided to come see what you've been up to."

"You would've seen what I've been up to if you'd been here," I state.

"I know you missed me," he smiles when he sees the expression on my face, "but I had to go supervise a new job and get some paperwork taken care of. I'll be here the rest of the week."

Oh goody.

"You still haven't answered my question," I push.

"I thought that'd be obvious. I told you to call me. You never did, so this is me trying to pick up where we left off," he says as his voice deepens. In this moment he looks predatory, like a hunter, as he waits for me to respond.

"I was busy," I shrug as nonchalantly as I can. "But I'm sure I can make an exception. My place or yours?" I'm proud of myself for getting right down to the true meaning of this visit.

"I was actually hoping I could take you to dinner tonight."

"Dinner?" I can't help but keep the confusion and surprise out of my voice.

He laughs as he responds. "Why do you always look so confused every time I bring up dinner?"

I can't stop the honesty from ripping out of my mouth. "Well, why go to dinner first? Don't you want to...you know?"

"Trust me on this, Mac," he says as he steps closer to me, "I definitely want, but the reason I want to go to dinner is because I haven't had a chance to eat yet. I'm starved, in more ways than one. And besides..." he trails off as he looks at me.

"Besides what?"

"You're going to need all the energy you can get for what I have planned for you." He says this in the most serious voice, his words low and heated.

"What do you have planned?" I can't help the whisper that leaves my lips.

"Just you wait and find out, darlin'." He winks at me and I feel my pussy clench at his words.

I'm tempted to beg him to show me now but swallow the words and ask instead, "What should I wear to dinner?"

He looks pleased that I've agreed to have dinner with him. "Whatever you'd like, darlin'. Just make sure it's easy to take off."

He's deadly serious, and I can't find the words to respond

because they're stuck to the roof of my mouth. He gives my body another glance and leans in to whisper, "I'll be inside waiting. Don't keep me waiting long or I'll come find you, and this time I won't be as nice."

With those parting words, he turns and heads toward the house.

I stand here and try and pull myself from the maelstrom of lust overriding my senses. What is it with this man and his ability to walk away while I'm left as a quivering bundle of desire? I can't even be mad because I know he'll be delivering on his promises later. I shake my head and walk toward the house as well, thinking about what I have to wear. I smile to myself as I head inside because I'm about to give Lawson Westbrook a run for his money.

THE LOOK he gives me when I come downstairs and twirl for him is worth the extra time it took for me to get ready. I have to mentally pat myself on the back for pairing my midnight blue jersey shift dress with black cowboy boots. From the front the dress is perfectly respectable, but the back is a bit more naughty in that it's low-cut and held together by a multitude of thin straps. I almost went with a bandeau top in lieu of a bra but decided to listen to my inner vixen and nix the bra entirely. My shopping trip the other day was definitely a good idea.

I know as soon as I complete my rotation and get a good look at Lawson's face that he wholeheartedly approves of my wardrobe choice. He's usually so charming and well-spoken that I take extra delight in the fact that I've managed to leave him tongue-tied, even if for a few seconds. I want to stick to my plan of having him experience a little of what he makes me feel, so I sway my hips right on out of the house before he can say a word.

We've been in the car for about thirty minutes, and my curiosity is increasing the farther away we get from Starwood. We listen to country music during the drive and eventually turn onto a main road in Fontaine, one of our town's neighboring cities. A few more minutes pass before we pull into the parking lot of a restaurant called Southern Silo. I turn to Lawson and find that he's already smiling at me.

"You read my mind," I say. "I haven't been able to stop getting my fill of Southern cooking."

"Considering the way you devoured our last meal, I thought this would be a safe bet," he teases.

I feign indignation and let out a small huff of laughter as he comes around and opens the door for me. We head inside, and I can't stop the feeling of surprise and giddy hopefulness that blooms in my chest when Lawson grabs my hand. I feel my cheeks warm as my attention shifts solely to the way his large hand grips mine and his fingers swipe over my skin, warm and calloused. I'm grateful for the setting sun and can only hope that the warm rays of fading sunlight mask the blush in my cheeks.

We enter the restaurant, and I'm impressed by the classy and comfortable atmosphere. I notice the hostess eyeing Lawson as we walk up to her booth and can't even bring myself to get upset because honestly, who can blame her? Lawson is a veritable feast for the senses. Between his insanely good looks, deep Southern drawl, and charming personality, he's a force to be reckoned with. I pity the female population and take comfort in the fact that I'm not the only one who seems to be under his spell.

"Hi, I have a reservation under Westbrook," Lawson says politely.

"Oh, it was me that took your reservation down when you called yesterday. We're happy to have you here, Mr. Westbrook."

At her words I turn to look at Lawson, my eyebrow raised quizzically. All I get in the form of an answer is a smirk as I stare at his chiseled profile.

"Yes, sir. Right this way. I'd be happy to take you," our hostess says eagerly.

I'm sure you would, honey. I'm sure you would.

We are led to a table that seems to be a bit separated from the rest, which I don't mind at all. It'll be nice to have Lawson all to myself with no distractions for a bit.

"Here's your table, Mr. Westbrook. Is there anything I can get you?"

"No, thank you. We'll be fine."

The hostess struts away, and Lawson pulls out my chair and gently seats me. When he comes around the table to take his seat across from me, I decide to call him out.

"So, a reservation huh? A reservation made yesterday? Am I a backup date?"

"Yeah, my regular couldn't make it so I figured why not? I know there's no way you can resist me," he says. His face is completely serious but a decidedly impish gleam lights up his eyes.

My response is immediate. "You betcha. You're a sure thing, Lawson. Who would resist in the first place? Although I'm slightly offended that I'm a benchwarmer."

His lips twitch slightly, but he maintains his straight face. "Sure thing, huh? Funny, I thought that about you. As far as your benchwarmer status, I need to be sure you can play hardball with the big leagues before I graduate you to the starting line."

"I assure you that I belong in the big leagues. I'm happy

to show you once you stop giving me little league equipment to play with," I fire back sweetly.

We stare at each other for a moment, neither of us blinking, before Lawson cracks and starts laughing. The hearty sound fills me up with warmth, and I find myself joining in.

"Ouch, darlin'. You wound me." He splays his hand over his heart and tries to appear hurt.

"Don't tell me I'm a benchwarmer, then I won't have to say such things," I grin.

He holds his hands up, both palms facing me, as he continues to laugh. "It won't happen again. But really," he says, "I made the reservation hoping you'd say yes. If you couldn't make it, I would've either brought Langley with me or canceled."

"That's actually really sweet," I admit.

"I know. What can I say? I was raised right." He smiles at me, and I can't help but agree. The Westbrooks did a stellar job raising their children.

"They did alright," I tease.

"Oh, did they now?"

"You know I'm just pulling your leg, Lawson. They did better than okay."

"You can pull something other than my leg," he says in a low voice. The combination of his words and that sexy smirk are downright lethal, so much so that I feel goosebumps start to spread across my skin.

"Oh, stop," I laugh. I try to discreetly rub my arms to chase away the tingling sensation he's caused. Not to mention, I'm also trying to distract myself from crawling under the table to find what he's referring to. I need to at least stay somewhat classy during this dinner.

"You walked right into that one, darlin'," he chuckles.

His voice is back to normal, and he's dialed back his smolder just a bit. Thank heavens.

Dinner is a sumptuous feast, and I'm surprised by how easily conversation flows between us, especially now that we've already slept together. I was under the impression that most of our dinner talk would revolve around sex. Instead, we swap stories and talk about our lives while our sexual attraction quietly simmers beneath the surface. It's beyond nice, and I find myself getting more and more drawn to the man underneath the sexy exterior that my teenage and current self swooned over.

"So, Lawson, last time we had dinner there was an awful lot of talk about me. I know we talked about the house you're building, but tell me something else, please."

He looks pleased that I remember our conversation about the home he's working on. He leans in closer to me over the table and asks, "What would you like to know?"

"Whatever you'd like to share. I'm not picky," I smile, curious to hear what he has to talk about it.

He seems to mull over his words for a few moments before he speaks. "I love and hate our town," he reveals.

Okay, that's a little surprising.

"Why? You're the town's golden boy. Everyone looks up to you and thinks you're awesome." I'm a little embarrassed by my choice of words and can feel my cheeks color, but it's the truth. Everyone in Starwood loves the Westbrook family; they may as well be royalty.

"That's exactly why," he says. He looks a bit surprised that he was so forthcoming with his response, but I don't press him to continue. Instead, I spear a piece of grilled shrimp with my fork and glide it through the creamy cheddar grits. I almost moan with pleasure as I pop the food in my mouth. *I'm really going to miss this food when I go back home*, I think to myself.

Lawson takes his own bite of his chicken fried steak as he thinks before he speaks again. "I grew up in this town, and I love everyone in it. This is home for me, and it's where I can see myself living for the rest of my life. I feel connected to the town like a beating heart. Now that I own my own construction business, I've had even more opportunity to get to know the residents better."

"That's wonderful," I say, because it is. There's something so charming about Starwood that big cities like Chicago just can't compete with or replicate.

"It is, but it's also horrible. It seems like everyone wants to know what's going on in my life. I know they mean well, but there are times when I feel *too* connected to everyone," he explains. "I feel like every mother is tryin' to set me up with their daughter or granddaughter or whoever is available. Being a single, successful man in our hometown has its disadvantages, especially when you come from a family as well-known and as well-connected as mine."

The sad thing is, I know he isn't boasting or exaggerating. Finding a handsome, accomplished man from an affluent family is like hitting the lottery for mothers who want to ensure their daughters marry well. Our town is lovely, but sometimes it can feel like you're living in an Austen novel and every mommy matchmaker is looking for a Mr. Darcy.

"You're the Mr. Darcy of Starwood," I blurt. How embarrassing. Hopefully he doesn't get the reference and we can move on.

"Oh good, as long as I'm not Wickham," he smirks. "I'd even take Bingley, but I like being the leading man. I just wish I could do it with more privacy."

Color me surprised. Lawson just earned major kudos by understanding my Darcy reference. Damn him. I'm trying not to like the guy's brain as much as I do.

"I applaud you for staying unattached this long, old man," I joke.

"I plan on staying unattached for much longer," he admits seriously. "I don't like the idea of being tied down right now. I want to focus on me and my business. If the right woman happens to come along later I'll know it and can change my plan. My intentions will be loud and clear when I'm serious about someone because I'll be able to breathe easy knowing everyone will back off when that happens. Until then, I plan on having fun and keeping things casual. I feel like all the scrutiny everyone puts me under makes it hard for me to pursue anything at my own pace."

His words shouldn't hurt, but they cause a slight twinge in the area of my heart. Dammit, I thought I was in the clear. It's probably just my natural reaction to being unintentionally rejected. I may not be his forever woman but I'm going to enjoy being Ms. Right Now while I'm in town.

"Do what makes you happy, Lawson," I say with honesty. Really, please do whatever makes you happy. Preferably me.

"Thanks, Mac. I appreciate you being so understanding."

"Of course."

We're momentarily saved from continuing the conversation when our waiter comes by to refill our wine.

"Would you fine folks like some dessert this evening? Tonight's specials include house-made peach ice cream, praline bread pudding with vanilla sauce, and bananas foster with house-made vanilla ice cream."

Lawson and I stare at one another before we both

respond at the same time. "Peach ice cream to share, please."

Our waiter walks off with our order as we laugh over our jinx. We steer our conversation back to lighter topics, and by the time our dessert arrives the twinge in my heart feels like the distant memory of a dull ache.

I pick up my spoon and scoop up some of the peach ice cream. It smells divine and the texture looks velvety and delectable. Lawson follows suit and we both bring our spoonfuls to our mouths at the same time. Unfortunately, I completely miss his reaction because my taste buds are being attacked by the sweet flavor of fresh peaches. I swipe the ice cream off the spoon with my tongue and have to stop myself from moaning out loud at the taste.

I look up and see that Lawson is watching me, his darkened eyes fixated on my mouth. "What? Do I have ice cream on my face?" I bring my fingers to my lips and check for ice cream.

"No, your face is perfect. I mean, perfectly fine." I swear I see Lawson shake his head before he continues. "I never thought I'd say this, but the expression you just gave when you tried that ice cream makes me envy your spoon."

He chuckles darkly, and I feel my nipples harden from the deep sound.

"Oh, really now?" I swipe more ice cream up with my spoon and bring it to my lips. Feeling daring, I dart my tongue out and taste the peachy goodness. "How so?"

"You know why," he growls. He's still watching my mouth, his ice cream all but forgotten.

"I think I have an idea," I murmur. My own voice has lowered, and the attraction that was so well-behaved up until this point is beginning to blaze to life with the intensity of a forest fire.

"I think you do too, darlin'." His hands are now clenched into fists on top of the tablecloth, and I can see the rise and fall of his muscular chest as he watches me.

"Mmmmm," I moan lightly. "I don't know how you're ignoring this ice cream, Lawson. It tastes incredible." I continue to slowly lick away at my spoon and revel in the obvious approval and attraction blazing in Lawson's eyes.

"I'd rather taste that sweet pussy of yours for dessert instead." His simple, straightforward statement almost makes me drop my spoon as desire crashes through me. Just thinking about the devastating pleasure his tongue can inflict has my nipples hardened to painful points and my panties uncomfortably wet.

I glance back at him, and he has his bottom lip held captive between his teeth. We stare at one another, and the low hum of the restaurant disappears as we eat each other up with our eyes. I'm not sure how much time passes, but we're dragged back to reality when we hear our waiter clearing his throat.

"Is there anything else I can get you tonight?"

I look at Lawson and a genius idea flashes across my mind.

"Just the check, please. Thank you," I say, keeping my gaze locked on Lawson's while I speak to our waiter.

A gleam of triumph fills Lawson's eyes as the waiter leaves. I may be turned on like a backup radiator in winter but I finally found a way to give Lawson a run for his money. This is going to be too much fun. He won't know what hit him.

13

W e're back in Lawson's truck, and he looks at me expectantly as he turns the key in the ignition. "Where to next, Mac?"

I plaster what I hope is a sweet, innocent smile on my face when I respond. "Shady Layne Orchard, please."

To Lawson's credit he doesn't look upset, confused, or disappointed. He simply nods as he smiles and says, "Whatever you'd like, m'lady," before heading out of the parking lot. His words make me smile, and we head back to Starwood to the soft strains of music floating from the radio. I marvel at how easy it is to have quiet moments with him. Usually I feel the need to fill a silence, but being with Lawson now, the only words between us those from whatever song is playing, make me feel comfortable and at peace.

I glance over as he's driving and feel my pulse spike as I take in his handsome form. He looks so strong and capable at all times, and I feel the urge to see his calm exterior rattled. I bite my lip and look out the window as I try to convince myself to move forward with my plan from the restaurant. I catch a peek of his profile in the reflection of the glass, and seeing him so cool and collected makes my decision for me. I'm doing this.

"Whatever I'd like?" I ask innocently.

"What was that, darlin'?" He tilts his head and shoots a quick glance my way before turning his attention back to the road.

"You said whatever I'd like just now. I was just making sure that's what you meant."

His brow furrows slightly as he processes my words. "Of course I meant it. Why, is everything okay?" The obvious concern coloring his tone makes me smile even more.

"Yes, it's just a little warm in here." To make my point, I fan the area around my face with my hands and touch my cheeks as if checking for warmth.

"Here, let me turn on the air condition—"

"No," I interrupt as he reaches out to turn the dial for air on. "I have something else in mind." As the words leave my lips, I place my hands on my thighs and start running my palms up and down, all the way from the hem of my dress to my knees and back.

I can feel Lawson's eyes track the movement of my hands and, with each pass up and down my thighs, I move them higher. I see Lawson's focus shift between the road and my hands in my peripheral vision. With each swipe I move closer and closer to my center. Inch by inch my dress rides up, and the combination of cool air and heated glances that kisses each sliver of exposed skin causes me to shiver. I shimmy in my seat and am finally able to bunch my dress around my hips so that my legs and panties are completely exposed.

"That feels a little bit better," I proclaim happily. I look at Lawson as I say this and am pleased to see his breathing has picked up. "I think I can do better though."

I hear him gulp and tear my gaze away from his profile as I spread my legs open on the seat. "Mmm, that feels even better."

"I think you can do better than that, darlin'." I'm surprised by Lawson's participation but am simultaneously turned on.

"How so, Lawson?" I ask as I place one had on my inner thigh and run the other over the soft fabric of my panties.

His response is immediate. "Show me your pussy. It's a shame to cover somethin' so perfect up, Mac."

I don't bother responding with words and instead follow his instruction silently. I push my panties to the side and bare myself to him. I turn my head to look at him and lift a questioning brow.

"Yes, just like that." His response is guttural, and he's gripping the steering wheel tightly.

Again, my response doesn't consist of words. Not taking my eyes off of his shadowed and clenched jaw, I cup my rapidly dampening center before gently gathering my wetness with my middle finger and bringing it up to my clit. The contact on my heated flesh has me closing my eyes in pleasure, and I can't stop the moan that comes out.

"Dammit, Mac. You're killin' me." Lawson sounds pained, and I know that he's having difficulty dividing his attention between me and the road.

My eyes are still closed, and I start to rub my clit in earnest. My own breathing is becoming ragged as I touch myself, the pleasure only heightened by the fact that Lawson is watching. I feel moisture leak out as this thought crosses my mind, and I arch my back in my efforts to reach a release.

"That's it, I'm pulling over."

My eyes fly open. "No, keep driving," I say breathily.

"What?" His response is a heady mixture of incredulity and lust.

"Don't stop. Take me home. Please," I beg as I continue to touch myself.

"Fine, but I want to touch," he says as he takes one hand off the wheel and brings it toward my spread legs.

"No, both hands on the wheel. Just focus on driving. Please, Lawson."

Instead of responding with words, Lawson draws his hand back and continues driving. I both hear and feel his groan of frustration at not being able to participate. Knowing that I'm having this effect on him causes a multitude of shivers to race up and down my body.

A few moments pass in silence as I quicken my strokes against my clit until I feel the start of an orgasm tingling deep inside of me.

"Spread that pussy for me, Mac. Show me how you like to be played with."

Oh God, Lawson the gentleman talking dirty to me may be my undoing. I must hesitate too long before responding to his command because a moment later he grits out, "I said spread it for me. Now."

With difficulty I give in and spread my lips with one hand so he can see all of me in the dim light of his truck, all while I continue to rub myself with my other hand.

"Fuck darlin', that's sexy. Yeah, let me see what you're doing to that pretty pussy."

I follow his orders and show him exactly what his words are doing to me. My greedy hands continually dip down into my wetness and swirl it back to my swelling clit. Somehow I have enough presence of mind to look out the window and see that we're pulling up to the entrance of my family's property. I need to come before we get to the house. I quicken my movements and increase the pressure of my fingers. My impending orgasm is so close that I find it hard to keep my eyes open.

"You better not come, Mac," he says harshly. "I told you that I'd be the one to take care of you. I meant it."

His words spark a surge of rebellion inside of me, and I insert a finger inside my tight passage while I quickly flick my clit.

"Oh God," I cry.

"Mac." My name sounds like both a warning and a plea as it leaves his lips. Hearing him say it like that, in a voice rough with desire, has the blackness edging into my vision. With a gasp I feel my orgasm burst, and I swear I see fireworks as my pussy flutters and my body jerks with its release.

I try to slow my breathing and am able to crack my eyes open once I hear the gravel shifting beneath the tires. We must be pulling up to the house now. I chance a look over at Lawson and his knuckles are white with tension, his body practically vibrating with frustration or desire or both. I don't have a lot of time. We finish pulling up the drive, and as soon as he puts the car in park I jump into action. I swiftly unbuckle my seat belt and, before he can so much as move, I'm across the center seat and am unzipping his pants.

"What—?"

"Shh, Lawson. Hands back on the wheel."

I'm beyond surprised when he groans and places his hands where I tell him to. I feel heady with desire knowing that this big, powerful man is at my mercy. I quickly unzip him and pull out his erect member.

"Oh baby, you look like you need some relief," I breathe. Before he has a chance to respond to my comment, I lower my head and lick him from the root of his thick erection to the throbbing tip that's already wet with a drop of precum. His low gasp and ensuing groan spur me on, and I grip him tightly before easing him into my mouth. He's so big that I have to go slow and gradually work his length inside.

"Fuck, darlin'. Just like that. Your sexy mouth feels so fucking good around my cock." His voice is strained, and the only other sounds I hear are his labored breathing and the slight squeak of the steering wheel's leather as he squeezes and releases his hands repeatedly.

Minutes pass as I worship his impressive length with my lips, tongue, and hands. I can feel the rock solid strength of Lawson's tense thighs beneath me and the tightening of his abs against my arm as he gets closer and closer to his own orgasm. I grip him tighter and run my tongue in random patterns all over his skin. He groans loudly and lifts his hips toward me as I swirl my tongue around the tip and follow it with an extra hard suck while twisting my hand at the base. Judging from his reactions, he seems to love this combination, and I quickly repeat it over and over as he sits through the erotic torture, his hands still on the wheel.

"I'm close, Mac. So fucking close," he grates.

His hips are straining as his cock grows even larger in my hands and mouth. Knowing that he's right on the edge, I repeat my combination and pay extra special attention to the small slit that's leaking precum. I want to make him lose control so I pop my lips off of him for a moment.

"Give me your come, Lawson. I want it all," I say as I put him back in my mouth.

He moans in pleasure and agony at my words and sucks in a ragged breath when I quickly follow this with a deep penetration of my throat. My efforts are rewarded when he lets out a long, low moan as he releases in my mouth. I swallow all he has to give me and gently suck him as he twitches and recovers from his orgasm. When he's finished, I sit back up and kiss the tip before letting him go.

"Thanks for dinner and dessert, Lawson," I say as I swiftly lean in and give him a peck on the cheek. I smile at his stunned expression, still languid from his orgasm. "Have a great night. I'll see you later." I smile sweetly and can't help adding in a playful wink before turning and quickly exiting his truck.

I'm walking away with a huge smile on my face. I bring my fingers to my swollen lips and want to shout in joy at the way I made him lose control. I think it's safe to say I did a great job of keeping things strictly physical.

I walk with an extra pep in my step and am almost to the porch when I hear his truck door open and slam shut.

14

My heart stutters in my chest at the sound of the slamming door and hurried steps. I turn and look over my shoulder; I need to make sure I'm not hallucinating. Instead of seeing Lawson driving away in his truck like I hope to see, he's eating up the distance between us in long, determined strides. The easygoing, charming man I'm used to is gone, and in his place is a force of will bent on getting to me. The hunger shining hotly from his eyes and in every rigid muscle makes it abundantly clear that he wants to do something, I'm just not sure what. I shiver in anticipation because I have an idea, but instead of stopping and allowing him to catch me, I quicken my pace.

Behind me I hear Lawson's steps speed up in response, and the dark chuckle he makes reaches my ears and sets my body afire with tingles of awareness. I manage to make it to the porch and up the first step before I feel his hand firmly grab my wrist and pull me back into his hot, hard body. He keeps one hand at my wrist and the other on my stomach, right above my pelvis. His touch is rough as he runs his hand up my body from my belly button, the fabric bunching as it travels through the center of my cleavage and up to my neck.

"Gotcha." His victorious whisper is rough in my ear as he swirls his fingers in soft patterns over the skin of my throat.

I swallow audibly at his touch. "Oh yeah, what are you going to do with me now that you've caught me?" My words are whisper-soft and sound entirely too eager.

Another wicked chuckle tumbles from his lips, and the vibrations it causes in his chest create an electric thrill I feel in every inch of my body. I want nothing more than to be tipped over into the undeniable vortex that is Lawson West-brook and revel in his touch like an addict.

"Ah ah ah," he tuts. "I let you have your turn in the truck. It's my turn now."

Oh God.

I don't have a chance to respond because he's stepping forward, his feet guiding mine up another few steps. The hand at the front of my throat moves to the nape of my neck and, the hand at my wrist moves to my lower back.

"Bend over, Mac," he whispers as he presses his hands down. "Put your hands and knees on the steps for me, and spread those long legs of yours." He presses a little harder against me before he steps back.

I'm drowning in desire and whimper in response because I am helpless to do anything else. Right now all I want to do, all I *can* do, is comply with his demands. My body is trembling and waiting as I place my hands at the top of the steps and touch my knees down a few steps below that. I can feel his presence behind me, laced with so much lust it's like he never stopped touching me.

His deep breaths blend with the sounds of the night around us. I wait for him to do something—anything—to me. I close my eyes when I hear him undo his belt buckle and slide the soft leather open. I bite my lip when I hear the muted sound of his zipper being undone. I subtly tilt my hips toward his body in a silent plea and fully expect him to take me up on my offer. Instead I gasp in surprised delight when he smoothly joins me on the steps, not from behind me but from *under* me. His front is facing my front, and he's sitting on a step lower than where my knees are at, the angle putting his face right in front of my pussy. I glance down and stare at his head between my thighs and almost fall over from desire.

His hands confidently move up the skin of my inner thighs, up my dress, and to the straps of my minuscule thong. In my next breath he rips my panties off, stuffs them into his jeans pocket, and then he settles into position. For good measure, he brings his hands up and around each of my thighs, gripping and squeezing my skin, before taking a deep breath of my aching, wet center that's laid out in front of him.

"Lawson, I was returning the favor from earlier. Please don't feel obligated..." My voice trails off in a gasp because as soon as the last word leaves my mouth, Lawson brings a heavy hand down on one of my ass cheeks. I'm confused, breathless, and so needy I could weep.

"Darlin', this is the last time you're allowed to second-guess me eating your pussy. This," he leans in and kisses my slit, "is all for me. I'm going to make this quick because of where we are, but don't ever doubt that I want to lick your sweetness all day, every day."

Oh God, we're on the front porch. The front porch of my parents' house. Outside.

"But—"

His other hand comes down swiftly on my other ass

cheek. "Stop. The only words I better hear from your mouth are 'Don't stop,' 'yes, more,' or 'give me your cock.' Now, where was I?"

His hands resume their place on my thighs, and I feel my eyes roll in the back of my head when he eagerly attacks my center with his lips and tongue. When he went down on me last time, he took his time and was slow and gentle in the pursuit of helping me reach my climax. Right now, he's voracious and determined to get me off as quickly as possible. My hands and arms tremble with the effort it takes to hold myself up. He continues to lick me, and I almost come apart when his tongue enters my tight passage. I don't even realize that one of my hands has moved to his hair and is pushing him further into my center.

He stops his ministrations briefly, and I want to sob at the loss of contact. "Hands back on the steps, darlin'."

I grip his hair tighter and try to push myself back on his lips to no avail.

I feel the rumble of his laughter against the lips of my sex. "Oh baby, you look like you need some relief."

The bastard is throwing my words back in my face. I breathe deeply, and he teases me by giving me a short lick across my clit that doesn't have nearly the amount of pressure I need.

"I'll take care of you," he licks me briefly again, "if you put your hands back on the steps. Turnabout is fair play, darlin'."

He sounds entirely too amused and smug for his own good, but I'm past the point of caring. I need to feel his mouth on me again. With effort, I remove my hand from his hair and place it back on the step next to my other hand. As soon as my hand touches down on the worn wood, I hear

Lawson's groan of approval as he dives right back into my pussy and licks me as if he never paused.

"Please, don't stop," I beg.

My words spur him on, and he thrusts his tongue back inside of me more strongly than before. I'm grinding down onto his lips, my legs still on either side of his head, seeking as much contact as I can. I almost cry when he removes his tongue, but I almost scream in pleasure when he moves those luscious lips around my clit and sucks harder than he's done before. The intense suction makes me slam my eyes shut because my senses are on overdrive.

He briefly lets up on his suction to circle and flick my clit with his tongue. I'm right on the edge of my orgasm when he inserts two fingers deep inside of me as he circles and flicks, circles and flicks, circles and fucking flicks. I tiptoe the line of pleasure and tip right over into ecstasy overload when he crooks his fingers inside me, spanks my ass hard with his free hand, and returns to sucking my clit in a way that makes it feel like pulsing jets are massaging me over and over again. I can't help the shout that escapes as I come all over his face, the pleasure so intense that I'm not sure if I want to press myself more firmly against his lips or lift myself away from the pressure.

Lawson makes the decision for me when he sits up and carries my body with him. He stands and I have enough presence of mind to marvel at his strength as he lifts me over his shoulder, one hand cupping my pussy and the other holding my lower back in place, and walks to the side of the house. As he steps into the shadows, he moves me so I'm pressed against the wall and he wraps my legs around his waist. I don't know what it is about this man and pinning me against walls, but I fucking love it.

LAWSON

I FEEL myself losing control as I pin Mac against the wall with my hips, my cock throbbing and heavy. If I hadn't unzipped earlier, I'm pretty sure it would've punched a hole through my jeans. I look at her beautiful face, still flushed and rosy from her orgasm, and feel pride at the way she came apart against my mouth. I can't wait to do it again and have her at my mercy in a fucking bed. For now, I have to sate the raging lust I feel and can't wait any longer.

I push Mac's arms to the side and give her a hard kiss as I grind against her still wet pussy. She kisses me back hungrily, and I'm turned on even more at the thought that she can probably taste herself on my tongue and she not only doesn't give a fuck, she kisses me with increasing fervor. I take one hand and guide my cock out of the confines of my briefs before rubbing it up and down her slit a couple times.

"Give me your cock," she begs in a whisper.

I smirk as I drive into her and take immense satisfaction in her sharp cry of pleasure. She's incredibly wet from my mouth and her orgasm, but her pussy still grips my thick length so tightly, so perfectly. I told her on the front steps that this would be quick because of where we are, and I intend to keep that promise. I roughly piston in and out of her tight sheath with hard, heavy pounds as cries of passion spill from her lips.

"Yes, more," she gasps over and over. Fuck, it's so hot that she listened to my command earlier. I haven't heard her say anything else and decide she deserves a reward for being such a good girl. I don't let up my pace as I pound into her, but I take one hand from her hip and move it in between our joined bodies. I quickly locate her swollen clit and start to rub it vigorously. Her moans increase in volume and her breathing becomes even more labored.

My balls start to tighten as I continue to use her body. A small voice in the back of my mind tells me to be gentle, but she feels too fucking good and she doesn't seem to mind. Her head is thrown back in pleasure, and her eyes are closed as she leans back against the side of her house. She's bouncing eagerly on my cock and gripping the back of my neck tightly with one hand and clawing at my back with the other. I can tell she's close to having another orgasm, and I want her to come with me. I shift my hand at her pussy and press my hand against it so it almost serves as another cradle for my cock. I press close and insert my middle and ring fingers, which are under my cock, inside of her and resume rubbing her clit with my thumb.

At the intrusion her eyes fly open but she's so slick, so wet, that I know she's only feeling intense pleasure at the added fullness. The force of my hips as I saw in and out of her tight body moves my fingers. She's surprised, but once she gives in to the extra sensation I know she'll be done for. I bend my knees and thrust in at a different angle, all while my fingers are rubbing her clit and her inner walls, and she comes apart like a bomb that's been detonated.

I manage to press my lips against hers and swallow the scream that leaves her throat in a hoarse, overwhelmed cry. The combination of her twitching pussy milking my cock and her shuddering cries spilling into my mouth trigger my own orgasm. I remove my fingers and bury my face in her neck as I continue to bury myself in her body, my thrusts becoming progressively gentle as we both come down from our shared release. I pull my head back and look at her as I shallowly push into her pussy. She looks sated and happy. She has a smile pulling at the corners of her lips, and the light misting of sweat on her skin gives her a sexy glow.

I lean my forehead against hers and place a tender kiss on her lips while I unhook her legs from around my waist. I set her legs down and make sure she can stand before I step back and push myself back into my jeans. She's still smiling and looks utterly relaxed as she supports her body weight against the wall. I feel a surge of affection hit me with the force of a wrecking ball and am confused by the rush of unfamiliar feelings.

We stare at one another as we try to regulate our breathing and while I try to analyze what I'm feeling. It can't be anything serious. That'd be ridiculous. It must be the high from my orgasm. *But you've had orgasms with other people and never felt this feeling*, an insistent voice in the back of my mind says. *She's different.* I push the voice further back in an effort to silence it. This must be a side effect of sleeping with someone who I see regularly, someone I'm not bored of. That's it. This is a new experience for both of us, and I'll enjoy it while it lasts, which will only be for the summer. It won't ever turn into anything more. I can guarantee that.

I paste my trademark smirk on my face and can't help stepping close to her once again. She glances up at me but doesn't move to touch me.

"Thanks for dinner and dessert, Mac." I can tell that it drives her a little crazy to hear her words repeated back to her. "Have a great night," I teasingly say. "I'll see you later."

She's shaking her head when I drop a quick kiss to her lips, wink, and walk away from her to my truck.

"Make sure you rest up. You're gonna need it for next time," I laughingly say.

"If there is a next time," she tosses back my way with a smile as she starts to saunter toward the front of the house.

I laugh at her words and hop into my truck. I watch her enter the house with a small wave in my direction and feel a tightening in my chest as I watch her disappear.

15

It's a gorgeous summer Sunday, and I'm working my family's booth at the local farmers' market. I liked working the booth as a child but find myself enjoying it even more now that I'm an adult. It's given me a chance to familiarize myself with everyone in town again. As I stand here waiting for customers, I think about all that has transpired with Lawson.

Over the past few weeks we've fallen into a routine: work, dinner, sex, repeat. Again and again and again. Even on the days when we aren't painting the barn's exterior or he isn't working on the barn's roof, he makes sure to stop by and take me to dinner before things get heated. I never tell him but I'm incredibly thankful that he doesn't want to get together for just sex. I know our arrangement isn't anything more than that, but it makes me feel like I'm more than just a good time.

Between working on the interior of the barn and spending long, sweaty nights with Lawson, my mind and body are sore, sated, and serene. Being back at my family's orchard and getting involved with something that has been in my family for generations has helped instill the sense of purpose I've been missing. Working at my family's booth has also validated my goal to get the barn fixed and cider made because there's definitely a large, vested interest from everyone I've talked to. I smile to myself and don't even realize I've zoned out until I see a hand waving in front of my face.

"Hey Mac, you home?" a teasing, amused voice says.

I shake myself free of my musings and focus on the lovely woman in front of me.

"Hey Langley! Sorry about that. I was just thinking about how nice it is to be back home. I didn't realize I missed it so much."

"Mmhmm, I'm sure that's what gave you that goofy look on your face."

"Goofy look?"

"Yes'm. You look like this." She adopts an expression that looks like a cross between sappy and zoned out.

"Rude! I do not look like that." I try to feign indignation, but it's hard when my laughter is moments away from bubbling to the surface.

"I'm callin' it like I see it, sugar. You so did, and to save you some embarrassment I won't even go into *why* that look was on your face," she says as she gives me a knowing look.

The laughter in my chest immediately disappears. I try and fight the blush I can feel suffusing my cheeks, but it's no use. I choose to ignore her comment instead and change the subject.

"So how's your booth today? Busy?"

The smug look she graces me with is not lost on me because the resemblance is uncanny. It looks too much like Lawson's.

"Yeah, it's been pretty steady, but I decided to take a little break. I almost feel bad because I think half the high school football team bought some baked goods. They're sure going to regret it later this week when they're running those extra calories off at practice," she laughs.

"Half the team? Langley, I'm pretty sure the entire team bought something. You're gorgeous and can bake, so I'm sure they're not going to regret a thing."

"Oh stop," she says, looking embarrassed. "Anyway, there's another reason I stopped by. What types of apples do you have left?"

"Let's see," I say, looking behind me at the large baskets filled with apples. "I still have at least three dozen each of Red and Golden Delicious, Jonagold, and Granny Smith. I also have about two dozen each of Winesap, Rome Beauty, and Gala."

"All right, that's a lot. Too bad that doesn't mean a lot to me. What's going to be good for baking?" she asks, curiosity coloring her tone.

"Hmm." I grab a Red and Golden Delicious, Granny Smith, and Jonagold. "I'd probably recommend any one of these. They hold up really well when baked, have great coloring, and are sweet in flavor."

I proceed to quickly cut the apples into wedges and hand her a sample of each. It's slowed down so I eat some samples with her and enjoy the flavors dancing on my tongue. The only thing that could beat seeing the bright skin of an apple, feeling the smooth, waxy skin, or smelling the crisp, tart smell is tasting one. It'll never get old for me.

"Mmm, oh goodness, these are all so good," Langley groans around each bite. "Which one is this again?" She's gesturing to her current sample, which has both a deep red and shiny golden color.

"Ah, that's the Jonagold. That's one of my favorites. It's a newer apple and is nice and sweet."

"It's so juicy!" As if to prove her point, she takes another bite and the clear juice runs down her chin just a bit.

I burst out in laughter and feel satisfaction swell in my chest that she's enjoying my family's apples so much. "Definitely juicy. Here," I say as I hand her a napkin.

"Thanks," she says as she pats her chin and smiles. "I'll take all of the Jonagolds, Golden Delicious, and Granny Smiths, please."

I'm not sure I've heard her right. "I'm sorry, what? You need nine dozen apples? *Nine*?" I can't keep the shock out of my voice or off my face.

"Don't sound so shocked, Mac. I do a lot of baking and am actually donating an ungodly amount of pies to a charity event this weekend and another charity fundraising auction that takes place in September. I need to get to it. Also, now that I think about it, could I please also get two half pints of the Golden Delicious apple butter? That stuff is to die for."

"You're crazy," I shake my head as I start to bag up her apples. I also grab the half pints of apple butter she requested, the mason jars smooth and heavy in my hands. "Is the apple butter for the auction, too?"

"Okay, you're the crazy one. The apple butter is all for me," she giggles. "I slather that stuff on some homemade biscuits and don't regret that choice one bit. I'll probably drop off one of the jars at Lawson's though. He loves that stuff, too."

A furious blush heats my cheeks at the mention of his name and only gets worse when Langley winks at me. The two are too much alike for my peace of mind.

"I have a better idea," she drawls, mischief clear in her voice.

I dread the words that are about to escape her lips.

"How about you give him the jar? I'll be much too busy making all these desserts to even stop by his place. Besides, you see him more than I do."

I'm pretty sure my face is redder than some of the apples behind me. "I do not." Does she know about our arrangement?

"But sugar, you do. He's still working on the barn, right?"

Oh, thank goodness. "Yes, he's still working on it. But seriously, I'm sure you'll have a chance to deliver it before I do," I say as I try and push the spare jar toward her. She doesn't take it, so I just toss it into her purse and smile in triumph when she doesn't take it out.

She completely ignores the jar and my expression when she changes the topic. "How much do I owe you, Mac?"

"Nothing. They're on the house, Langley."

Her bewildered expression makes me laugh. "That's not right! I want to pay you! How much?"

"Seriously, they're free. Consider the apple butter my thanks for the free pie when I came back to town. As far as the apples go, the day is almost over. I need to get rid of them, so you're actually doing me a favor. If they don't sell, I won't know what to do with them. Besides, I know you'll be using them for a good cause. It's my good deed for the day. If you need more apples for the fundraising auction, just let me know. I'm happy to pitch in."

That's a tiny little lie because if they don't sell I would've donated them anyway, but she doesn't need to know that.

"Aw, Mac, thank you! I'll make sure you get one of the pies I make," she says as she gives me a dazzling smile filled with gratitude.

"Anytime, Langley!" I tell her as I start to bag up the apples. "Also, how are you getting these to your car? Do you need a hand?"

"I'll help," a deep voice to our left says.

The blush that just managed to escape my face comes back in full force. Seeing him in public and knowing what we do in private makes me more aware of him physically. My mind officially went from innocent to gutter in less than one second flat. It doesn't help that he's looking at me like he wants to devour me.

"Oh, Lawson, there you are! You're such a dear. Thank you," Langley gushes.

She leans in and gives him a hug. Seeing the two together is like looking at a painting; the Westbrook siblings are too attractive for their own good and for the sanity of Starwood.

"Anything for you," Lawson says back to her, but his eyes haven't left mine. I'm not sure if I should read more into his words or not. I can't help but feel they're meant for me and not Langley. I mentally slap myself and force my mind back to reality. Of course they're for his sister. I'm not even sure what those words would mean for me. Lawson isn't looking for anything long-term or committed. Neither am I, for that matter.

I hold my breath as Lawson comes behind my booth and stands too close for comfort, his body bumping against mine.

"Sorry, darlin'," he mutters for my ears only. His words belie his tone and smirk because he's obviously anything but sorry, the rogue.

I roll my eyes in response and he just chuckles as he lifts all of the apple bags. After throwing another heated glance my way and saying bye, he heads to the parking lot. I try and fail at not watching the play of his muscles in his tight shirt, but damn, the view sure is nice.

"I'm gonna get goin', but it was great seeing you! We'll have to get together soon."

I tear my gaze away from Lawson and grin in embarrassment when I see the twinkle in Langley's eyes. She knows I've got it bad, so I guess there's no use in hiding it around her.

"Definitely, it's always great seeing you. Let me know if you need help at the auction when it comes around. I'd be happy to help."

"Oh, that'd be wonderful. I'll text you, Mac!" She leans in and gives me a quick hug before she heads off after her brother.

I watch them for a moment and turn back to my booth. The day is just about over so I start to pack up. As I glance back down, I notice a lone jar of apple butter where Langley's purse had been sitting. That little sneak. I pick up the jar and roll it between my hands. I have no choice now than to deliver the apple butter myself. A smile blooms on my face at the thought. I'll never admit it, but I'm glad she left it behind. I can't wait to give this to him myself.

EACH DAY I spend in Starwood starts to feel more and more like home. Granted, this was my home growing up, but Chicago is starting to feel like a small blip on the radar that is my life. After the farmers' market, I went home and spent some quality time with my family. Now I'm upstairs and am browsing through my cell. The only things I really miss from the city are Cade and some deep-dish pizza, so I decide to text my friend and see how he's doing.

Me: CC!! How are you?!

Cade: I'm sorry, who is this?

Me: Ha ha, very funny. How are you? I miss you.

Cade: Everything is good. I miss you, too. Ollie doesn't share his food.

I laugh out loud at his text. Ollie is his business partner and other best friend. I'm not surprised he won't share his food because he eats just as much as Cade does. It's a miracle they look as good as they do with all the food they eat.

Me: LOL. I'd be down to share a pizza with you. I have a craving.

Cade: Mm, pizza. Giordano's?

Me: Ugh, yes. You should bring me some.

Cade: Ha, it probably wouldn't be very good.

Me: I don't mind cold pizza. Or you can just bring yourself.

Cade: I guess I can do that.

Me: Wait, what?! Really?

Cade: Yeah, my assistant keeps telling me to take a vacation.

Me: You must be driving her crazy.

Cade: Maybe.

Me: But seriously, can you visit? I'd go but the barn isn't done.

Cade: I can be there Saturday.

An unladylike screech leaves my lips when I read his text.

Me: YES!! Please!! I think you'll like it here.

Cade: I'm sure I will. I just put it on my calendar. I'll see you this weekend.

Me: You rock.

Cade: This I know. You tell me all the time.

Me: *rolls eyes* Yeah yeah. Oh, and CC? Don't forget the pizza. I'm dead serious.

Cade: I know, weirdo.

Me: Thanks! See you Saturday, bestie face. :)

Cade: See you Saturday. :)

I drop my phone on my bed and smile at my ceiling. I'll have the best of both worlds soon, and I can't wait.

16

"Y ou're gonna be the death of me, darlin'," Lawson pants.

"And what a death it'll be, right?" I smile as I stretch my well-used muscles.

"You've got that right. No better way to go."

We both laugh and try and slow our breathing. After texting Cade, I texted Lawson and told him about the apple butter Langley got him and left behind. I was excited and pleased when he said he'd stop by and then proceeded to offer to take me to dinner. It may as well be code for good food and even better sex. I couldn't pass up the offer to see him, especially after seeing him at the farmers' market earlier today.

After another date in Fontaine, we went back to his place and had sex all over his living room. We can't get enough of each other, and now we're sprawled across his couch, naked and replete. I don't want to overstay my welcome, so after a few moments I get up to try and find my clothes. I don't make it off the couch before Lawson grabs my arm and pulls me into his warm embrace. I rest my head against his chest and am glad he doesn't see my expression because if he could, he'd see shock and hope warring with one another. Up until this moment, pillow talk hasn't been a thing. I really need to get it together.

He doesn't make it better with his next words.

"So Mac, last time we had dinner there was an awful lot of talk about me..." he trails off.

I lift my head and gently smack his chest. "How good is your memory? You are way too good at quoting me verbatim."

His laughter rumbles through his chest and causes it to vibrate against my palm. "I'm good at paying attention. Sue me. But really, how's your soul-searching coming along?" He sounds curious and is watching me with a genuine look in his eyes.

I can't look at him without my thoughts getting muddled, so I lay my head back down when I respond. "It's going better than expected," I admit as I run my fingers along one of his arms. "I came here hoping to find myself again, but I don't think I really expected it to happen."

His free arm is rubbing my back, and it calms and soothes me. "Why do you say that?"

"Well..." I pause as I try to figure out how to word what I'm feeling. "I think I initially wanted to come back home to hide from my issues for just a little bit. I wanted a change and, while I was hopeful, I didn't really expect anything to come of it. But now..." I trail off.

"But now what?"

I sigh. "I've actually found a sense of purpose again and some of that is because of you." His body tenses underneath mine, and I realize how my words must sound. I quickly add on, "If it weren't for you, I wouldn't have gotten so involved in getting the barn fixed up. It's given me something to look forward to, and I can't even begin to express how happy I am at the prospect of having cider brewing again at Shady Layne. It feels great to be part of something I'm actually invested in again. I have a sense of purpose here. Thank you for helping me with that."

His body is once again relaxed, and I can't help but feel disappointed at his initial reaction to my words.

"I'm glad I could help. So what comes next?"

I think about my next words and answer honestly. "I'm not sure. I feel purpose here, but I can't guarantee that it won't disappear when I'm back in the city. If it does, I know that it probably isn't me but what I'm doing. It might be a sign to look for something different. I'll have to discuss it with CC this weekend."

"Who's CC?" He sounds curious.

"My best friend. We'll actually be getting together this weekend," I say, the excitement clear in my voice.

"You goin' back to the city?" His tone is neutral so I can't gauge how he feels about this.

"No, the other way around. CC is actually coming to visit so we'll have to press the pause button this weekend."

"I understand," he laughs. "I'm glad you'll have a friend out here visiting you. But really," he continues on, "when you head back to Chicago, do something that makes you happy. If it isn't graphic design, don't do it. Or if it is, then find someone who appreciates you. You could even start your own business and be your own boss. I could never go back to working for someone else now that I own my company."

"I haven't thought of doing that, but it's definitely a great idea," I muse.

"Of course it is, I gave it to you."

We both laugh as I pinch his arm. "Oh stop. Really

though, was it scary starting off on your own?" I ask as I lift my head and look him in the eyes again, my chin propped on my hand.

He thinks about his answer before responding. "A little," he admits. "There's a lot of work and paperwork to get done. I think the toughest part was getting clients and establishing myself as my own person, but once you get someone who'll vouch for you and take a chance on you, you'll be fine. It took some getting used to, but it's a great feeling knowing that my business is doing well and that my hard work has paid off."

"That's really great, Lawson. Good for you. I'll have to add that to my list of options for when I go back. Thanks for the advice!" I lean in and give him a quick peck on the lips to show my gratitude.

"Anytime, darlin'," he says. My heart stops for a second as we look in each other's eyes. He's giving me a look that's filled with tenderness and warmth and I wonder, for the millionth time, if I'm imagining things or if he's starting to feel the same way.

I've internally struggled with my feelings for Lawson for years and am frustrated with my feelings. I thought I could handle this, but if my heart hurting at the thought of leaving him at summer's end is any indication, I'm already in too deep.

I break eye contact and watch my fingers as I splay them across his smooth, tanned skin. "I should probably get going," I say, happy I'm able to keep the reluctance out of my voice.

"Already? Why don't you stay for a movie? It's still early."

I look up at him again, and his smile takes my breath away and steals another piece of my heart. Before my brain can talk sense into me, my heart takes over and answers. "Okay, that'd be nice."

He smiles again, grabs the remote, and starts to look through movies on Netflix. As we watch the movie with our limbs entwined, I can't help but think about how I've fallen for this man. With each moment we spend together and each smile he carelessly throws my way, I fall more hopelessly intertwined with him. Too bad he doesn't feel the same. Damn you, Lawson. You make it so easy to fall for you, but you make it so hard to do anything about it.

17

I t feels like years have passed until Saturday finally rolls around. I'm a combination of anxious and excited because I can't wait to talk to Cade and get his perspective on things. After all, he is a guy and gives some brutally honest feedback if needed. Not only that, it'll be good for my soul to spend some time with my best friend. I'm downstairs cleaning up the aftermath of this morning's breakfast and am lazily scrubbing dishes as I try to organize my thoughts for our talks later.

"Whatcha thinkin' about there, sis?" My brother's familiar drawl snaps me out of my reverie, and I look away from the pan I've been mindlessly wiping.

"Nothing really. I'm just excited because my best friend is visiting from Chicago today. I just want time to pass as quickly as possible, you know?"

"Yeah, I know, but take some pity on that pan. Here," he says, grabbing the soapy pan from my fingers and rinsing it off in the sink. "You sure that's all you're thinking about?"

My brother's concern for me is sweet, and I realize I also

miss our close camaraderie. It's hard to stay close when you live in different states. Even though I'd love to unload some of my burdens on him, I can't. I can imagine Smith's reaction and it isn't pretty. *Oh yeah, Smith? I'm screwing your best friend and I'm not sure how he feels, but I'm pretty sure I'm falling for him. What should I do?* I'm pretty sure my brother would go kill Lawson and lock me up before I could even finish my sentence. Yeah, so not happening.

"Yep, that's it," I assure him. I need to change the subject. "So what are you doing today? Anything fun?"

"Yeah, I'm going fishing over at Stout Creek for a few hours. Lawson should be here to pick me up any minute now."

I try and keep my expression neutral as I respond. "Oh, you two are going fishing? That'll be fun."

"It should be a good time. Even though he's here working on the barn a lot, we don't get to hang out and shoot the shit as often as we used to. I was happy when he called me up. I've been trying to get together sooner, but he's been unusually scarce. Come to think of it, I think he might be seeing someone."

Keep your cool, Mac. Keep your cool. I take a deep breath through my nose and exhale through my mouth before I respond. I'm pretty sure the reason Lawson's been scarce is because we've been spending practically every night together. Having sex. In secret. Oh God, I'm going to hell.

"Well, at least y'all get to hang out. That's all that matters."

I mentally pat myself on the back for sounding so unaffected.

"That's true. Plus, knowing Lawson, it'll fizzle out

quickly. He'll never settle down. He's not the serious type. Whoa there, Mac. Watch it!" he yelps.

I didn't realize but at his words I roughly slammed a pot into the soapy water in the sink, splashing water and suds everywhere.

"Sorry about that," I murmur, completely flustered. I'm such an idiot. "It slipped." Yep, I'm so going to hell.

We finish the dishes together, and thankfully the subject has steered away from Lawson. Smith chats on happily and succeeds in making me laugh more than once with his crazy stories.

"Thanks for helping me with the dishes, Granny."

"Anything for you, sis. It's nice having you home, even if you do call me by that stupid nickname," he says.

I laugh because his nickname isn't going anywhere any time soon. "It's nice being back. I've missed you." I lean in and give him a hug before pulling back and punching him playfully on the arm.

"Hey! What was that for?"

"For not visiting me in Chicago. I know we both get busy, but it'd be great if you could visit me in the city if you get the chance."

"I'll visit every weekend if it'll keep you from hitting me," he teases. He clears his throat before continuing in a more serious tone. "Really though, I'd love to visit. It's just hard to pull myself away. You know how it goes. Besides, I keep hoping you'll decide to move back here. It isn't the same without you. But if you do go back, I'll make sure I visit and that we keep in touch more."

"I'll try and do the same. Don't get your hopes up though. My stay here is temporary, but if I can visit more I'll do it. I promise."

Smith reaches over and ruffles my hair like he did when we were kids. I squeal and we get into a brief tickle tussle in the middle of our kitchen, our laughter filling up the house.

"What's goin' on in here?" an amused voice asks from the doorway.

I breathlessly pull away from Smith's grasp and step away. My hair's a mess and, if my brother's face is any indication, my face must be as red as a Gala apple.

"My monster of a sister attacked me," Smith says dramatically.

"Oh, please, you little liar! You attacked me!" We can't help the peal of giggles that follow my words. It really is nice being back home.

"You two are hilarious," Lawson joins in on our laughter as he watches us with sparkling eyes.

"Well, I should probably get goin'," Smith says. "You ready man?"

"Ready if you are. Mac, did you want to join us this morning? We're goin' fishing," Lawson offers.

"It's nice of you to offer, but CC will be here soon. Thank you though. I still need to get ready, and then I'm sure we'll find stuff to do. We'll probably go shopping and catch up on things." I smile at the thought.

"Sounds like a good time," he smiles. "Anyway, we should get goin' while it's still pretty early. I'll be in the car, Smith." His words are accompanied by a smile and a walk out the door.

"Y'all have fun out there today and be safe," I say as I walk my brother to the porch.

"Always," he reassures me. "You have fun with your friend today. Maybe we'll catch y'all later."

"Yeah, maybe. Now get goin' before it gets too hot." I

playfully push him toward the stairs and watch as he makes his way to Lawson's truck where all their fishing gear is packed up. I watch him get inside and wave back as they drive off. Just as I see Lawson's taillights disappear, I hear my phone ping with a text notification.

Cade: GPS says I'm an hour away.

Me: Yay! I'll get ready and can meet you out front.

Cade: Sounds good. What did you want to do today?

Me: Up to you. If you wanna eat we have leftover breakfast. We can head out after.

Cade: Sounds good. I can always eat. See you soon.

Me: Drive safe. :)

I smile as I tuck my phone in my pocket, turn, and head back into the house. Today's going to be a great day.

IN MY EAGERNESS, I shower faster than normal and have a little extra time to spend on my appearance. I hear my phone go off just as I finish swiping on a coat of mascara. The excitement that's been simmering since I found out about Cade's visit bubbles over. I haphazardly apply some lip gloss before I grab my phone and run down the stairs at a pace that would have my mother shouting at me if she were home.

Shoes squeaking, I burst through the front door and run down the steps in time to see a black luxury rental car pull up to the house. I shake my head as I smile. Cade is such a city guy. If I didn't know better, I'd be worried that he couldn't cut it out in the country.

The car doesn't make a complete stop before I'm running to the driver side door. I practically dance on my tiptoes as the door swings open and launch myself into Cade's arms as soon as he steps out of the vehicle. I give him a fierce hug and smile wider when I feel his warm arms return the gesture. As I squeeze him, I can't help but think to myself that this hug is as much for me as it is for him.

I pull back and look up, up, up into his amber eyes. I think Cade is the only man I've met who is taller and bigger than Lawson. Dammit. There I go again thinking about him. I need to focus on my best friend. He's rumpled from the drive but looks happy to see me.

"CC!" I exclaim happily. "I've missed you. Thanks for visiting me!"

His deep laugh warms my heart, and he smiles at me as he holds one finger up in the universal signal of *wait just a second* before turning. He bends and leans his tall frame into the car. When he comes back out he's holding a square cardboard box. My brow furrows slightly as I look at it, but then I gasp when I see the name scrawled across the top of the box.

"You actually got me my Giordano's? Oh my God, you really are the best! Chicago Classic? Deep dish?"

He gives me a look as he arches an eyebrow. *Duh.* Of course he did. He's Cade.

"I should know better. Thank you! Let's go eat this," I say as I drag him by the wrist back into the house.

We heat the pizza up in the oven and easily fall back into

our old routine as we share the delicious, cheesy goodness. I knew I missed my friend, but I didn't realize just how much I missed having someone I could be around without having to worry about what would pop out of my mouth. I stare across the table at Cade and take in his wide shoulders and tousled, dark brown hair. He looks huge sitting in my family's kitchen and looks a little out of place in his button-up shirt and slacks.

"Your hair is getting long," I point out playfully.

"Yeah, yeah," he rumbles. He runs a hand through his hair and it draws attention to the unruly curls.

He doesn't say it but I think he's growing his hair out because he's self-conscious about his hearing aid. Cade served in the military for a few years because he wanted to do his part for our country. Unfortunately, he didn't come away unscathed. He lost almost all of his hearing in his left ear and wears a hearing aid. It's partly why his verbal responses are so short. He'll never say it, but he's worried about how his words sound since he can't hear himself completely. He'd rather listen, this one. Not only that, he lost part of his left leg overseas and wears a prosthetic. It still makes my heart hitch that someone so wonderful and outwardly confident can be uncomfortable in his own skin sometimes. I met him after all this happened and he's gotten better, but he definitely has some unresolved baggage. I decide to change the topic so he feels more at ease.

"So, what do you want to go do? Do you want to take a nap?"

He thinks for a moment as he chews some of the pizza he brought back with him. "No, I'm good," he says slowly. "Show me your town."

"You sure about this? Big city CC wants to see little ol' Starwood, Tennessee?" I tease.

"I might as well, it *is* my vaca," he says as he rolls his eyes.

"Anything in particular you'd like to do?"

A shake of the head is all the answer I need.

"Got it. Well, I hope you're ready. I'm about to show you every touristy thing this town has to offer. I'll even get you a shirt! But first, I want to show you around the orchard and show you what I did growing up!" I say, the excitement and pride clear in my voice.

He groans in response, but I can see the large smile breaking out across his face.

As we head back outside and toward his rental car, I can't help but think of how nice it is to have my two worlds collide. It's too bad that this can't be the norm, but I'll be thankful for this time with my bestie. Besides, showing him around town will be a good way for me to remember my hometown when I eventually move back to the city.

WE SPEND most of the day touring the orchard and visiting a bunch of the kitschy souvenir shops that border Starwood. We even took a nice long drive with the windows rolled down, basking in each other's company and the warm summer sun. We eventually work up another appetite so I decide to take Cade to Stella's, the local diner that I used to frequent as a teenager. Outside of a home-cooked meal, Stella's is the best he'll get when it comes to trying good ol' Southern food.

We enter the diner and are greeted warmly before we're taken to a booth. I slide in on one side and the vinyl squeaks under my thighs, the sound familiar and oddly comforting. Cade sits across from me, and I smile because his muscular frame is almost too much for this place. Come to think of it, he's probably too much for this place. I look around and, sure enough, everyone woman in the place is staring at him with doe eyes and slack jaws.

"What is it with me and knowing men who are unfairly attractive?" I mutter under my breath.

Cade cocks his head to the side, and I know he didn't really catch what I said. A faint blush steals over my cheeks as I shake my head and gesture for him to look at the menu. Our waitress comes by to take our order, and we both order Nashville-style hot chicken with mashed potatoes. I can feel my mouth water and, even though I ate half a deep dish pizza earlier, my stomach grumbles at the thought of my next meal. Note to self: avoid the scale.

"So, who is he?"

Cade's direct question, which comes out of nowhere, catches me by surprise and causes me to choke on the big gulp of sweet tea I just took.

"He who? There's no one," I sputter.

We both know I'm lying. Cade just smirks and crosses his arms as he waits for me to talk. He knows me too well.

"Fine, maybe there is someone. Let's call him...Salt," I say. Even now, I'm cautious about mentioning my non-relationship with Lawson and decide to refer to him as the first thing that lands in my line of sight. It's frustrating, to say the least, to have to be so hush-hush about something. I really, really don't like being someone's secret.

"You sure you want to listen to this?" I ask, hoping that he'll say yes because I really would like a man's advice.

Cade, the angel, nods his head and gestures for me to continue with my story. I speak as low as I can, and even though he tilts his head so that his good ear is facing me, I make sure to keep eye contact and speak at a steady pace so that he can read my lips if needed.

I launch into my story and can feel my face coloring with embarrassment when I explain the nature of my relationship with Lawson. Thankfully Cade just gives me a small, encouraging smile; he's a guy, so this probably doesn't shock him. I continue on and explain my frustration over having to be kept a secret and the constant struggle to keep my growing feelings at bay. As I tell him my story, our food arrives and we take a break from my wreck of a love life to eat.

We both bite into our chicken at the same time, and I smile around my bite as I hear Cade's groan of satisfaction. Hot chicken is one of my favorites, and I think I've created a fan for life. I gingerly hold the juicy piece of chicken and savor the crisp of the skin and riot of flavors on my tongue. We chew for a few moments in silence, each enjoying our food, before Cade gestures for me to continue with my story.

"I'm so confused. The sex is obviously spectacular, but he confuses me. He takes me out to dinner beforehand, and lately he's been wanting to talk and cuddle after. It wasn't like that before, and I feel like even though we aren't addressing it, we're crossing some sort of line or getting closer. I just..." I look up at the ceiling and try to think of how to word what I'm feeling. "I just know that I'm probably not handling this how I should. Should I say anything?"

Cade wipes his lips with a napkin as he thinks about his response. "What do you want?"

"Ugh. That's the million dollar question. Why is such a simple question so difficult to answer?" I ask. "I admit...I care about him more than I should. But I finally feel like I'm in a good place with myself again. I still plan on going back to Chicago."

"Then that's your answer."

"That's it?" I push. I'm not sure if I want him to convince me otherwise or not, and that thought alone terrifies me.

He nods and leans closer to me over the table. "You're leaving. He's staying. He's a guy. If he wants more, he'll either man up and say it or he won't. It's simple."

My heart drops a little at his words. "Is it that simple?"

Another nod answers my question. "Guys are simple. If he wanted more, he wouldn't set up this sex-only arrangement."

"But he never does repeats, Cade. I'm a repeat," I say as vehemently as I can while trying to keep my volume down. I don't even realize I'm tearing my napkin up into tiny pieces as a sign of my frustration until Cade reaches over and places a large hand over my fidgeting fingers.

"Mac," he says kindly. "It's still temporary. If he wants more, he'll tell you. Don't chase after a man who doesn't want you. You deserve better."

"I didn't say I was chasing him," I say faintly.

"No, but you want to. It's in every word you haven't spoken. If he cares, he'll come around. If not, he doesn't deserve you. Simple," he says as he leans back against the booth, taking the warmth of his hand and my hope with him.

"You're right," I try to admit brightly. "It sounds cliché, but if it's meant to be, it'll be. Okay, enough about me," I say as I slap my palm against the table top. "What about you? What's new?"

"Not much. Just busy with work," he says.

Cade briefly fills me in on what's been happening back home—it hits me now how wrong it feels to call Chicago home—before steering the conversation to what we're doing today. I start to throw out options and see that his gaze has drifted off my face to something behind me. I can usually tell when he's paying attention, and it's as obvious as the sky is blue that I've lost him. His lips are slightly parted, and a gleam of interest brightens his gaze as he stares at whatever has captured his attention.

I raise a quizzical brow and turn to look over my shoulder. It takes me a moment because nothing immediately stands out, but I feel my other brow join my raised one when I see what must have caught his attention. Walking out of Stella's is a tall, curvy woman with her hair in a high ponytail, the black strands swishing with each step. I look back to the hostess counter and see a tower of brown boxes that I'd bet my entire savings holds some baked goods. The bell attached to the door jingles with her departure, and I plaster an innocent expression on my face as I turn and face my friend again.

I smile inwardly when I see his glazed gaze fixated on the door.

"Something, or *someone*, catch your eye?" I ask nonchalantly.

My words seem to break him out of his daze because he shakes his head and turns his attention back to me.

"Nope."

"You sure about that?"

His eyes flicker toward the door and back to me so quickly I would've missed it if I hadn't been paying such close attention. I smile at him, letting him know in my own way that I caught his action.

"Yep," he answers curtly.

Interesting, I think to myself. Usually Cade is very open about women who catch his eye, and I'm pretty sure that's what Langley just did.

"Okay, if you say so." I let it slide and decide not to

pursue it because he could have been momentarily stunned by her looks. Also, he gave me some honest advice so I figure it's okay to let him off the hook for right now.

I look down at my wrist and check the time. "I think we can head back to my parents' house," I say. "I'd like you to meet my family and figure we can just relax tonight. You've had a long trip."

Cade simply nods in agreement, so we pay and leave Stella's. As we exit and walk out into the sunshine, I loop my arm around Cade's and give him a quick squeeze. With my other hand, I reach over and tug his shirt down a tiny bit at the shoulder so he knows to look down at me. Once he glances down and makes eye contact, I decide to speak.

"Thanks again for visiting me, CC. It's so nice to have you here. It means the world to me."

In response, he pulls his arm free from my grasp and loops it around my shoulder. He pulls me close to his side as he says, "Anything for my best friend."

I smile at his sweetness. I'm so lucky to have him in my life. It really is like having a second older brother and I love it, so much so that Smith would probably be a little jealous. "I guess I should be honest and say what I'm really thanking you for."

He looks at me expectantly, and I fight the smile that's trying to bloom on my face.

"Thank you for the pizza. That really hit the spot," I say seriously, my expression neutral.

Cade throws his head back and laughs loudly at my words, the rich sound ringing happily in the air as we walk toward the car. As his chuckles die down, he gives me one more tight squeeze before opening the door for me like the gentleman he was raised to be.

I enter the car and can't help but feel a tingle of awareness zip down my spine. It feels like I'm being watched. Goosebumps break out across my skin and the hair on the nape of my neck rises. I look around as Cade shuts me in and walks around to the driver side door. I don't see anything and decide to ignore the odd sensation. It's probably all in my head.

18

LAWSON

I'm losing it and am not sure how to feel right now. Smith and I just got done fishing and have made it back to town. We stop to fill up on gas and as soon as we step out of the truck, we are approached by two old biddies. I swear these women must have been ninjas in their past lives, they move so silently.

"Oh, good day to you, Smith Layne! You too, Lawson dear! Do y'all have a moment?" one of the women asks. As they get closer to us, I realize they're two of Starwood's biggest gossips. Great.

"We have more than a moment for two beautiful ladies such as yourselves," Smith says. "Good day to you both, Ms. Saunders and Ms. Garber."

I struggle to not roll my eyes, but the two women swoon and preen at Smith's words.

"Likewise, honey. We have a question for you. Why didn't you tell us your sweet sister has a beau?" Ms. Garber asks.

I freeze at the words and wait for them to turn their eyes on me as they wait for a response. I am surprised and not as relieved as I thought I'd be when they both keep their gazes locked on Smith.

"A beau?" Smith asks, confusion clear in his tone.

"Oh yes," chimes in Ms. Saunders. "And he's handsome, too."

"I'm sorry, but Mac doesn't have a 'beau' in her life."

"Oh, she sure does, darlin'. I dare say he is one of the most handsome men I've ever seen in my life."

Both women titter like birds, excitement clear in their eyes.

"Yes, they've been spending all day together. We saw them cruising around in a black car earlier—a fancy car, mind you—and then about an hour ago they entered Stella's."

"They sure did," the other woman says. "We stopped by to get some water and saw them gazing at each other with stars in their eyes. He had his hand on top of hers, and they just looked so cozy."

Without skipping a beat between breaths, the conversation continues without input from me or Smith.

"I know, it was just precious. I've never seen him before. You can't forget a face like that. I hope he ends up staying."

"I'll keep my fingers crossed for a spring wedding for the two."

Wait, what?

"Oh, yes, that sounds delightful."

The two women are lost in each other as they talk while we just stand here, completely clueless.

"Well, Ms. Saunders," I nod in her direction. "Ms. Garber," I say with another nod. "We need to get going, but thank you so much for stopping by to say hello. We hope you both have a wonderful day," I say as I tip my baseball cap to them.

"Thank you, Lawson. Thank you, Smith. We should get goin'."

"Yes, you're right. You sweet boys have a good day now, ya hear?" With those words, the two gossips leave as quickly as they came.

Now I'm standing here and am looking at Smith, waiting for him to fill the ensuing silence. I don't want to press him for information and raise suspicion, but if Mac is really seeing someone I'm sure as hell not okay with it.

"Well, that was weird," he says as runs his hand over the back of his neck.

"Yeah, it was," I agree. "Well...if she gets married let me know so I can buy a tux," I laugh, hoping that it covers up the anxiety I'm feeling in the pit of my stomach like a dead weight.

"Ha, funny. We may not talk as often as I'd like since she moved away but Mac isn't seeing anyone. I'd know if she was. The only person she ever really talks about regularly from back in Chicago is her best friend, CC. These women are crazy, man." Smith shakes his head and starts walking toward the gas station. "I'll be right back. I gotta take a piss. Let me know how much I owe you for gas."

I nod absentmindedly as I walk to the pump. I swipe my card and lean against my truck as the tank fills. I think back on my previous talks with Mac, and my gut twists at the realization that she's never confirmed her single status. I may be a lot of things but I refuse to be any type of homewrecker. I close my eyes and savor the cool metal against my back as I think. I know Mac, and she isn't the type to cheat. She'd tell me if she was seeing someone. By the time the tank is full and my receipt spits out I've decided that Ms. Saunders and

Ms. Garber, gossip extraordinaires that they are, must be mistaken. That's gotta be it.

Smith shows up just as I'm rounding the truck, and we hop in at the same time. "Hey Law, you got plans tonight?"

"No, I've got nothing. What d'ya have in mind?"

"If you wanna stay for dinner you're welcome to. My parents are makin' a feast for the mysterious CC's visit. They're beyond excited to meet Mac's best friend from the city."

I turn the key in the ignition and think for all of two seconds before I respond. "That'd be nice. Thanks, Smith." I hate to admit it but I'd like to see Mac again, even if we aren't having sex. I like spending time with her. Jesus, something really is wrong with me.

I'm back on the road when Smith's comment pulls me out of my self-chastisement. "Awesome! It's still early, so you can hang at the house until then if you want."

"Maybe. I'll play it by ear and see how I'm feelin'."

We ride in silence through the town's main street for a few minutes before getting held up at a railroad crossing.

"What the?" Smith says in a voice filled with shock.

I turn and look at him curiously. "You okay, man?"

In answer, he points across the street and says, "Who is that?"

I follow the direction of his hand and take in the large, vintage-looking sign for Stella's. I didn't realize it but we have a clear view of the parking lot from where we're waiting. My eyes scan the surrounding area before zeroing in on what must have undoubtedly captured Smith's attention.

What in the ever-loving fuck?

I can feel my blood pressure start to rise and an uncomfortable heat start to creep up my neck as I take in the sight before us. Instead of spending time with her best friend like she told me, Mac is leaving Stella's with a man in tow. I squint and try to get a good look at the guy. He's definitely not from around here. I watch as they walk into the parking lot arm in arm but feel myself tense up like a motherfucker when I see him pull his arm free and loop it around her shoulders. I'm tempted to undo my seat belt and go find out what the hell is going on but am dragged back to reality when I hear Smith muttering his confusion under his breath beside me.

We watch as the two laugh and smile, happiness clear on their faces. It doesn't take a genius to know that they're comfortable with one another. I've seen a lot of different expressions on Mac's face and have been the cause of some of my favorites: loose and relaxed when we talk, sassy when we banter, and replete from the multiple orgasms I've given her. But now I see a different look on her face that hasn't been directed at me before: pure contentment. I swivel my eyes toward the railroad crossing and see there's still a long line of train cars that have yet to pass.

I look back at Mac and this mystery fucker. I didn't think it possible but I tense up even more when they get to a luxury car and he draws her into a tight hug. Mac wraps her arms around this guy's waist and looks up at him, her smile radiant and unaffected. He opens the door for her and I see Mac stop, turn, and scan the surrounding area with her eyes for a few brief moments before entering the vehicle. As if he's the luckiest man in the world, the guy walks around the car with a huge fucking grin on his face. *He is*, I think to myself, *because he's with her.*

I shake my head and tear my eyes away from them when I hear cars start to move ahead of me. It looks like the train has passed completely. I start to drive again and can't stop replaying what I just saw in my mind as I drive back to Shady Layne Orchard.

"Maybe those women were right," Smith chimes in after a few moments. "It sure looked like the two were close, right man?"

"Yeah, I guess." My answer is terse, but I can't bring myself to sound remotely polite right now. I'm not sure why I'm all worked up, but I feel the urge to hit something.

"I wonder why she didn't just tell us CC wasn't visiting. I'm assuming her friend was her cover," Smith muses out loud. "Oh well, I guess we'll have to meet him tonight and find out what's going on. Mac wouldn't dare flake on my parents, especially since they've been preparing a big dinner."

I make a noncommittal sound in the back of my throat. The conversation dies after this and before I know it, we're back at the house.

"I'll be back later, Smith. I'd rather get cleaned up and wind down from our fishing trip before coming over for dinner," I say as I pull up and put the truck in park.

"No problem, Law. I'll catch you later." He tips his hat in my direction as he exits the vehicle and walks into the house.

"Later, man."

I'm pulling away from the house and catch sight of the barn in my peripheral vision. I head toward it and park on the side. I didn't realize until it was too late that I had left one of my ladders outside the other day when we were painting. I locate it quickly and am in the process of putting it in the bed of my truck when I hear another car in the distance. I lift my head in the direction of the sound, and the same black car from Stella's pulls up the driveway.

I feel like a fucking creep as I stand here and watch from

the side of the barn, but I can't pull myself away. When the car parks mystery asshole exits, walks around to open the door for Mac, and puts his hand on her back as they head inside the house. They're still smiling and laughing as if they never stopped. I feel my jaw clench and unclench repeatedly at their closeness. I can't tear my eyes away from the scene and watch on as something I never thought I'd see, or even thought would bother me for that matter, unfolds before my eyes. With a loud shriek of laughter and a giggle that carries on the breeze to my heated ears, Mac hops onto her secret lover's back. His hands grip her thighs, and he easily turns her body and hoists her over his shoulder. The last I see of Mac's face is her smile before it's covered by her long hair that falls in a glossy cascade, the sun hitting it so it shines like molten milk chocolate.

As they enter the house, I try and get my breathing under control and don't even realize that I've gripped the sides of the ladder so hard that my hands are red, the indentations etched deep into my skin. I flex my palms and try and get a handle on my feelings. Never in my life have I felt so out of sorts. I told Mac that this wouldn't be anything serious, so I'm not sure why this bothers me so much. I didn't care in the past if women I've fucked were screwing around with other guys when they were seeing me, as long as they weren't in a committed relationship. Even if this is just a guy she fucks around with back in Chicago, why should it be any different with Mac?

Because everything's different with her, you dumbass, the increasingly prominent voice that speaks from deep inside says.

I try and ignore this persistent thought and groan as I lean my head against my forearm. So what if she's sleeping with someone else? Why do I care? I huff in a deep breath and try to rationalize the emotions rolling through me like an angry, unfettered storm.

Am I bothered that she's fucking someone else? Fuck yes, I am.

Why does it bother me that she's fucking someone else? If I'm being honest with myself, it's because she'll be going back to this fucker in Chicago. This realization is enough to make a sweat break out across my brow and a chill run down my spine. I did not sign up for this shit.

Have my feelings about being in a relationship changed? No, they sure as hell haven't.

Am I going to do anything about this new discovery? No, because I shouldn't care. I shouldn't be bothered.

I take one last fortifying breath, and just when I'm about to turn and enter the truck, I catch movement in an upstairs window of the house. It's still bright out and I can see inside clear as day, even from this distance. An aching feeling erupts in my chest and my body goes rigid when I see Mac and mystery douche enter a bedroom. I watch with bated breath and, contrary to everything I've thought over in the last few minutes, I pray that one of them leaves the room.

Instead, I see the unknown usurper unbutton his shirt slowly as he stalks into the room, backing Mac into it further. I swing my gaze over to Mac as she approaches the window and pulls the curtains closed, effectively blocking my line of sight.

As the curtains cease their fluttering and finally go still, a hot rage erupts inside my chest. Fuck everything I told myself. I'm not okay with this, and I'm going to make sure Mac knows it before the night is through. I told her I'd be the only one to take care of her. I fucking meant it.

19

A gentle rapping sound wakes me up from the nap I took after getting back from Stella's. I didn't realize until the car ride home from the diner how tired I was and was relieved to know that Cade was sleepy as well. I was tired from our day of heavy food and sightseeing, and he was tired from his trip here, so thankfully he was game for a nap. As soon as we got back to my parents' house I showed him his room, shut his curtains, and immediately went to my room for a nap of my own.

I keep my eyes shut as I stretch my limbs and pull my blanket over my head.

"Ugh, yes?" I groan out in response to the continued knocking. Waking up from a great nap is the worst.

I hear my door creak open slightly before my mother speaks. "Mac, baby, dinner will be ready in half an hour."

"Thank you, Mama. I'll be down soon," I say, my voice muted slightly by the blanket. This means I only have twenty-eight more minutes of time in bed before I have to get up, brush my hair, and head downstairs.

"Perfect. I'm excited to meet your friend, dear."

"He's excited to meet you, too," I smile. She's too cute.

When she doesn't immediately respond, I pull the covers down a bit and turn on my side. The quiet rustling of the cool sheets as I shift my legs and downy softness of my pillow are about to send me into another nap. As if she can read my mind, my mother speaks up again.

"Oh, and Lawson is coming over for dinner, baby. Smith invited him earlier today. I'll see you soon," she says as she clicks my door shut.

At her words, my eyes fly open and I'm hit with a mixture of feelings all at once. I'm excited to see Lawson and have him meet Cade because I think they'd get along. However, a feeling of anxiety eats at me because of my talk with Cade earlier. I'm having a hard enough time fighting my feelings for Lawson, and seeing him interact so effortlessly with my family and best friend won't help any. Still, that doesn't change the fact that he's coming over and that I'll just have to deal with my rampant emotions.

I turn to look at my clock and see that I now only have twenty-six minutes until dinner, which means I have even less time until Lawson is here. I wasn't going to put in a lot of effort to look nice for dinner before, but my mother's news changes things.

"Thanks, Mama!" I shout as I fling my blanket off my body and bolt out of bed. I scurry on over to my closet and try to figure out what to wear. I need to pick something cute but not so cute it seems out of place for a dinner at home. I seriously hate being a girl. Lawson will probably show up in jeans and a tee and will somehow manage to still look like the physical embodiment of sex.

Since time is running short, I quickly decide on a dark pair of skinny jeans that does wonderful things for my butt and a Chicago Cubs tank top. I throw my outfit on in record time and twist my hair into a messy bun on the top of my head. I apply some lip gloss and evaluate my look in the mirror, pleased at how my cute and comfortable look came together. I shoot Cade a text to make sure he's up and will be ready for dinner. He responds right away and lets me know he'll be down in a few but that I can head downstairs without him.

As I walk downstairs, my mouth starts to water at the smell of Southern beef stew and homemade biscuits. Between my dinner dates with Lawson, my parents' cooking, and Langley's baked goods, I'm positive that I've gained some weight. Not that I care, but every single pound is definitely worth it.

I'm almost to the bottom step when I hear a knock at the front door.

"Can someone grab the door, please? I'm a little tied up in here," the muffled sound of my mother's voice drifts over from the general vicinity of the kitchen.

"Sure thing, Mama. I've got it!" I call back.

I head to the front door and nervously run my hands over my hair and outfit. I reach for the door and swing it open to reveal none other than Lawson Westbrook, the itch I can't seem to fully scratch. My face is already halfway to gracing him with a megawatt smile, but my lips freeze in place at his expression. I've known Lawson for years, so between that and knowing him in the biblical sense, I can tell right away that something is off.

He stands on the porch and although he has a relaxed expression on his face, every line of his body is etched with tension. He's all hard edges, the only warmth emanating from him coming from the burning intensity of his eyes. I can't pinpoint his current feelings, but it is obvious that something is wrong.

"Lawson, are you okay?" I ask in concern.

He doesn't immediately answer, but when he does his words are chilly, brief, and lightly laced with sarcasm. "Just peachy."

"You're such a liar," I scoff quietly so that my voice doesn't carry. The last thing I need is for someone to hear us and wonder if there's more than meets the eye. "I'll take it for now since dinner is about to start. Besides, there's someone I want you to meet." I try and inject some excitement into my voice in hopes that it'll help improve his mood.

I step to the side to grant him unfettered access into the house, and as he steps by me I swear I hear him mutter, "This'll be good."

I'm not sure I heard him right, but if I did I'm not sure what he means. I shrug a shoulder in confusion and make a mental note to check on him later. I can only hope that this strange, sour mood of his doesn't last the rest of the night.

I follow him into the house and right into the dining room where my father, Smith, and now Lawson have decided to congregate. As soon as Lawson is within eyesight of my family, he appears to be back to his usual, charming self. I watch him interact with them for a moment and realize that although he's behaving, his easygoing manner seems forced. I'm going to figure out what's going on whether he likes it or not, it'll just have to wait a bit.

I look around and notice that Cade isn't downstairs yet, but I figure now is as good a time as any to set up his introduction. He's always on time so he should be here any minute now.

"Hey guys, could I get your attention for a second, please?" I ask the group of men in front of me. Once they all turn to look at me, expectant looks in their eyes, I continue.

"I'm glad we could eat as a family tonight and Lawson, it's nice having you here as well." I chance a glance at him and notice that his hardened gaze is on me. "I'm excited to introduce y'all to my best friend and roommate in Chicago, CC. I'm sure you'll all get along famously," I say hopefully.

My father is smiling, but the looks Smith and Lawson are throwing my way are strange.

"What are the looks for, you two?"

No sooner are the words out of my mouth before I feel a presence right behind me. As I'm turning to greet Cade, I see Smith and Lawson turn and share an unreadable glance. I decide to ignore them for now and give Cade a side hug as he steps forward so we're standing side by side.

With a smile I announce to the men, "Mama's already had a chance to meet him, but everyone, this is CC!"

The expressions flickering across the faces of Smith and Lawson are comical and confusing. Smith looks shocked and relieved, while Lawson looks shocked, relieved, and...angry? The look of shock and relief quickly give way to the stony expression he graced me with earlier, which is now firmly back in place.

"That's CC?" Smith blurts out in surprise.

Cade just shakes his head in amusement at the nickname I gave him and steps up to my father with his hand outstretched. "Cade Carson, sir. It's a pleasure finally getting to meet you."

My father is grinning and is clearly impressed by Cade's manners. "Pleasure to meet ya, son. My daughter has nothing but great things to say about you."

Cade smiles and moves to stand in front of Smith. "Nice to meet you as well, Smith."

My brother shakes his hand and, never one to be subtle, asks, "Does she call you CC because those are your initials?

I'm tellin' ya, Mac," he says as he glances at me, "you're losing your touch with nicknames."

I snicker and Cade just groans. He knows what's coming.

"I mean, that works, but that's not why I call him CC," I say smugly. I love this story. "I call him CC because it stands for Cade Commando."

At my words, Lawson looks like he's vibrating with some unknown feeling. My father and brother, who are completely oblivious to this, look surprised and confused.

"Aw, come on, what's the story?" Smith asks.

"When we first moved in together Cade had a housekeeper. I know, it's unreal," I address everyone's surprised expressions at Cade's wealth. "Well, said housekeeper turned out to be a little obsessed with my friend here. Cade was grumbling one day about missing boxer briefs, and it turns out that she was taking them. He set up a camera feed and caught her in the act."

"Dude, creep alert!" Smith exclaims.

I laugh, and Cade just gives an embarrassed chuckle.

"I know, right? Well, Cade of course fired her as soon as he found out, and she lost it. She decided to march right on into his bedroom and set his drawer of boxer briefs on fire. This happened in the morning so after this was all settled, Cade had to go into work commando because he didn't have time to shop. And that, guys, is how Cade Commando came to be."

There's a slight pause before my father and brother bust out in boisterous laughter. Cade joins in, and then I cave and join in as well. I laugh along with them as I wipe the tears from my eyes. It's at this moment when I realize the only person in the room not truly joining in on the fun is Lawson. His smile looks fake, and all he contributes in the way of laughter is a single, curt "Ha." I manage to catch his eye, and his pretend smile vanishes. Now he stares at me with a fierce look in his eyes with his arms crossed over his chest. I lift my brow in his direction as if to ask "What's your problem?" and all he does is give me a very small shrug in response.

As the guys get it together, Cade makes his way over to Lawson. As the two stand in front of each other, practically toe to toe, I notice the differences between the two. Cade is taller and broader of shoulder, but is a little leaner through the hips. Lawson, on the other hand, is stockier throughout, but he is still solidly built and just a few inches shorter. Both are incredibly good-looking, but the biggest difference between them is their expression. Lawson's polite expression looks strained and I realize, not for the first time tonight, that his usual charming personality seems forced. Cade, on the other hand, is smirking, and for reasons unknown to me is giving Lawson a challenging smile. I watch Lawson closely, and his nostrils flare slightly at my best friend's expression.

As they reach out to shake hands, I have a feeling in my gut that their grip is so hard that it must hurt both of them, even though neither of them wince at the contact.

"Cade Carson, best friend. Nice to meet you. And you are?" Cade asks coolly.

"Lawson Westbrook, family friend."

My heart sinks a little at Lawson's words, and I want to smack myself. Why would I expect him to own up to anything happening between us in front of my family if he won't even do it in front of anyone else in town?

"That's what I heard. I'm sure you've been a good...friend...to Mac," Cade says. He steps back from Lawson and now addresses the room. "I hope you all know she's one of two best friends I have. You raised a wonderful woman," he tells my father, who beams proudly. "And," he says as he turns to look at Lawson before saying his next words, "I hope you know she's in good hands. Whatever she needs back home, I make sure she's taken care of. It's my personal duty as best friend and roommate."

Oh God, Cade. What are you up to? After spilling my guts at Stella's about everything that's happened, my friend knows the significance and meaning of the words he just uttered.

Cade smirks at Lawson before moving to stand beside me again. I look up at him because I don't know what he's trying to do or achieve. My best friend looks back down at me and the expression on his face tells me to trust him. I roll my eyes and look in Lawson's direction. He looks ready to combust, as if he's barely hanging on by the thinnest thread, and I'm surprised that my family hasn't noticed or at least called him out on his atypical behavior.

It's at this moment that my mother bustles into the room, and the change in demeanor in Lawson is immediate and noticeable. As soon as she comes in he tears his eyes from mine, takes a breath, and plasters on a smile. I fight to keep the frown from forming on my face at his transformation. *What is his problem?* I ask myself.

"Okay, y'all," my mother happily says. "It's time for dinner. Please take a seat. Mac baby, I need your help," she says as she zips back out of the room and heads toward the kitchen.

I follow in her wake and help her grab the food.

"I'm so glad your friend is here, Mac," she says as she grabs jars of butter, apple butter, and jam for the biscuits.

"Thanks, Mama. Me too," I say.

"You sure he's just a friend?"

"Yes, I'm beyond sure. He's like another Smith to me."

"Got it. Now don't tell your father this MacIntosh, but if I were young and single like you I'd be all over that. Cade is definitely a looker," she says as she waggles her eyebrows.

"Ew, Mama! Please stop," I exclaim on a giggle.

My mother laughs mischievously at my reaction. "Just kiddin', baby. Your father is the only one for me. Can you grab the stew, please?" she asks. "Although I wasn't lyin' about how handsome he is. Lawson's mighty handsome as well, Mac..." her voice trails off.

I fight to keep a straight face as I walk around the island but know my cheeks must be flushed. "Is he?" I say as nonchalantly as possible.

The arch look she gives me is full of a mother's intuition. "Mmhmm. That man may as well be another son to me, but I can honestly say he's beautiful. He's a catch. It's too bad he's already taken."

My arm, which is stretching over the oven to grab the stew, stops in midair briefly before I can reign in my surprise.

"Taken?" I can barely choke the question out.

"Mmhmm, by you baby," she smiles.

"Mama, I love you, but you're crazy. He and I are just friends who work together on the barn."

"Okay, I'll let you think that. But baby, the way he looks at you when nobody is watchin' tells a whole other story."

My mother's words are confusing me. "He looks at me? Wait, you've been in here the whole time."

"Mac, I'm a mother. I see *everything*. And yes, he looks at you just as much as you look at him."

My shock is obvious, and she continues to laugh. "You both won't admit it and probably don't see it yet, but you will. Eventually."

My mouth is opening and closing like a fish in desperate

need of oxygen. I think my failure to form words is a sign that my brain is short-circuiting from the need to correct her and the hope that she's right.

I'm still unable to say anything when my mother claps her hands and puts me out of my misery. "Just let that marinate, baby. Now, that room is fit to burstin' with handsome men right now, don't you think?"

"They're okay," I deadpan, finally able to form words.

"Let's go feed them, baby," my mother says as she whisks out of the room with a twinkle in her eyes.

I follow her back into the dining room and see there are only three available spots at the table: the other end of the table opposite my father, beside Cade, or beside Lawson. I look around for my brother and see that he's not in the room. Damn. I was hoping he'd be here to make the choice for me. I'm not sure if it'd make more sense for me to sit across from my best friend or next to him. On one hand, if I sit next to Lawson I'll have to endure the intensity rolling off him up close. On the other hand, if I sit next to Cade I'll have to face Lawson and deal with his looks of anger or disapproval or whatever he's feeling.

My choice plays ping pong between both options, so I finally decide to just sit down next to Cade because I'd rather see Lawson's expressions. At least this way I can try and decipher them. I walk over to the seat, but Cade stands up and pulls out the chair for me before I can get to it.

I smile as I sit down. "Thank you, CC. You're such a gentleman. The South is rubbing off on you," I tease.

"Don't tell anyone back home," he says.

I shake my head in laughter and smile up at him as he helps me push my seat in. As Cade sits down, I peek over at Lawson from beneath my lashes and see his eyes flickering back and forth between me and Cade. His expression is polite and neutral, but the hardness of his jaw and slight tick in his cheek are giveaways that something is off.

I look at him for a few seconds, and my attention is drawn away when Smith reappears and takes his seat next to Lawson. "I've been thinking about this meal all day," he says, excitement clear in his voice as he pats his stomach. "Thanks, Mama!"

"Yes, thank you, Mama. There's nothing that beats a home-cooked meal," I say.

After this statement, the rest of the men at the table chime in and express their thanks. My mother just brushes off their gratitude and orders them to eat.

"It's my pleasure. Cade, it's nice to have you visiting. We've heard great things about you," she says warmly before turning to the man who's been driving me crazy. "And Lawson dear, thanks for joining us as well. It's always a pleasure to see you. Now, let's eat!"

We all start serving ourselves and are all piling hearty portions of my mother's stew onto our plates. My mouth waters as I inhale a deep breath of the delicious scent. I'm definitely going to miss this. We eat in silence for a few minutes before the conversation picks back up. The dinner talk is directed toward Cade since he's our guest of honor, but it's only a matter of time before the focus shifts to Lawson.

"So, how's business going, Lawson? I know you're always very busy, and I feel awful knowing that I'm pulling you away from other work to fix our barn roof," my mother asks, the worry clear in her voice.

"Business is great, Mrs. Layne. It's definitely keeping me busy and please, don't feel awful. You're all practically family, and I'm happy to help out in any way I can."

"Oh, you're such a sweetheart. Thank you, Lawson."

"It's my pleasure, it really is. I can't turn down a pretty woman such as yourself, especially if she needs help," he says, turning on the charm.

"Watch it, son. I don't want to have to shoot you for stealing my wife," my father chimes in jokingly.

The table laughs as Lawson banters easily with my parents while everyone eats. I feel slight annoyance spark to life at the easygoing way he's talking to everyone else but me. He's focusing on them and rarely looks in my direction, but when he does his eyes dim and there's a barely noticeable tightening of his mouth. It's become clear to me that he has a problem with me, but I can't fathom what it could be.

"All I can say is that it's such a shame to keep you locked away, working all the time. The poor women of this town must not to know what to do with themselves," my mother says.

"Ha! The women of this town don't stand a chance, Mama. Lawson doesn't date," Smith chimes in.

Oh God, why are we on this topic?

"You don't date? Like at all?" My mother sounds genuinely surprised, and I look at her to make sure she isn't meddling. Her face is the picture of innocence, and her eyes don't even flicker my way. Oh yeah, she's meddling all right.

"No, he doesn't!"

"Hush, Smith. Your name isn't Lawson, is it?" my mother asks. She shifts her focus back to Lawson and asks, "Now, what's this all about? You're young and available, Lawson James Westbrook," she practically scolds.

A heavy silence hangs in the air for a few moments as we wait for him to respond. With bated breath, I finally force myself to look at him. He looks as if he's thinking about how to word his answer. When he finally responds he simply says, "I'm just not looking for anything serious."

Before he can continue, Smith interjects quickly with, "Yeah, I'd bet all my savings that it's because you're seein' someone." My brother chuckles at his words, not knowing that my heart has lodged itself in my throat.

I fight to keep my gaze on Lawson's face. The myriad of emotions that play out across his face range from surprised and disbelieving to guarded and weary, all in the blink of an eye and all without looking at me.

"I am not," he replies.

"I call bull," Smith laughingly says. "We rarely hang out anymore. If you're just out having fun you usually tell me about it, but you've been close-lipped. It must be serious because you're not tellin' me anything."

My chest tightens when I hear this. *False hope*, I think repeatedly. *Don't get false hope.*

Everyone else at the table is looking at Lawson expectantly, and he chooses to respond after finally looking my way with a look I can't read.

"Fine, I'm maybe seein' someone. It's nothing serious." He says these words while looking me straight in the eyes, and I feel the rising heat of a blush fight its way up my neck.

"I knew it!" Smith crows in triumph. "If it's not serious then why didn't you say anything till now?"

"Not worth mentioning." He pulls his gaze from mine, and I feel my spirits drop with the loss of visual contact.

Ouch.

Cade senses my inner turmoil and lifts his arm so that it's resting on the back of my chair. I feel a gentle squeeze on my shoulder and know that he's offering his support and probably restraining himself from punching Lawson in the face.

I look up at Cade and smile in gratitude and as a sign that I'll be okay. I'm still looking at my friend when my attention is captured once again by the man across from me.

"And to further answer your question, Mrs. Layne," Lawson continues, "I don't know if I'll ever want to settle down. I haven't met the woman yet who makes me want to do that." He pauses as he thinks about his next words. His eyes move back to me and they turn a glacial shade of jade when they land on Cade's arm around my chair. His nostrils flare slightly, and I see a slight furrow start in his brow before he swings his piercing gaze toward my mother when she clears her throat.

"What type of woman would make you settle down, Lawson?" my mother asks, genuinely curious.

"Not entirely sure. I haven't thought about it much. I just know I want her to be honest. There isn't anyone yet who's caught my eye, let alone captured my trust. Women will say stuff to make you believe one thing," he says as he looks at me again, "but they eventually show their true colors. Besides, I don't know a lot of women who really want to settle down. They're also content to play the field, so to speak, and aren't comfortable at the thought of one man taking care of them."

What the hell? His face is serene, but his eyes are blazing at me in accusation. What in the heavens is he trying to say?

I look back at him, unable to voice my confusion or ask him what he means. He looks away yet again and addresses the table with words much warmer than the look he just pinned me with.

"And of course, I hope she's beautiful," he chuckles.

"Don't lump all women in the same group, dear," my mother chides gently. "Mark my words, you'll find someone when you least expect it, and it'll happen sooner than you think." Her words are airy, but her tone is filled with confidence and wisdom.

"We'll see, Mrs. Layne. We'll see," he says. "Enough about me and my bachelor ways," he laughs charmingly. "Those aren't changing anytime soon. What I need to know," he looks to my father, "is how Smith learned to fish, Mr. Layne. His skills are nothing compared to yours. He's putting a smudge on the good family name," he says good-naturedly.

His words cause a roar of laughter to erupt from my father's throat and an indignant huff to leave Smith as he begins to defend his honor.

Cade squeezes my shoulder again, and I catch the sympathetic look my mother sends my way. She must've been wrong earlier in the kitchen because whenever my gaze clashes with Lawson's, there is nothing warm and fuzzy about it; in fact, it feels colder than a Chicago winter.

The conversation at the table continues, Lawson's teasing and subject change alleviating some of the earlier tension building in the air like an oncoming thunderstorm. He doesn't look at me again, but I vow to give him a piece of my mind the next time we are alone.

20

The rest of dinner passes by without any additional awkwardness, probably because I completely avoid looking at Lawson. The conversation also steers clear of anyone's love life or lack thereof. I'm beyond relieved when Lawson announces that he's leaving shortly after dinner is over. With a parting smile and a promise to stay longer next time, he's out of the house and in his truck, the taillights winking goodbye in the night. I inhale and breathe deeply, instantly feeling less tense. I thought I was confused before, but it's nothing compared to how I'm feeling now.

I offer to help my mother clean up and she staunchly refuses, saying I should focus on my guest. Not a bad idea.

I turn to Cade and raise an eyebrow in question. "Since we didn't get to it earlier, do you wanna see the barn I've been working on, CC?" My voice is eager and filled with pride; I can't wait to show him how hard I've been working.

One long arm extends away from his body, palm up, as he gestures toward the front door. "After you."

"We're not quite ready yet." I walk deeper into the house and beckon him to follow with a tilt of my head.

I lead him to the enclosed porch that runs the length of the back of the house where the sharp, tangy sweetness of apples blends with the fragrant, pleasant scent of applewood.

"I need your muscles," I say over my shoulder. We step over slats of wood and around empty barrels that have a light smattering of sawdust as we make our way to the shelves on the other side of the room.

"That's what all the ladies say," I hear from behind me.

"Oh stop," I laugh. I place my hands on my hips as I stop in front of the racks. Dozens of mason jars glint brightly, the lights making them shine in a way that contrasts beautifully against the worn, aged wood of the shelves.

Turning around to face Cade, I gesture toward the contents of the room. "I don't need all of this, but I could use your help in carrying some of this stuff, please. My father made some bowls out of applewood and some frames that I want on display in the barn. Not to mention," I point with my thumb behind me, "I'm going to need a lot of this jam in there, too. It'll only take one trip between the two of us."

Cade's taking everything in and a smile lifts his lips when he looks back at me. "Only you, Mac, would make me work on my vacation."

"Hey now! I'll pay you."

"You can't afford me."

"Ew." I shake my head in mock disgust. "I'll pay you in apple jelly and apple butter. I promise you either is worth its weight in gold."

"Fine," he rolls his eyes playfully, but I know he's secretly pleased at doing something that requires physical activity. Cade isn't one to stay idle.

"I'll take the bowls, frames, and some of the jars if you don't mind taking the rest of it. I can handle a few jars no problem, but when carried together they're awfully heavy."

"Well," he flexes his arms and the sleeves of his shirt strain against his biceps, "you asked the right guy. Let's do this."

It's my turn to roll my eyes and laugh. "You're such a nerd," I say with affection in my voice.

We quickly get to work and have everything packed up so we can easily make it in one trip. I'm grateful for the help and take advantage of Cade's strength, packing more jars of jam than I originally planned on taking. When we make it to the barn I swing the door open dramatically.

"I present to you," I flourish, "the newly renovated, not quite done but almost there, apple cider barn of Shady Layne Orchard."

The barn lights up as the doors open and we step in with our haul. I survey the room, and my heart swells with satisfaction at the sight before my eyes. What used to be a neglected, dirty space is beautiful and welcoming once again. When I'm not passing out from orgasmic bliss with Lawson, the rest of my time is spent in here, hard at work. Everything is now pristine, and Lawson finished the interior part of the roof, ensuring nothing else can get in now. All that's left to do is fix the shingles up top, make some cider, and open for business.

"This is it," I say as we make our way over gleaming wood floors. I set down the frames on the counter and walk around, my hands gliding over the smooth surface. "You should've seen it before. What do you think?"

Cade looks around and doesn't answer as he starts to explore the large space. I let him look around without interruption but can't help the small knot of nervousness twisting in my gut. Once I realize I'm wringing my hands uselessly, I decide to occupy them and put them to better use. I start shelving jams in neat little rows on a counter display and on the built-in racks behind me. I get to the jars of apple butter and smile as I swipe my thumb across the labels I created. *I wonder if Lawson has tried his apple butter*, I think before halting that train of thought. I need to stop thinking about him, even though it's difficult when everything around me right now reminds me of him.

My fingers are grazing the smooth, pocked wood of the bowls my father made when Cade finally answers my question.

"This is awesome, Mac. I'm impressed." His tone is genuine, and he's still looking around the space with assessing eyes. "The setup you have is really nice, and it has a warm ambience. Customers are going to love it. Did your dad make this, too?" he asks, running his hands over a long table on the far side of the room.

I smile because I love that table so much. "He sure did. He's definitely talented. He made the table years ago, but it's just been sitting in the back of the house. I was so excited when they said I could move it in here," I say as I grab a jar of jelly and walk over. I roll the smooth container between my palms and, once I get to the table, set it down so I can trail my fingers over the chairs my father made from apple barrels. "He's a crafty one. Now that he's older, he sticks to the small stuff but he made all the shelving, the countertop, and the furniture here."

"Wow," Cade breathes in awe.

"I know," I agree. "All that's left to do is put a few more products out and get the cider going, which should be easier than cleaning this place up."

Cade lets out a large yawn as he nods and says something unintelligible. I think he said he can't wait to try it, but I can't be too sure.

"You've had a long day, CC." I reach over and rub his back for a few seconds. "You should head up to bed."

"I'm okay, I want to help." His helpful words are followed by another yawn.

Laughing, I start to push him toward the barn door. "Not tonight, mister. I'm going to put the frames away and will be right behind you."

"Fine," he grumbles, his fatigue finally getting the better of him. "You better be in bed soon."

"Yeah yeah, Mr. Bossy. I'll be in bed soon. Now go." I give one final push and watch for a moment as he heads to the house and disappears inside.

I turn back into the barn and notice the lone mason jar of apple jelly I left on the table. I grab it and smile as I think about the exciting changes in store for the orchard now that the barn will be up and running again. I can only hope someone keeps things running after I leave.

"You sure you don't want to get to bed, too?"

I almost drop the jar in my surprise as I spin around and find Lawson leaning up against the doorframe.

"Seriously, stop doing that!" I shout. "Not cool. You're going to give me a heart attack." My heart is still thumping wildly as the wheels in my head start to turn. "And where the hell did you come from? Have you been here the whole time? I didn't see your truck."

"I wanted to double check my supply count for the roof before leaving. I parked on the side of the barn." He straightens away from the door and lazily prowls into the room, his eyes pinning me in place. It's the subtle anger I see brewing in his gaze that ignites my own ire from dinner.

Time to give him the piece of my mind I promised I'd give him earlier.

21

"Y ou!" I seethe. "What the fuck is your problem?"
I stalk toward him and shake the fist holding
the jelly.

"I'm not sure what you mean."

Oh, you fucking know, you asshole.

His brow arches as his eyes burn brighter. "Oh, I do?
And asshole?" he says, a slight tinge of amusement coloring
his tone.

Shit, I didn't mean to say that out loud. Oh well. Now
that it's out there, I refuse to take it back. This is not funny.

"Yes, you do! You've been acting cold toward me all
night. Something is off. You're polite to my family, but every
time you look at me I feel like I did something wrong, like
key your truck or offend you somehow. What's your
problem?"

I don't realize until now that we're practically standing
toe to toe in front of the table and away from the barn door.
Good. If we shout I don't want our voices to carry and alarm
my parents.

My words seem to prod the beast in Lawson's eyes that's

been tethered up and pacing about in his head tonight. "My problem," he growls, the sound sending shivers racing up my neck, "is you."

"No shit, Lawson! What about me?" I challenge.

"You conveniently left out that you were fucking someone else."

My mouth pops open in confusion, and I'm momentarily at a loss for words. After a moment, my brain starts to work again and I fire my questions at him. "What? Who? What makes you think that?"

"CC," he says, practically fuming. "I didn't know you were fucking your 'best friend,'" he uses air quotes around the words, "who, by the way, we all thought was a damn woman. I saw you two earlier." He must understand the look of confusion on my face because he clarifies. "I saw you two leaving Stella's all lovey-dovey. I saw y'all again after dropping Smith off when I came to get my ladder. I looked over at the house and saw you in the window when he took off his shirt. You closed the curtains before I could see more, but it was pretty clear what y'all were about to do."

Lawson's anger is causing his chest to rise and fall rapidly while my own mind is trying to process what the hell is happening. I'm not sure if I want to laugh, shout, or cry at how wrong he has things. I open my mouth to correct him but stop myself because he should already know the type of person I am. Instead of accusing me and jumping to conclusions, he should've just asked me. Besides, he has no right to be angry.

"What the hell does it matter, Lawson? Why do you even care?" I call him out, my voice rising higher with each question. "You told me from the beginning that this was just a temporary arrangement for the summer." I realize I'm gesturing wildly with the hand holding the jar of jelly, so I set it down on the table beside us before I hit him over the head with it. "Why do you care if I'm fucking Cade, huh?" I taunt, pushing him to answer.

My outburst and lack of denial seem to catch him off guard. After a second, a scowl mars his features and he looks larger than life as his outrage builds higher and hotter than an inferno. I watch him, and the detached part of me that isn't lit up with frustration is acknowledging how sexy he looks right now, all manners and pleasantries forgotten in his anger.

"I care," he says as leans in closer to me, "because you said you weren't looking for anything serious, but something serious is obviously going on. I. Don't. Fucking. Share," he spits out. "I don't ever mess around with women who are taken because shit gets complicated."

"He's not my boyfriend, Lawson! And neither are you! I'm not yours!"

"True, I'm not your boyfriend, but I fucking told you countless times, Mac, that I'd be the only one to take care of you," he shouts.

"Oh, like you're not out fucking other women?" I challenge.

"No. I told you I don't do repeats. I don't have double standards either. I fuck one person at a time, Mac."

"Lawson." I close my eyes and rub the bridge of my nose in agitation. "Who I sleep with is none of your business. At the end of the day, I'm moving. You don't want anything serious. Let's leave it at that. I honestly think you're just jealous of Cade."

I open my eyes and see his smirk, which is usually so playful and charming, look full of disdain. "The only thing I'm jealous of is the fact that he lives with someone who's a guaranteed lay."

I don't even think before my hand whips out and slaps him hard across his cheek. His face has turned slightly at the impact, and he glares at me in surprise. My palm and fingers sting, each nerve screaming and tingling, the evidence of my reaction clear in the angry-looking hand-print left on Lawson's cheek.

"You watch how you talk to me, Lawson Westbrook. You may not like what I do or agree with it, but you will fucking respect me."

We don't speak as we stare at each other. Even though we're both pissed off, I can't fight the invisible pull of attraction that still connects us. This man makes it impossible to see or think clearly.

"You know what," I finally say as I take a step back from him. "I'm going to bed. We obviously have very different thoughts on the matter. This isn't working. I'm done," I say in parting as I move to leave.

I barely make it two steps before his hand is on my arm, halting my progress.

"Let me go," I glare at his offending hand.

"No." He's removed his hand but he sounds resolute.

I raise my eyes and am face to face with his chest when I speak again. "I told you I was done, Lawson."

"But I'm not done," he says.

"You are unbel—"

My words are cut off with a hard, bruising kiss. Even though I'm angry, even though I am beyond frustrated, I'm held captive by Lawson's demanding lips and tongue. His exasperation is coming through in his kiss because he isn't gentle. Instead, I feel like he's branding me with each swipe of his lips, claiming me as his with each pass of his tongue. I moan at the sensation of being dominated by him through this small point of contact. He groans in response as he moves one hand to my waist and the other to the back of my head where he deftly removes the pins, causing my hair to fall free of my bun and tumble over my shoulders. The pins fall to the floor in dull thuds as Lawson drops them before gripping a handful of my hair and tugging my head back.

I force my eyes open and drink in Lawson's fierce expression.

"Law—" I start to say before he tugs my head back the tiniest fraction.

"No, you've said your piece," he grates. "Now it's my turn, Mac."

I open my mouth to retort but snap it shut at his expression.

"I probably didn't make myself clear when we set up this arrangement, Mac," he says as he stares me straight in the eyes. "But you," he lifts me up and swings me around so I'm sitting on the table, "and this," he spreads my thighs with his hips and grips my pussy over my jeans, "are mine." He leans in so his temple rests against mine before he tilts his head to speak against my neck. "Only mine. No one else's," he breathes, the feeling of his lips against my tender flesh causing goosebumps to break out across my skin.

He pulls away and his hands are everywhere, branding my skin with their heat and intensity. He doesn't ask permission as he jerks my tank top over my head, and he doesn't need to because angry, passionate Lawson has me aching in ways I never saw coming. I whimper as he unhooks my bra and roughly palms my breasts before tugging on my nipples with the hardened pads of his fingers. It's obvious we're both still running high on emotion, but lust is overriding everything. In this moment we are both animals, slaves to our baser desires, and there's no room for gentleness or sweet words.

I reach my arms around and slide my hands up his back, clawing at his skin as he continues to torture my nipples. With each rake of my nails against his back he tugs harder. I can't bring myself to stop chasing the feeling that's a direct line to my throbbing clit.

Just when I think I can take no more he pushes me flat on my back, hastily unbuttons my jeans, and drags them down my legs. His hands travel from my ankles to my hips with a heavy touch, and in seconds his hands are wrapped up in the strings of my panties.

"This is going to be rough," he pants as he tears my panties in half and away from my body in one swift movement.

I can only nod and whimper a desperate sound as response.

"This isn't for you." He runs his fingers over my exposed slit, and I buck on the table when his fingers briefly circle my clit before pulling away. "This is to remind you of who you belong to," he says as he plunges two fingers inside of me, his fingers sliding easily into my drenched center. He may say it isn't for me but his expert touch still sets all my nerve endings on fire in the best way.

I may be naked and exposed as I lay before him but I feel a small rebelliousness well up. "I belong to no one," I manage to gasp out with difficulty as I fight the drugging effect of his touch.

My words incense him, and in the next instant he removes his fingers from my body. "You're mine, Mac. You're going to admit it before I'm through with you," he promises darkly in a voice made of pure gravel and smoke, his drawl more pronounced.

I've always been yours, my mind screams. *I'll always be yours*, my heart cries. I refuse to admit it though, taking selfish satisfaction in Lawson's possessive streak that I'm sure we both didn't know was there.

His hand moves lower between my legs and finds the part of me that can't lie to him, no matter how much I wish it would. His stance widens and pins my thighs to the table's edge as his fingers dip in and swirl around my wetness before entering and working me like a tool he uses on a daily basis. He knows my body better than I know my own, and I'm soon delirious with pleasure. His touch alternates between slow, rough pumps and pinches or slaps to my clit with his wet fingers. He's still got ahold of my hair, so I close my eyes and run my hands down my body and over my breasts and stomach, savoring each poignant touch. I reverse the path and travel by hands back up my body before I raise them above me and claw at the smooth, textured surface of the table in a futile effort to keep the oncoming orgasm at bay. I want to prolong this erotic torture as much as possible, I never want it to end, but I don't know if I can hold off. My hands do another sweep and bump against something, the sound of it thumping back into place jarring me momentarily. The sound causes Lawson to suddenly withdraw his hands from my body just as I'm about to detonate into pleasure.

I whimper and close my eyes in frustration because I was so close. Lawson is still standing between my legs, the only contact between us his jean-clad thighs against mine. A few moments pass before I hear him chuckle seductively as he reaches for something behind me. It must be the offending object that stopped the flood of pleasure Lawson was giving me. I'm still catching my breath when I hear the sound of something opening. A moment later, I feel Lawson run a single finger from the base of my throat all the way down to my clit. He does this again a few times, occasionally making a detour to circle his finger around my painfully erect nipples. He finally pulls his finger away, and I wait in anticipation for him to repeat the action again.

My eyes fly open in surprise when his finger returns because this time it's sticky. He's putting something on me and tracing his finger in an entirely different pattern. I look down and see he's writing on me. Just as the scent hits me, I realize what the stickiness belongs to: apple jelly. He starts at one nipple and makes a few jagged strokes before ending at my other nipple. His finger dips back into the mason jar and comes back to my skin, where he firmly makes a straight line done my stomach, the gleam of possession in his eyes bright.

As he starts the next shape over my belly button, I realize he's writing letters. I imagine what it looks like from his point of view and gasp as his last letter ends right over my pussy. He licks the remaining jelly from his fingertip and looks down at me in satisfaction, obviously pleased with his handiwork.

"What's that say, Mac?"

I look again and finally see the letters he's painted across my skin: M-I-N-E.

"It says 'mine,'" I respond faintly. I should probably be upset that he's essentially branded me, but all I feel is giddiness.

"That's right, darlin'. You're mine. Every inch of you. *Mine*." His words ring with confidence and finality. "Now, who do you belong to?" he asks.

I squeeze my lips together and refuse to answer, holding on to the last bit of stubbornness left and curious to see what he'll do next. I shake my head up at him and glare. I expect him to send me an answering glare, but instead he smirks. This can't be good.

He doesn't say anything as he leans down and covers my right nipple with his mouth and sucks, hard and hot. My back bows away from the table at his ministrations. He follows the path of the apple jelly he put on my skin and kisses, grazes, nips, bites, and licks it all away.

By the time he's done with the first letter, I'm shaking. By the time he's finished with the second letter, my pussy is leaking arousal everywhere. By the time he's finished with the third letter, I'm crying out at the pleasure that is borderline painful because there's so much of it. Before moving to the last letter, he looks back up at me and his expression is wicked and serious.

"These letters don't need to be on your skin for me to know you're mine, Mac," he says right before he dives in and attacks my center with his wet lips and tongue. Most times he's gone down on me before now have been unhurried because he enjoys taking his time to taste me at his leisure, ensuring I have a long, slow buildup to my orgasm. Now, though, he eats my pussy greedily with every trick he has in his arsenal.

By the time he's done with the last letter, I'm screaming out in orgasm and my body is wracking in waves of pleasure, tears streaming down my face at the strength of my release. He's right; I feel like he's etched himself into every molecule of my skin and I fear I'll never be free of him or the way he makes me feel.

I'm barely coming down from my orgasm when he flips me over so I'm laying on my stomach, my body flush with the tabletop. One hand cracks down like lightening on my ass cheek, and the other grips a handful of hair and tugs my head back, pulling roughly. *Oh heavens*, I think to myself as I arch my back and neck to get closer to him, *this is incredible.*

It's almost too much but yet, at the same time, not enough. Never enough.

I hear his pants unzip and hear the sound of a condom wrapper opening. I brace myself, beyond ready for his hot length to enter me. His hand comes down and smacks my other ass cheek, the sweet sting of it soothed by his calloused hands rubbing my skin and squeezing the flesh there. He alternates between each cheek and occasionally dips down to touch my pussy, wet and wanting with the need to be filled. With another tug of my hair he grips my hip and enters me quickly and roughly. I cry out at the intensity and fullness of it. Even though I'm soaked, he's still so big and is more than a snug fit. Instead of giving me time to adjust like he normally does, he pulls back out and rams back in, slamming into my body at an unforgiving pace. The slight sting kicks my pleasure up another notch and I'm crying out, trying but failing to push back against him because I'm still flush against the table and pinned in place by his hard body.

He continues to tug my hair and slap my ass between his punishing, heavenly strokes. He's never been so rough with me and I love it, exalt in it, want to live in it for as long as I can handle.

"Play with your clit," he orders in a gritty voice heavy with desire.

I try to touch myself with one hand but have difficulty getting my hand underneath me, the intensity of his thrusts making my body bounce. He notices because he moves his hand from my hair and maneuvers one arm underneath my hips to support me, lifting just enough so I can squeeze my hand between my legs.

"I've got you," he growls against my back.

I successfully bring my hand to my clit and play with

myself, the sensation of Lawson using my body for his plea-sure and me seeking my own relief almost too much to bear. I can feel myself getting close to another orgasm and my pussy tightens.

"Fuck, your pussy squeezes my cock so perfectly," he groans. "Who do you belong to, Mac?"

I'm surprised at his words but ignore him, instead focusing on my fingers. Lawson makes a sound of displea-sure and halts his movements. He's still seated deeply inside of me, his cock twitching, but he is no longer moving back and forth. I cry out and try to push back against him, eager to feel his thick length entering me, but he squeezes my body tight with the arm that's around me, the tight band of muscle effectively halting my movements.

"I said," he repeats, "who do you belong to?"

"No one," I pant.

"Wrong answer, darlin'," he says as he withdraws and enters me again in one rough thrust. I gasp at the hard intru-sion and want to curse at him for not moving again, but my brain can only do so much. "Now," he breathes against my ear, "who do you belong to?"

"Who do *you* belong to, Lawson?" I ask. I try to sound confident and sure, but my voice comes out sounding vulnerable.

He groans against my back at my words. I don't think he's going to answer, but he surprises me when he says, his voice low and borderline inaudible, "You, Mac. Only you."

His words and the tone in which he says them, as if they are being ripped out of a secret place against his will, tear down the walls around my guarded heart. I feel unshed tears well up in my eyes and, as one breaks free and travels down my cheek, I surrender.

"I'm yours too, Lawson. Only yours," I whisper.

The words are barely out of my mouth before Lawson is slamming back into me, his cock feeling impossibly larger and harder than before.

"Fuck, yes. You. Are. Mine," he punctuates each word with a hard thrust.

Before long I'm at the brink of orgasm again, my fingers working my clit madly as he continues to press against the spot inside me that has me seeing stars.

"Almost there, Lawson. I'm almost there," I manage to get out.

"Me too, darlin'. Let me help you get there," he says as he continues his expert thrusts.

I'm not sure what he means, but his meaning is soon clear when I feel his hand join my hand from behind. I think he's going to enter me with his fingers like he did before, but I'm wrong, oh so wrong.

His fingers tangle with mine briefly before he scoops some of my wetness up and drags it back up to the untouched pucker of my ass.

"Lawson...what? Oh my God," I cry as he begins to circle my most private place with his thumb.

"Has anyone ever done this?" he grunts, still circling his thumb, getting closer and closer with each swipe.

"No," I gasp when he makes brief contact and flutters his thumb there before resuming the circular motion.

He groans at my response and reaction, his own words coming out guttural. "Fuck yeah, that makes me so fuckin' hard." As if to prove his point, he pulls his hips back and thrusts again, his cock a hot brand of steel inside me.

I fight for breath as he starts to rotate his hips before taking both hands and pulling my hips and ass up into the air. My chest is still pressed tightly against the table and my lower half is now on full display, propped up high for

Lawson's inquisitive touch. He moves one hand to the center of my shoulders, holding me in place, and moves his other hand back down to play with my pussy and ass.

"Yes," I hiss, biting my lip in ecstasy at the way he makes me feel.

"That's it, darlin'. Take me," he whispers darkly against my back before he pushes his thumb into my ass and two fingers in my pussy to join his cock, all while continuing his thrusts.

Between Lawson's length hitting my g-spot and the added tightness from his fingers, my own fingers pinching my clit, and his thumb in my ass, I'm done for. I shatter and come, long and hard, with a harsh cry.

"Fuck yes, Mac. So fucking good," I hear Lawson say, and it sounds as if he's in some far-off place as I come undone beneath him. His orgasm follows as I shatter to pieces, and the feeling of his cock growing and twitching inside of me as he comes kicks me off into another orgasm.

I'm a sweaty, replete, and boneless mess as I come down from my release. Lawson is still twitching inside of me, but his movements have slowed and he's removed his thumb from my ass. Once he stops coming, he pulls out of me and I hear him remove the condom before wiping me with the soft fabric of his shirt. Funny, I didn't even realize he had taken it off.

He gathers my body in his arms and sits down in one of the chairs with me in his lap. I sigh in contentment and snuggle into his chest as he rests his chin atop my head.

"You okay, darlin'? Was I too rough?" The concern is clear in his voice.

I smile weakly and answer honestly. "I'm great. Never better. You were perfect," I say.

His low laugh rumbles through his chest and warms me

from the inside out. I hear him inhale a breath as if to speak, but I cut him off before he has the chance. There's something I need to clear up.

"Lawson, there's something you need to know about Cade." I feel his body tense beneath mine, and his hands grip my body tighter as if he expects my best friend to come in here and fight him for me. "I never slept with him. We are just best friends. I swear. What you saw in the window the other day was just him showing me his new tattoo. I closed the curtains for privacy and left right after. I hope you know me better than to think I'd be sleeping around."

A moment of silence passes as Lawson digests my words. "I believe you," he admits sheepishly. "I know what type of person you are, Mac. If I thought about it instead of jumping to conclusions, I would've remembered that or at least asked you about it before going off. I'm sorry for everything I said earlier. It's no excuse, but I obviously wasn't thinking clearly."

"Apology accepted," I say. "But don't be too sorry because what we just did was all worth it."

My words cause him to break out in another round of laughter and I join in, happy that we are able to clear things up.

"So, you and Cade never..." he trails off, the unanswered question hanging between us.

"Never. I swear he must be a long lost brother, because it's like I'm with Smith when we hang out. I can guarantee he feels the same as I do."

Lawson sighs happily in relief and loosens his grip on my body at my words.

"So, Lawson, what's this mean for us?" I ask.

"It means that while you're here I'm yours, and you're mine. I mean it. I don't want us fucking other people."

My heart squeezes unhappily at his words. He's still set on a temporary arrangement and just doesn't want to share while I'm in town. I feel tears begin to well and snuggle further into his chest so he doesn't see. He holds me for long moments and I soon start to drift off, the stress and activities from the evening finally catching up with me. My eyes are closing and I'm toeing the line between drowsiness and slumber when I feel warm lips press against my forehead and strong arms squeeze me close. I'm not sure if I hear it, but I'm pretty sure "I wish I could keep you" is whispered in the quietest of voices. Knowing me, it is only in my dreams. I snuggle closer and give in to the fatigue, peaceful in the fact that my dreams can't disappoint me like real life can.

22

September

I'm standing over a large stockpot of boiling water, the steam causing a fine sheen of condensation to form on my forehead. I use both hands to stir the batch of cider, my fingers gripping the stainless steel paddle as I breathe in the delicious scents of cinnamon, allspice, and sugar that marry with the array of apples I added in earlier. This is the first batch using my grandma's tried and true recipe, and I'm thrilled at the thought of bringing this tradition back to Shady Layne. Not only that, the cider has been boiling for about an hour and the back porch smells like heaven. The warm, earthy smells are bringing back memories of my childhood. I'm lulled into a trance by my stirring in this little world where it's only me and these ingredients, and my thoughts begin to drift away from the past and toward my current predicament.

August rolled into September quietly, and I have no idea where the time is going. I've been back in Starwood for a month and, in just a few weeks, I'm supposed to head back to Chicago. With each day that passes in my hometown, the more pain and indecision I feel at the thought of moving back. It doesn't help that things have improved with Lawson either. Ever since the night I christened the barn with him, things have been much easier between us. I'm not even sure if he's sensing or even aware of the change. Although we still have sex just as often, if not more than before, we spend more time talking in our post-sex recovery time than we used to before Cade's visit. He wrapped up work on the roof of the barn, so whenever he's free he'll invite me over and we'll spend hours getting to know each other. We'll talk about life or just enjoy the silence as we lay intertwined in his sheets. It feels like we have more than just a temporary arrangement. It's...wonderful. Wonderful and terrifying because I find it increasingly difficult to keep my growing feelings to myself. I know we agreed that I'd tell him if things changed, but I'm afraid this beautiful thing we have growing between us will disappear in a puff of dreams and yearning. If possible, I'd like to continue lying to both of us a little bit longer.

I cover the pot and turn the dial on the burner to low so it can simmer and the flavors can develop further. In two hours I'll come back, remove the cheesecloth filled with spices, and drain the cider through a sieve to remove any remaining solids before moving it to the fridge to cool. I wipe my forehead with the outside of my wrist and smile. This feels right and the part of me that was missing feels full again. I step away from the large stockpot where I've spent a large chunk of my day and head out through the screen door a few feet away. I walk over to the large tree in the backyard and take a seat on the swing my father built when

I was a kid. The grass at my feet is dappled with pale sunlight that filters from the tree top overhead, my skin warming each time it touches one of the sunny rays.

I grip the rope, the once rough fibers softened from years of use, and push off the ground with my feet as I close my eyes. I swing back and forth to pass the time and listen to the gentle breeze rustling the leaves overhead as if secrets are being shared while the old seat creaks slightly under my weight. I lean further back as I swing and extend my legs to the sky, swinging higher and higher with each pass. I feel weightless and free, like a bird soaring without a care in the world. Just as I'm closing my eyes again, I hear my phone ping with an incoming text. I reach back to remove my phone from the pocket of my jeans and unlock the screen, holding my arms over the ropes and toward my center so I don't drop it. I smile when I see who it is.

Cade: I'm going to need you to send me more apple butter and jelly.

Me: I can bring some back with me.

Cade: No, I'm going to need it sooner. I'm all out.

Me: LOL you little glutton!!

Cade: Shut it. The stupid store-bought stuff is crap and doesn't compare.

Me: Told you you'd love it. ;) I'll send some to you tomorrow. Deal?

Cade: Deal! Good lookin' out, Mac. How have things been since I left?

Me: Things are great, actually. Really, really great.

Cade: But?

Me: Why does there have to be a but?

Seconds after his text pings through, my phone rings with an incoming video call. I shake my head and laugh as I swipe to answer.

"You're too perceptive, you know that right?"

Cade smirks at my words and I smile wider. He's wearing a suit and I can see the Chicago skyline behind him, which means he's at work.

"Mac, I know you. There's a but. Blame it on me being a shrewd businessman and amazing best friend. Now tell me, what's the but?"

"I just..." I try and think of a way to vocalize how I'm feeling. "I'm happy here. My first batch of cider is almost done and I just feel more...fulfilled...from everything I'm doing here."

"Then it's simple. Stay."

I fidget as I look at him. "It's not that easy."

"But it is, Mac."

"Is not."

"Mac," he says. His tone is stern and brooks no argument. "It is. You quit your job and you live with your best friend. I'm not going to penalize you for moving, and it's not like I can't afford to live on my own." He ends his words on a laugh because we both know he's richer than Croesus. He does make a point, but I find myself staring at my phone in silence, unsure of what to say.

"Just tell me one thing."

"What?" I sigh.

"Do you want to stay for you? Or do you want to stay for him?"

I pause before responding and take my time to really think about my answer. I need to be honest with Cade and, more importantly, with myself. Cade was only able to stay another day because he got called back in for a work emergency but he was able to see Lawson again briefly. I smile at the thought of Lawson owning up to his behavior and apologizing to Cade. After watching them interact, I wanted to pat myself on the back; I knew they'd get along. When we had a moment alone, I gave Cade a glossed over version of what took place in the barn and all he said was, "I knew it." I mull over Cade's question and smile at my realization.

"I'd be staying for me." My words ring with truth and purpose.

Cade presses for my answer to make sure I'm not trying to delude myself. "You sure?"

I take a deep breath and stare him right in the eyes as I respond. "Yes. Even if things don't work out with him, which would suck, I'm happy here. I feel like I have a sense of purpose again. The only reason I really moved in the first place was because of Lawson, and look where that got me. I'm not going to let him influence my decision again. I've thought about it. If I stay, I'll run the cider shop and help my parents since they're getting older, but I'll get my own place. Also, I'm going to set up an online graphic design company and work for myself. This way I have another form of income. I've talked to a few people in town and they've expressed their interest in rebranding, and I know a few clients in Chicago who will follow me. I checked my email and I feel good knowing that I still have support from old clients. Plus, I can stick it to that bitch, Lindsay. Karma!"

Cade's deep chuckle floats from the phone at my last words. "That sounds like a solid plan, Mac. I'm proud of you."

"Thanks, I'm proud of me too. I'm just scared," I admit, my words trailing off into a whisper.

"I know, but you know what they say about risk and reward. How're things with Lawson?"

"Easy. I feel like we've gotten closer since you left. I'm falling, Cade. Falling harder and faster than the apple that hit Newton's head."

"You fell a while ago, you nerd." He's shaking his head but his words come out gentle. "You're just now admitting it."

"What do I do?"

"Since I'm a guy and I'm also your best friend, I'm going to tell it to you straight," he warns.

Oh God, should I be scared about what he's about to tell me?

"Noted," I say, which is all I can manage to get out as I wait in anticipation for his advice.

"Tell him how you feel, and tell him you plan on staying. You don't know how he'll react unless you tell him. He'll either tell you he feels the same and that he's happy you're staying, or he'll deny how he feels. It really is simple, Mac. Women overthink everything."

"We do not!" I say. He gives me a skeptical look, so I amend my statement. "Okay, maybe not all of us. But I can't just do that, Cade. What if he tells me I'm crazy and that he doesn't feel the same?"

Cade scoffs at my words. "If he does he's lying to both of you. He wouldn't have freaked out and gone all possessive alpha on you if he didn't feel threatened by my sexy alphaness or care about you." He's smirking again and I dramatically roll my eyes at him.

"Oh my God, you are too much."

"That's what the ladies tell me," he quips with a wink and a flash of dimple.

"EW STOP!" I cry out. "I can't deal with you right now."

Cade is laughing as he swivels in his chair. "Just tell him. If worse comes to worst, don't let him keep you from seeking your own happiness. You deserve the best, Mac," he says in a voice filled with sincerity.

"Thanks, Cade," I say warmly.

I hear Cade's assistant speak in the background, and he removes the ear bud he is using to listen to me so he can hear her. A few seconds pass and he replaces the ear bud before giving me an apologetic smile.

"I need to head to a meeting but keep me posted. And please, for the love of God, send me some apple condiments!"

His plea jolts me back into delighted laughter. "You got it!"

I hang up and turn my phone's screen off. I know he's right in that I should speak up about how I feel, but it isn't as easy as he makes it out to be. Part of me is hopeful that Lawson feels the same, especially considering how close we've gotten, but the other part of me still thinks he's just being his normal, charming self. I guess I can try and gauge how he's feeling before saying anything. I was invited to dinner at his parents' house tonight and can feel things out then. Granted, Langley said her mother invited me when she heard I was back in town, so I'm curious to see how Lawson will treat me in front of his family.

I tuck my phone back into my pocket and continue swinging, content to let the breeze carry my worries and doubts, if only for now.

23

My nerves are eating away at me as I pull up to the Westbrook family's sprawling, two-story estate. Rows of dogwood trees, their scarlet leaves reminiscent of rich wine, line the long road leading up to the elegant house at the top of the hill. My pulse beats faster the closer I get. I realize I'm not nervous because of the quiet air of affluence that hangs in the air, but because I'm not sure how tonight will go. My doubts from earlier plague me as I worry about Lawson's attitude toward me in front of the people he cares about most in this world: his family.

I round the circular driveway and park my car, smoothing my palms over my dress and down my thighs in an effort to remove any wrinkles. I'm almost to the huge front door when it flings open and Langley greets me.

"You're here! Thank God," she says as she grabs me by the wrist and hauls me inside. "I was gettin' bored." Her eyes pass over my body quickly as she takes in my dress. "Sugar, you look amazing. My brother is gonna have a tough time keepin' it together tonight," she winks.

I deny her statement, even though I can feel the tell-tale blush form on my face. "We're just friends, Langley. I don't know what got into your head, but that's all we are."

"Yeah, and I hate to cook and am the worst baker in three counties," she scoffs, sarcasm dripping from each word. "You're delusional, Mac. It's okay though. Y'all have your little secret, and it's safe with me. Things will pan out eventually."

I don't have a second to respond because just then Langley's parents show up to greet me. Mrs. Westbrook steps up and gives me a warm embrace before Mr. Westbrook steps up to do the same.

"Oh Mac, it's so great to see you! It's been ages," Mrs. Westbrook says in her kind voice. "I'm so glad you were able to make it. It'll be so nice to catch up."

I smile, feeling happy from their warm greeting. My eyes flicker between the two, and it's obvious where the good looks come from in this family. Lawson is the spitting image of his father, and I know he's going to age well if Mr. Westbrook is any indication. The silver strands in his full head of hair add an even more distinguished air to his already impressive looks. Langley looks like a taller, curvier version of her mother, having inherited her height and eyes from her father's side of the family. There's no doubt about it, this family has some fantastic genes.

"Thank you so much for having me. I didn't realize I was so remiss in visiting until I came back and saw everyone." This causes both of Langley's parents to chuckle. "It's great to see you both as well." My words are genuine; every time I've talked to the them, they've always made me feel at home. Lawson and Langley are lucky to have such kind, down-to-earth parents that don't see their wealth and status as a pedestal to stand on.

"Yes, it's great to see you too, Mac. We hope you know you're always welcome to stop by. Why, Langley and Lawson can't stop talking about you," Mr. Westbrook says, a sly grin on his face that matches the twinkle in his eyes. Langley definitely takes after her father.

I can't help but feel like he's insinuating something, but I'm afraid to push and ask. Before I can think of something else to say I feel a strong, muscular arm loop around my shoulders from behind. Startled, I look up and feel my breath catch in my throat when I see it's Lawson embracing me...in front of his parents...like it's no big deal. My cheeks heat in embarrassment and surprise.

"Hey Mac, nice to see you again," Lawson says in a voice loud enough for everyone to hear. I'm sure my cheeks turn crimson when he whispers out of the side of his mouth, just loud enough for my ears only, "You look good enough to eat. I can't wait for dessert."

"Nice to see you too, Lawson," I manage to cough out.

Lawson laughs at my attempt to speak and keeps his arm around me, all while his family looks on and smiles at our exchange.

"Now, why are we all standin' here? Let's go eat!" Lawson cuts the silence again and moves his arm from around my shoulders to my lower back. His palm is like a hot brand against me, the heat of him cutting through my dress and warming my skin.

We all make our way into the dining room where Lawson pulls my chair out and takes a seat next to me. Dinner starts without a hitch, and the conversation eventually steers toward me as we begin to eat.

"So Mac, tell us, how long are you in town for?" Mrs. Westbrook asks.

"The plan is to leave at the end of the month," I

begrudgingly admit. As much as I'd like to say it out loud, I'm afraid to tell them that I've considered staying. Truth be told, I'm hesitant to mention it in front of Lawson because I'm worried about how he'll react.

"That's too bad, we'd so love to see you more," Mr. Westbrook adds.

"That's the truth," Langley chimes in. "There aren't a lot of girls in this town I get along with and want to actually hang out with. Sorry, Mom," Langley says in response to her mother's embarrassed expression, "but it's true. Besides, it's amazing to see someone who can keep Lawson here on his toes."

I wait with bated breath as all eyes swivel to Lawson, awaiting his response.

"Too true," he replies. "Mac here sure likes to keep me guessing." He smiles as he lifts an arm and places it on the back of my chair behind my neck. My body starts to immediately respond to his even closer proximity, humming like a fine-tuned weapon of lore that can only be used by who it was meant for.

"A woman after my own heart then," Mr. Westbrook chimes in jokingly. "My boy here needs to be kept in line."

I'm not sure how to respond so I try and make light of the situation. "I'm not sure I can do all that work, Mr. Westbrook. I'm not a miracle worker."

Everyone at the table laughs at my comment, but my laugh dies in my throat when Lawson's fingers start to toy with a lock of my hair.

"If there's anyone I'd want to keep me in line it'd be you, Mac. You're one of a kind. I'm sure gonna miss having you around."

Did he just say that out loud in front of everyone? I lift my eyes to his and see him looking down at me, a smile on his face. He looks as charming as ever and his tone is light-hearted, but there's a seriousness about him as we gaze at one another. It feels like we're the only ones left at the dinner table, and that inevitable pull I've only ever felt around Lawson tugs hard at his words, causing my heart to squeeze tightly. He's still twirling my hair around his fingertips, and I maintain eye contact as hope swells once again in my chest. We continue to look at one another, the unspoken message in his eyes eluding me.

"That's got to be the smartest thing I've heard you say in a long time, Lawson," Langley says, breaking the silent conversation between the two of us.

Lawson dips his gaze to my lips and back to my eyes one last time before turning and responding to his sister's comment. "Yeah yeah, Langley. Shut it," he says playfully. "I never asked, but how'd the auction you volunteered for go?"

His attempt to change the subject is successful because Langley corrects him, reminding him the auction is tomorrow. I'm certain he knows when the auction is, but I'm grateful for the change in subject. Langley launches into a colorful retelling of how all of the preparation went. I ended up helping her prep some pies and enjoy listening to her express her excitement. As I'm listening, I notice Lawson has removed his hand from my hair. Before the feeling of disappointment can settle, he takes the same hand and partially places it on top of mine on the table top. He isn't holding my hand but his thumb is making lazy swipes over my skin, sending tingles of warmth up my arm and stirring up feelings of arousal in my core.

I look down at our hands and can't believe what I'm seeing. Langley is still regaling the table with her story, but as I glance around I see both Mr. and Mrs. Westbrook look at our hands and exchange a knowing look, smiling at each other all the while. I'm not entirely sure what this means, but my heart drinks up the display of affection. Up until this point, Lawson hasn't acknowledged our relationship or arrangement in public and, although this isn't necessarily public, the fact that it's in front of his family makes it seem more profound and intimate. I try not to get my hopes up, but it's proving difficult.

All too soon, dinner is over and I'm thanking the Westbrooks for having me over. "This was wonderful. Thank you so much for having me. It was a pleasure seeing y'all," I say as I give each of them a hug.

"Oh honey, the pleasure is ours," Lawson's mother says as she hugs me back. Before I can pull away completely she leans in and whispers in my ear. "If my boy's reaction to you is what I think it is, I have a feeling we'll be seeing you again soon. We hope you consider staying."

I blush furiously as I pull away and take in her knowing smile. If his mother thinks something is going on between us, then I really don't know what to think. What does she mean, his reaction to me? And does she want me to consider staying because of what she thinks is going on between us?

I'm confused as I'm stepping over the threshold to leave but am even more confused when Lawson accompanies me out the door.

"Are you leaving, too?" Mr. Westbrook asks him.

"I'm going to follow Mac home and make sure she gets there safely."

"Oh Lawson, that's not necessary," I say. "I can make it home."

"It's late. I'd hate for anything to happen to you," he insists.

I open my mouth to retort when his father responds. "He's right, Mac. It's dark and we'd feel better knowing you got home safely." His twinkling eyes keep me slightly suspicious, but I graciously give in to the show of chivalry.

"That is very kind of you, Lawson. Thank you," I capitulate. "Thank you again, Mr. and Mrs. Westbrook. Langley, it was also great seeing you. Let me know when you want to get together again."

"You got it, sugar!" she replies in a cheery voice.

I'm stepping out the door but now Lawson is at my side. He leans in slightly and whispers in my ear as we walk out, "I'll follow you to your house, but then I'm taking you to my place. You got it, darlin'?"

I give a slight nod, thankful that my back is turned to his family so they can't see my reddening face.

"Don't wait up for me," Lawson calls back. "I'll be heading home after following Mac home."

I hear his parents laughter echo behind us as we make our way to our respective vehicles, Lawson still behaving himself. The anticipation builds up inside me because I know my night is only just getting started and, by the wicked gleam in Lawson's eyes, it's going to be a long night indeed.

24

From the moment I set foot inside of Lawson's apartment, I know something is different. Every time we've been here, our encounters have been frantic and wrought with enough sexual chemistry to cause the apartment to simultaneously combust from the sheer energy of it all. While the attraction between us burns hotter and brighter than ever, it is now simmering and burning through my system like a shot of the finest whiskey, slowing things down to an almost idle pace. My thoughts are running rampant, and I feel like I'm in a dream as he leads me into his bedroom by the hand, his skin hot against mine. Without a word, he stops and turns back to me. Instead of tearing off my clothes like I'm used to, he runs one long finger over my lower lip before passing it in a gentle sweeping motion over my cheek. His hand slides into my hair and he steps closer, his eyes never leaving mine as he steals my breath and causes my heart to beat erratically.

We continue to stare at one another, and the entire world could cease to exist around us and I wouldn't know or care. Every cell of my body is attuned to his, and I'm tempted to blurt out my feelings for this man as I look in his eyes, searching for a glimmer of the same chaotic bliss he stirs in me. He feasts on me with his eyes, their mossy depths burning with more than desire and, if I'm deluding myself, more than passing affection.

I'm not sure how long we stand here devouring one another, me with my heart in my throat and his hand in my hair, but I finally manage to say something.

"What are you staring at?" My attempt to sound playful fails and comes out breathy.

He leans in the few inches separating us and whispers, "You. I'm trying to commit how beautiful you are to memory since I was clueless and failed to realize it before." He pauses and takes a deep breath before adding on, "I'm gonna miss you like crazy when you leave, Mac." His words tumble from his mouth, almost as if against his will, but he doesn't take them back.

Oh God, this man. My heart aches painfully at the thought of leaving not only my newfound sense of purpose behind, but Lawson. In this moment, I'm hit with a burst of clarity: I'm staying. I'll figure it out and I'll make it work. A heavy weight lifts off my chest at this revelation, and my second epiphany quickly follows: I love Lawson. I really, truly love him. I may have been infatuated with him growing up, but he's embedded himself in my heart as deeply as the roots of an apple tree, making it so I couldn't help but fall in love with him this summer.

I feel a smile start to form on my face, but it slows when my earlier text conversation with Cade flits across my mind. This would be the perfect time to tell Lawson my plan and how I feel about him. I should tell him he won't have to miss me because I'm not going anywhere but I'm afraid, so freakin' afraid. I feel my brow furrow slightly at the war going on inside my head while Lawson watches me with a sweet smile on his lips.

"Cat got your tongue?" he teases. I simply nod as he leans in a fraction of an inch closer. "Let me help you then." He finishes this sentence with his warm, soft lips pressed against mine. We kiss for an indeterminable amount of time, our tongues dueling almost lazily, while our hands roam each other's bodies.

"Mmm," I moan.

"Mmhmm," he groans in return.

My world tilts sideways when he momentarily stops our kiss to sweep me off my feet and carry me toward the bed, one arm cradling my neck and the other my knees. He sets me on my feet gently, and my hands reach down to the hem of my dress before he halts my movements.

"Please," he says as he places my hands back at my sides. He runs his fingertips up my arms and down the center of my chest, causing goosebumps to erupt everywhere like blossoms in spring. "Let me."

He then proceeds to peel off my dress and undergarments slowly, as if he has all the time in the world. He places a reverent kiss on each sliver of heated skin he reveals. By the time he's done, my breaths are ragged and my core is a blazing inferno of dripping wet need.

"So perfect," he whispers in awe as his eyes skim my now naked form. "Do you have any idea what you do to me?"

I give a minute shake of my head and reach out to unbutton his shirt. He lets me remove his shirt, and I take a moment to admire the hard slabs of muscle on display. I admire each ridge of his abs and flutter my fingers against the deep vee leading to his thick member. In my excitement, I fumble slightly as I unbutton and unzip his jeans. Lawson helps me by shucking his jeans and boxer briefs so that he's left standing gloriously, mouth-wateringly naked.

"This," he reaches for my hand again and places it on his erection. "This is what you do to me." I run my hand over the steel encased in softest velvet. My core clenches hungrily as I marvel at the long length and thickness. I'm mesmerized by my movements but am surprised when Lawson pulls my hand away and places my hand right over his heart.

"And this," he says, his voice guttural. "This is what you do to me, too." My open palm rests over his heart, and I can feel the rapid *thump-thump-thump* of his heartbeat. "Only you, Mac," he says. "Only you manage to do this to me."

My heart lurches at his words, and joy and hope explode in my chest. I pull his hand to rest over my heart and repeat his words. "Only you, Lawson. Only you manage to do this to me."

My words spur Lawson to move, and he places his hands on my hips and lifts me so I'm placed on my back in the center of his bed. He follows and props himself on one elbow so he's leaning over me. I savor the crisp, cool sheets against my back and the blazing heat at my front that comes off Lawson in waves.

He leans down and peppers my face with sweet kisses, starting at my forehead and covering my eyelids, nose, cheeks and, finally, my lips. My tongue tangles with his for a few moments before he continues his descent down my body. The further he gets, the lengthier his kisses become so that by the time he makes it to my aching nipples, his tongue and teeth have come out to play.

"So responsive, darlin'," he says as he nips my skin and soothes the slight sting with his tongue. "I love it."

I love you, I think but don't dare say out loud. Instead I say, "Only for you, Lawson. I'm yours."

My words cause him to growl deeply, a sound so dark and sexy that I get wetter at the memory of the way he took my body to new heights in the barn. His lips are already moving down my stomach and past my belly button to my dripping center. He places a kiss on top of my mound and raises his eyes back up to mine.

"Fuck yeah, you're mine," he says as he extends his tongue and gives a long, thorough swipe through my slit. "I love this pussy, too. So sweet," he licks me again. "So wet," he gives another pass of his tongue and gives a slight nibble on my clit that has me bucking off the bed. "And so fucking tight," he growls against me, the vibrations making me tingle as he inserts two fingers inside me.

I don't even attempt to respond, the only sounds coming from me incoherent moans and gasps. He eats my pussy slowly and drags his tongue through my folds as if he were French kissing my mouth. He removes his fingers and places his hands beneath my hips. He lifts me higher so he can focus his ministrations on my opening. I come undone on a strangled cry when he roughly pinches my clit between his fingers and inserts his tongue into my pussy, thrusting in and out and wriggling inside like he can't get enough of my taste.

I'm coming down from my high, and Lawson continues to slowly lick up my juices. When I'm finally able to catch my breath, he lifts his head and smiles at me, his lips wet and swollen. He crawls back toward me and sits so his back is against the headboard. He wraps his arms around me, lifts me like a rag doll, and positions me so I'm straddling his lap. My drowsiness fades when I feel the firm, insistent pressure of his length under me. I place my hands on his shoulders and rub my wetness all over his cock to the symphony of our combined moans of pleasure. Lawson reaches for the nightstand, and it's then I know he's reaching for a condom.

"I'm on birth control if you want to forgo the condom," I whisper.

His body stiffens momentarily, and his cock twitches in interest at my words.

"I've never gone without a condom." I can see the excitement and hesitation warring in his gaze.

"Me either. I had my yearly exam a few months ago and haven't been with anyone since then except you. I'm clean," I say.

"So am I."

A few moments of silence pass and I decide to let it go. I reach for his nightstand to grab a condom, but he stops me.

"We don't need it." His voice sounds strained from lust and anticipation.

"You sure?"

"Yes," he says as he bucks up against me. "I can't wait to feel this pussy bare and feel your tight heat swallow my cock. Put me inside of you, Mac."

My mouth has gone dry at his words, so I lean in to give him a kiss as I grab his length with one hand and notch the head at my entrance. I groan at the insistent pressure and feel ready to come again when I shift my hips and feel him begin to slide into me. It takes a few tries, but eventually he's seated inside me to the hilt.

"Fuck, darlin', you're squeezin' me like a vice," he chokes out.

I manage a shuddered gasp in response and revel in the feeling of being impaled by him, my legs spread wide and my pussy filled to the max.

"Ride me, Mac," he grits out. "Move. Show me what you like."

I can't help but respond to his command, and I begin to grind my hips against his. I lift my hips in shallow thrusts and swivel so I'm rotating my clit against his abs. The feeling of pleasure is intense, and I can feel another orgasm start to build deep inside.

"So sweet," Lawson groans as he thrusts up, deeper than what I've been doing.

"Oh my God, yes," I cry out. "Lawson, please..." I say, eyes clenched tightly shut.

"Please what, Mac?"

"Please, fuck me. Make me come, please," I plead.

"I'll make you come, but I won't fuck you." His words surprise me and as my eyes fly open, he shifts and turns so I'm laying on my side on my hip. He's still inside me, but the new angle has me writhing in need.

"Why not?"

"Because," he leans down and sucks one of nipples into his mouth as his hand snakes down between our bodies to flick my clit. "Calling this fucking won't do this justice and is a disservice to you."

I'm shocked speechless and can only respond by widening my eyes. He doesn't seem to mind because he starts to thrust slowly, yet heavily, into my tight heat. As he continues to enter me, he doesn't let up the pressure of his fingers around my clit and the oncoming orgasm I sensed earlier is building in strength.

I look at him pumping above me and can't believe how incredibly lucky I am. I reach up and place my hand over his heart again so I can feel his heartbeat. His smooth skin feels like a furnace, and his pulse is more erratic but still steady and true. His gaze follows my hand and watches it for endless moments before he looks me in the eyes again and places his own hand over my heart.

I push back against him as he continues to make love to me, both of us with our hands over the other's heart. Our heartbeats have synced up, and his thrusts match the steady thumping as well. We keep our eyes locked on each other, and the air between us hangs heavily with unspoken words.

I love you, I love you, I love you, my heart calls out to his.

Lawson starts to speed up his pace and, on a particularly heavy thrust, he grits out, "I'm yours." He punctuates his words with a rapid tapping against my clit and, after a few more heavy thrusts, we reach the pinnacle of our release at the same time.

My back arches at the sweet release, and Lawson continues to thrust, gentling his strokes as my pussy milks him for all he's worth.

"Wow," I say.

He chuckles from above me as he pulls out. "I know."

He starts to move away, but I stop him. I push him down with what little strength I have left and rest my head on his chest as I trace his strong muscles with lazy kisses and fingers.

"I've never come at the same time as anyone," I muse, wonder clear in my tone.

"Me either. You know why that is, right?"

"Why?" I ask on a yawn, the intense orgasms catching up and making me sleepy.

"Because," he leans down to place a kiss on the top of my head, "we're a perfect match."

My face breaks out in a smile at his words as I start to succumb to sleep.

"Lawson?" I ask drowsily.

"Yeah, darlin'?" His voice sounds far off and groggy as well, though not nearly as bad.

Darkness is creeping into my vision and the walls around my heart are falling faster than my eyelids. My words come out whisper-soft and feather against his chest. "I love you."

25

LAWSON

uck fuck fuck fuck fuck. I don't know what the hell I'm doing anymore. Last night I made love to Mac —a first for me—right before she passed out and whispered the three little words that shredded up my insides with more feelings than I know what to do with. I'm not even sure if she remembers saying them, but her words dragged me out of my post-sex lethargy real quick. I lay there for at least an hour, staring at the ceiling as she slept peacefully against my chest. She ended up staying the night, and in the morning I couldn't hold a decent conversation so I fucked her roughly in the shower, as if I could simultaneously fuck and wash away her tender words.

I just got back from dropping her off. Although she didn't say the words again, I can't get the vision of her sweet, trusting smile and eyes filled with affection out of my head. Right as she kissed me goodbye, she said she had something important to tell me later. She sounded so hopeful and excited. I'm pretty sure she wants to tell me how she feels, and I'm not sure I can handle hearing the words again. I'm not sure what I'll do if she says them when she's completely lucid, so I told her I had plans. It's not that I don't care for Mac. I do, way more than I've cared for anyone before. When I'm not near her, I feel anxious anticipation that's only soothed when I see her again. She's my best friend's little sister and I know her family, so that's gotta explain my stronger than normal feelings for her. That and the fact she's the first woman I've fucked repeatedly. That must be it.

I don't know why I got all emotional and shit last night. I basically told her I was making love to her, but I need to stop whatever this is. I'm not looking for anything and don't want to be tied down, and I definitely don't want to lead her on. I'm happy being single...*right*? Right. Sure, I'm gonna miss her, that wasn't a lie. I'm sure I'll get over it when I bury myself in someone new. My body immediately reacts, and I try to ignore the churning and self-disgust in my gut at this thought and brush it away before I can dwell on it further.

I'm going to need to find a way to end things as cleanly as possible. I don't want to hurt her, but I'm not sure how to reconcile everything I thought before summer with the turmoil going on inside my head now. *You're a cowardly, lying piece of shit*, my conscience whispers. I ignore that nagging voice and push it away. I'm not prepared for the unknown and need to go back to something familiar.

As I pull back up to my apartment my phone rings, and when I see the name on the screen I see my way to get things resolved. It isn't my smartest idea, but it's all I've got right now.

"Hello? This is Lawson," I answer the call. I listen for a few seconds and steel my resolve. "Yeah, okay. I'll be right there. See you soon."

I hang up and head into my apartment to prepare for

what I need to do. I'm in and out quickly, eager to escape the memories of last night that plague me. I ignore my rebellious heart as I drive away and crank the music to drown out my thoughts. This may not be the best way, but I know it'll work. God forgive me. Mac...please forgive me.

I WALK with an extra bounce in my step as I think about all that's in store for me. I feel weightless and heady with the relief of finally making a decision and putting my fate in my own hands. I'm staying in Starwood, and nothing is going to change my mind. I grin at the thought and feel an extra surge of happiness when I think about Lawson. I'm doing this all for me, and I'm excited to tell him I plan on moving back here. When he dropped me off I told him I had something to tell him later, and I can't wait to tell him I'm not moving. I want to shout the words from every rooftop here. I'm not going to lie, my stomach flutters with nerves at how he'll react, but after last night I can only hope he'll respond positively.

I'm on the back porch at my parents' home and am putting together mini jugs of cider for the next farmers' market. I am equal parts elated and relieved that I didn't botch the cider and that it turned out sweet, its rich taste a delight on the taste buds. I'm hoping these little jugs of deliciousness will get the word out about the cider and will help drive business in a couple weeks. I've set the grand reopening of the barn for a little over two weeks from now so I can work on getting my life in order and so that I can ready the next few batches of cider. I look out the window and see the trees off in the distance, weeping under the weight of the ripe fruit hanging from their branches. Apple season runs through the end of October and, judging from the sheer volume of apples and cider I'll be making, there'll be enough cider to store for winter. My heart races in excitement and swells with joy at the thought of this next chapter in my life. It feels so incredible to be happy.

Just as I'm putting on the last of the Shady Layne Orchard labels on the jugs, my phone rings. I look down and see that it's Langley.

"Hey girlie," I answer. "How's it goin'?"

"Great! How're you, sugar? You busy?" She sounds breathless on the other end of the line.

"Not really. I just finished packaging some cider for the next farmers' market. Why, what's up?"

"I need a huge favor, please. I'll make it worth your while," she cajoles.

"That statement right there worries me," I laugh.

"It'll be okay! I need two things actually but was thinkin' we could knock out two birds with one stone. I need help takin' all these pies to the charity auction, and I need a date for tonight. Would you be able to help out and go with me, please? After we get done delivering the pies it should be a good time."

I think for a second before giving in. I had asked Lawson if he had plans for later when he dropped me off and he said he'd be busy but that he'd see me soon.

"Of course! I don't have any plans for tonight. When do you need me?"

"In about an hour. Will that work? I can drive tonight, but if you'd like you can come get ready over at my place."

At the mention of getting ready a thought hits me. "Oh God, Langley. What's the dress code for this thing?"

"Formal. Why?"

"You've seen my closet," I laugh. "I have nothing to wear

and an hour isn't enough time for me to shower and go shopping for a new dress."

"Don't worry about it," she says. "I'll have a dress for you."

I'm skeptical because we aren't the same height, and she's curvier than I am. "You sure?"

"Yes, ma'am. I've got a dress that'll look great on you. I got it when I was a cup size smaller," she admits. "I wish it still fit me, but you can have it as a thank you for helping me and going as my date last minute."

"Langley, that's so generous of you. Thank you!"

"No problem. I'm hangin' up now. I still have to get these damn pies packaged. I'll see you in an hour and we'll glam up before leaving. See you soon, sugar!"

"Sounds good. See you soon," I reply right before she ends the phone call.

I quickly put the cider away and run upstairs to get ready. I catch my reflection in the mirror right before I step in the shower and hope Langley can work her magic.

TWO HOURS LATER, I'm standing in Langley's bathroom and am marveling at my transformation. I've gotta give it to her, she's got some serious talent. As soon as I got to her place she yanked me inside and, after we transported the pies to the car, she set to work. I rotate on my heels and check out my reflection. I'm decked out in a beautiful, seafoam-colored cocktail dress that brings out the bluish-green hues in my hazel eyes. It's elegant and classy, the fit hugging me in all the right places. It turns out Langley and I have the same shoe size, so she also outfitted me in a pair of nude pumps. When combined with the hem of the dress, which hits me just above my knees, they make my legs look extra long. My hair is in loose curls that are clipped over one shoulder, and my makeup is fresh and flawless. I don't mean to toot my own horn, but I look amazing.

"I was going to decline accepting this dress from you, but I think that polite gesture went out the window," I admit. "I love this dress, Langley."

"Ha," she laughs. "Screw being polite. Keep it, please. I can't squeeze into it anyway, and it's too gorgeous to stay in my closet untouched. I have another dress in the same color since I love it so much, so I'm good. Besides, I'm sure it looks better on you than it would have on me. You look gorgeous, Mac."

"Thank you," I smile. "You look gorgeous as well."

And she does. She's in a cocktail dress as well, but this one is the color of rich, ripe plums. The bold color makes her look extra exotic and her lush, black hair falls in a long sheet down her back.

"Thanks, sugar." She winks at me as she swipes on one last coat of gloss on her lips. "Let's get goin'! I have the hottest date tonight and can't wait to show you off!"

We strut out to the car and she drives us to the venue, which is an upscale hotel that was recently built. As we pull up, I look down at my feet and back to the pies that are in the back seat.

"Langley?" I question.

"Yes, Mac?"

"Do you have an extra pair of flats? I don't want to fall on my face getting the pies inside."

"Oh, Mac," she laughs. "Don't worry. We won't be taking the pies inside. Our job is to get them here. I was told by the coordinator to give my name to the valet and they'd have some of the event workers come out and grab them. Our job now is to have fun," she ends with a smile.

She pulls up to the entrance and speaks to the valet and, sure enough, a few men show up a few moments later to grab the pies and take them inside. As they grab them, they shoot us interested, sidelong glances. It's obvious they're checking us out. I'm not interested in them, but it's always nice to be noticed.

We make our way inside arm in arm and wave hello to people we know. We're greeted by the event coordinator, who thanks us warmly for the pies and for coming before telling us to have a fabulous evening. As we enter the main event space, which is in a huge auditorium, I gasp. The space is decked out beautifully, and the chandeliers glittering above add a little extra pizzazz to the event. I look around at the tall centerpieces made of fresh flowers and feel my blood start to pump at the lively music being played. I'm turning back to look at Langley so I can thank her for bringing me when my eyes land on something that makes my blood run cold.

Off to my right, standing among a small circle of people, is Lawson. He looks delectable in a tuxedo the color of midnight and an emerald green bow tie that matches his eyes perfectly, making them pop more than usual. His hair is combed to the side and his scruff lends him a mysterious, extra sexy edge. However, it's not just the fact that he's here that's shocked me. I shift my eyes slightly to his right and there, plastered against him like a second skin, is Della Du Bois. Della *fucking* Du Bois. Her bottle blonde hair is pulled back in an elegant updo, and she's wearing a garish dress the color of burnt oranges. A small part of me feels sick satisfaction that she's not wearing green like Lawson is but another, much larger part of me, is seething with jealousy and confusion. I wouldn't think they were together, but the way she's all over him and the self-satisfied smile and possessive hand hooked around his bicep have me bristling. He's at a very public event, in our town, with a woman who is clearly his date. I don't understand what's happening, but I want to rip her hands off of him and slap him across the face. Again.

I don't realize I've stopped in my tracks until Langley turns back to me.

"Mac?" she asks, confusion clear in her voice. She follows my gaze, and once her eyes land on Lawson she cusses under her breath. "Holy fuck, what's he doing here? And what the hell is he doing here with *her*?" she says with disdain.

It's as if he can feel the intense scrutiny of our stares because at that moment, Lawson turns and looks at both of us. His eyes are unreadable, but they stay locked on mine. I feel like I could tug on the connection between us and draw him to where we're standing, but he stays still before moving his gaze away from me dismissively.

I'm not sure what's happening, but I'm going to find out and try to ignore the rapid fracturing of my heart in my chest.

26

I f it weren't for Langley holding onto my arm, I would have marched right over to Lawson and demanded answers. With more muttered curses under her breath, she drags me toward our table. After pushing me down into my seat, she sits in the chair next to mine and scoots closer.

"My brother is a dumbass," she says bluntly.

I can't form a sentence at the moment, my mind still running a million miles a second as it tries to process what I just saw.

"Do you know why he'd be here with Della, of all people?"

I shake my head and search my brain for any reason, any at all, to explain why he's here with someone else. I don't even try to deny anything in front of Langley because she obviously knows there is something going on between us.

"I don't know," I finally manage to get out. "He's been so adamant about not dating anyone in town. This goes against everything he's told me. Things were so great last night, too. And this morning. I'm not sure what's happening."

I feel cold inside and am thankful that I'm managing to keep it together as well as I have been.

"What happened last night?"

"We made love," I say in a hushed voice. "I'm sorry in advance for any oversharing on my part. He initiated it, too. He kept telling me he'd miss me. I thought..." I pause, embarrassed at my next words. "I thought we had reached a turning point. He made me feel cared about. Now...I don't know. He won't even take me on dates in town because he doesn't want people seeing. I don't know why he's suddenly on a public date with someone else, especially after last night. Now I just feel...dirty." I can feel my eyes start to shine with unshed tears, so I look up at the ceiling and try to will them away.

"Don't let him get to you," Langley urges as she reaches out to rub a hand up and down my arm. "I know he cares about you, Mac. There's got to be an explanation. My guess is he's probably freaking out right now cause he's a guy and doesn't know how to handle feelings. I know my brother better than anyone, and I've seen how he looks at you. He's never been happier and he never, ever brings anyone home."

"He didn't bring me home, Langley. Your parents invited me," I say miserably.

"You know what I mean. He would never have acted the way he did last night in front of my parents if he wasn't serious about you."

I find it hard to believe in her words because I can't scrub the thought of Della on his arm out of my mind.

"I don't know, Langley. Being here with her at this event makes its own kind of statement."

"We'll get you answers, don't you worry. Just try and have a good time, sugar. And whatever you do, ignore him. Don't let him see that he's gotten to you. We're gonna focus on us tonight and show him what he's missing. If I know my brother—and I do—he won't be able to stay away for long."

I smile half-heartedly at her enthusiasm and attempt to cheer me up. I try to follow her advice and ignore Lawson, but I can feel his presence in the room, calling me to him. A few minutes later, we are approached by two handsome men who ask us if we'd like to dance. Before I can decline, Langley accepts for both of us. I try and shoot her a subtle glare, and she just smiles in return as she's led away to the dance floor.

"I'm Deacon," the man left standing in front of me introduces himself. "If you'd prefer, we can stay here at the table while our friends dance."

I look up at him and have to admit that he's handsome in a wholesome, boy next door way. He's tall, with golden hair the color of sunshine, and his eyes are a warm brown color. He isn't looking at me with lust in his eyes. Instead, he exudes a friendly vibe, and I find myself softening toward him.

"No, dancing would be nice. Thank you," I smile.

He leads me to the dance floor, and my anger from earlier soon fades to the background. It's still there but is no longer simmering so close to the surface, ready to boil over at any moment. Deacon is a great dance partner and maneuvers me easily around the dance floor as he tells me joke after awful joke.

"What's a pepper that won't leave you alone?" His eyes are twinkling, and his lips are already twitching at the corners.

I feel an answering smile form on my face as I think about it. "I don't know. What?" I ask.

"Jalapeño business." He says the words with extra flair

and the expression on his face matches the ridiculous punch line.

I throw my head back in laughter at his joke. "Oh my God, that was terrible. It's so bad, it's actually good," I say as I wipe a tear or two from the corners of my eyes.

"Just wait, you're going to be sharing that one with people. I'll let you borrow it."

"How generous of you," I say as I roll my eyes playfully at him.

We continue to dance and smile, erupting in peals of laughter every now and then at another of his bad jokes. I notice him looking over my shoulder periodically and decide to ask him what he's looking at.

"What's grabbed your attention, Deacon? You keep looking behind me. Do you see another unsuspecting person to practice your comedy routine on?"

"Ha, very funny. Actually, I'm staring at a man who looks like he wants to walk across the floor and punch me in the face. For my own safety, I'm keeping an eye on him."

My face blanches slightly at his words. "What's he look like?" I can't help but ask.

"Tall, brown hair, wearing a tux. I think it's Lawson Westbrook. He owns a construction company in town. Why? Do you know him?" He's looking between me and Lawson, shifting his eyes back and forth. "Oh, you do. What's the story there?"

"No story to tell," I say bluntly. "We just know each other's families." Even saying the words makes my heart break a little more.

"As much as I'd like to believe you, I don't think that's the truth," Deacon replies honestly. "Besides, he's on his way over here."

"What?!" I exclaim in an annoying mix of disgust, fear, and shock.

"Yep. His date in the ugly orange dress walked off with a bunch of other women in hideous dresses. Incoming in three...two...one," he counts down in a whisper.

Right on cue, I feel a solid presence behind me.

"May I cut in?" Lawson's words are terse and barely polite.

"Yeah man, take care of her. She's fantastic." Deacon winks at me and I mouth "traitor" at him before turning and stepping into Lawson's arms.

We hold onto one another stiffly but soon his dancing skills and our unfailing attraction to one another prevails, enabling us to move across the floor fluidly. It's only a matter of moments before Lawson breaks the silence between us.

"Who was that?" Wow, he wastes no time in getting straight to the point.

"Are you kidding me, Lawson?"

"What? I saw you two all cozy and laughing together. You two looked close."

Oh, he's a fucking crazy hypocrite. "Excuse me? If we looked close, then I'm sure we don't hold a candle to you and *Della*," I spit out her name as if it leaves a foul taste in my mouth.

Lawson's mouth tightens, and I feel him stiffen at my statement. "Oh, you can bring up who I'm dancing with, but I can't do the same?" I taunt. "Those are some double standards, Lawson. Why are you here now, dancing with me?"

"I didn't like seeing you dance with him," he admits in a voice low enough that I have to strain to hear.

"Well too bad, Lawson. You obviously came here with someone else. Cut the mind games and confusing shit. She's your date, right?"

He looks at me and his eyes are blazing. "Yes."

"I didn't know you two were so well-acquainted. I also didn't know that when you told me this morning you'd be busy, that you'd be busy with her. Besides, I thought you didn't screw around with more than one person at a time."

"I don't," he says, making me feel more confused. "And we aren't...yet."

I want to cry at his confirmation that he's on a public date with someone else, someone who isn't me, and at what his words insinuate. Does this mean he's done with me? "I thought you didn't date women in our town."

"Yeah, well, Della is different."

Those five words effectively confirm my suspicions and kill the hope that had flared to life after we made love last night. While I'm still feeling sad, I also feel white-hot rage start to build deep inside of my chest. I thought I was different, but I guess I'm wrong.

"Lawson, last night..." I pause and try to keep my composure intact. "What was last night all about then? I got the impression that this was different, that there was *more* between us."

He stares at me for an indeterminable amount of time before he answers. "It was a different experience, Mac, that's all. I care about you, but not in that way. I told you this was temporary."

"But...what if I? I..." I trail off. I won't beg, but I'm just so confused. "Just to make things clear, you don't see this going anywhere?"

His expression is stoic and I can't read it at all, so much so that his next words surprise me and catch me off guard. "Mac, do you love me?"

I can't lie to him or myself anymore. "Yes," I breathe. "I

love you, Lawson." I want to kick myself at the way my voice cracks slightly when I say his name.

His expression doesn't change as he responds. "I know. I'm sorry, but I don't love you back and I never will. This summer was just about fun."

His words slice through my heart and cause the pieces that have broken apart to explode into tiny, miniscule shards. Thankfully, the anger that's been brewing inside sparks some life into my body and my words.

"Fuck you, Lawson. Fuck you and your stupid arrangement. And fuck you for throwing me aside like this just so you can chase some new piece of ass." I rip my arms away from his and step away from him. Keeping my voice low I say, "I don't love this asshole that's saying this shit. That's not the man I've grown up admiring. I don't know what happened to him, but the Lawson I love is the one who made love to me last night."

"He's gone," is all he says in return.

"Who's gone?" a whiny voice says from behind my back.

Lawson's eyes glint in irritation as they look behind me. I turn and see that Della has returned from her trip to the restroom.

"No one," Lawson mutters.

Della saunters up to Lawson and places her claw-like hand on his bicep again, clearly staking her claim.

"So good to see you, Mac. My mother said she ran into you at the grocery store recently. How long are you in town for?" She's smiling but her words are disingenuous, her eyes cunning and cruel.

"Only a few more days," I say, not bothering to add that I still have every intention of moving back. Lawson lost every right to information about me when he broke my heart.

"Oh? Well, that's too bad," Della crows, the satisfaction

in her eyes belying her words. "If you were staying longer, I'd have loved for you to go on a double date with us," she squeezes Lawson's arm.

"Oh, how nice of you," I say, sarcasm clear in my voice. "I need to go find my date. Have a good night, Della." I give one final look at the man who has stolen my heart and handled it so carelessly. His face is impassive, and his body is tense as he watches me. "Goodbye, Lawson," I say with finality.

Without another word, I turn on my heel to go find Langley. I need to get the hell out of here.

Chicago—One Week Later

"Another glass, please," I gesture to Cade to pour more of my favorite wine.

He obliges and grabs the bottle off the coffee table to pour me a generous amount. I'm back in our apartment and am sprawled out on our couch in the ultimate comfort clothing: my unicorn onesie and fuzzy socks. He knows I need to numb myself a little bit as I try and forget Lawson, which is next to impossible when I can't stop cursing the bastard's name.

After my run-in with Lawson at the charity event, I found Langley and we left early. She spent the night with me and we gorged on an ungodly amount of ice cream as we binge-watched too many episodes of reality television to count. She tried to reassure me that everything would be okay and made a valiant attempt to convince me of Lawson's feelings, but I couldn't forget his cold words. The next morning, I booked my ticket back to Chicago and flew out that night, not wanting to chance seeing Lawson and Della out in public. I surprised myself by doing a nice job of holding it together, but as soon as I saw Cade I broke down and sobbed, all of my pent-up emotion from the past couple days finally boiling over.

"I'm gonna be okay, CC," I slur my words just a bit. Perhaps I've had too much wine. "Besides, I need to be back in time for the barn's reopening next week. My parents are selling the jugs at the farmers' market and getting the word out, but I want to be there. I *need* to be there. I worked hard," I say, feeling that same spark of anger that's kept me going the past week.

"I never doubted you'd be okay, Mac," Cade says. "Trust me, it'll all work out."

"It will, but I'm so confused."

"I'm sure he is too, Mac," he supplies. "I can't speak for him since I'm not entirely sure what the hell is going on in that head of his, but I'm sure there's an explanation for all of this."

"Wow, are you sticking up for him?" When I shared all the details of what had me coming back home sooner than planned, I thought Cade was going to explode. I'm still surprised he didn't hop on the first flight back to Tennessee to kick Lawson's ass.

"No," he reassures me. "But his actions that night don't add up to everything else that went on between you two. Something isn't right."

"Thanks for having girl talk with me. I know it must kill you," I smile weakly.

"You're my best friend. It's no biggie." He gives me an answering smile in return as he gets up from the couch to stretch. "I won't lie. I'm going to be dragging Ollie to some super manly activity to make sure I get my testosterone levels back up."

His comment causes me to snort in laughter, and it also lightens the heaviness in my heart. I'm thankful that he's here to support me but will restrain myself from expressing it so he doesn't get embarrassed.

I get up from the couch as well and walk my empty wine glass to the sink. "Speaking of plans, guess what I have planned over the next few days?" The excitement I feel manages to peek through, and Cade must notice because he smiles and ruffles my hair with one hand.

"Besides packing?"

"Besides packing," I confirm.

He steps back and leans against the kitchen island, his hands resting on the countertop on each side. "No clue. What's going on?"

"I have a few meetings with clients that I've worked with in the past. I emailed them letting them know I was back in town, and they're excited to hear more about my plan to go solo with design. They've agreed to follow me, but I'm hoping they'll be open to referring me to fellow business partners."

"Nice, I'll also be sure to spread the word as well. You were wasting your talents at your old job. I'm excited for you." He smiles at me, and I know I'll get a few clients out of Cade's referrals. In the business world his word is gold, and if he likes a business enough to endorse it, then others will surely follow.

"Thanks CC, for everything." I walk over and give him a quick hug before stepping away and walking toward my bedroom.

I have a busy few days ahead of me, what with packing and the business lunches, and need to make sure I'm prepared. Even though Lawson ended things with me, I still feel excited to go back home because I know in my heart it's the right decision. I may not be getting everything I hoped for but I'm ready for what's in store.

LAWSON

"YOU'RE AN ASSHOLE," a disembodied voice reaches my ears as I try and blink my eyes open. I hear the clinking of bottles before the voice speaks again. "You should be ashamed of yourself."

"Ugh, who's there?" I scrub my hands over my head in an effort to dull the pounding in my skull. "And please, stop yelling," I groan. I feel like a jackhammer was used in an attempt to get to my brain, the pain is so acute.

"Your sister, you douche canoe!" Langley shouts. So much for some peace and quiet. "Do you have any idea what you've done?" Her voice gets progressively louder and as I lean up on the couch, I finally spot her. She's moving around my apartment with my recycling bin and is angrily tossing empty beer bottles inside in an attempt to clean up.

"What day is it?"

"Ugh, men! It's been two days since the charity auction, Lawson. And you know what happened right after?"

She's stomped over to me by this point and is glaring down at me with daggers in her eyes. Holy shit, when have I ever seen Langley this angry?

My thought is cut short when she continues. "I took Mac home, and I watched her heart finish breaking over your stupid ass. And you know what else?"

My gut clenches at the thought of hurting Mac the way I did. God, I'm so fucked up.

"No. What else, Langley?" I ask warily.

"She went back to Chicago yesterday, you self-absorbed prick! She's no longer in Starwood. How does that make you feel now, huh? Ugh, I can't even look at you. I love you Lawson, but I'm so ashamed to call you my brother right now."

I'm hit with a wave of nausea, and I know it isn't from all the beers I've been drinking since the night of the charity auction. Shame, hot and intense, washes over me. My skin crawls at the memory of what I said to Mac and how I ended things.

"She moved back?"

"That's what I said, Lawson. Honestly, what the hell were you thinking?"

I groan and bend so my head is hanging between my knees, my arms thrown over my neck. "I don't know, Langley."

She shakes the recycling bin threateningly, the clinking of the bottles causing my head to ache further. "Well, you best get to explainin' mister before I start breaking things, starting with your face."

I sit back up and put my elbows on my knees so I can rest my temples between my palms. "I freaked out, Langley," I whisper.

"No shit, Sherlock. God, I didn't think I got *all* the brains, but it sure seems that way now. She told me you made love to her and were telling her you'd miss her which, while a complete overshare, is completely misleading if you say you're not looking for anything serious."

I'm silent as I process her words.

"Do you want something serious with Mac?" she demands.

"I don't know what I'm feeling, Langley," I groan. "I don't

fucking know anymore. The other night was a mistake, but nothing happened with Della, I swear it."

More silence passes, and I glance up to see that she's sitting on the coffee table in front of me. She's looking at me expectantly and raises her hand for me to continue.

"Yes, we made love," I admit. "And it was me who brought it up. We agreed to keep our time together temporary and physical. I wasn't looking for anything more, Langley. You know how it is in this town. Everyone's in everyone's business, and when you come from our family it's multiplied tenfold."

"Mmhmm, go on."

"I told her this and even took her out on dates in other towns to avoid gossip in this town," I admit with chagrin, to which my sister mutters under her breath that I'm a tool. I can't help but agree. "I know, I know. But you know me, I've never had anything serious with anyone. I just never saw it in the cards for me. With Mac though...everything is different. I feel like something's tugging at me when I'm not near her, and when I'm near her I never want to leave. She got under my skin and when she told me she loved me—"

"She what?" Langley exclaims. "Oh God Lawson, don't tell me you didn't say it back."

"I didn't say it back." I still can't believe she said it in the first place.

"You are such a fucking ball sack!"

"Langley, I didn't want anything serious. I don't know how to deal with all these...emotions and shit. She told me the night before the charity auction as she was falling asleep, and I don't even think she remembers saying it. I freaked out and after I dropped her off, I got a phone call from Della. Her mother gave her my phone number, and she said her date got sick and she needed a date to the event. I went with her in hopes that the town would talk and word would get back to Mac, but I wasn't prepared for y'all to show up together and for her to see it in person. This is all so fucked up."

"You've got that right, Lawson. You fucked up. Now what are you going to do to fix it?"

"I don't need to 'fix' anything, Langley. It's over. It was never goin' anywhere with Mac anyway. We both knew that."

My sister stares at me for long moments, a skeptical expression on her face. "So you're telling me that you don't care if she's back in Chicago and finds love with someone else?"

I can't even bring myself to answer because I know if I say I don't care, it'd be a lie. A look of triumph sparks in Langley's eyes at my lack of answer.

"Exactly! Let me tell you somethin'. I'm not sure you realize it, but moments ago you said you *weren't* looking for anything more and you *didn't* want anything serious. Past tense, Lawson. *Past tense.* I think you're just afraid to have found someone who changes all that for you, and you're unable to get over having your private life in the spotlight for a little bit. I have one last question for you, Lawson. I know you mentioned you don't know how you're feeling, but if you're honest with yourself I think you know the answer. Do you love Mac?"

My stomach twists at the words, but the sensation isn't all that unpleasant, just foreign. I stare at her as I mull over the words. Do I love Mac? I don't know. I know that the thought of her with someone else guts me and, regardless of how I acted the other night, I meant what I said before. We're a perfect match, and even though I'm not entirely sure how I'm feeling, I know I fucked things up and regret lying to her.

"You know what, don't answer that now. It's clear you have some thinking to do. Seriously though, get your shit together before you fuck things up further and lose her for good."

And with those final words, my sister gives me a hug and leaves my apartment, the bin full of empty beer bottles waiting by the door.

28

I'm surprised by the nervous excitement I feel as I get ready. Yesterday I met with a couple of my old clients, and they've agreed to help spread the word about my business. I have my last business lunch today and find I'm looking forward to it the most out of all of them. Today I'm meeting with Oliver, Cade's other best friend and business partner. Not only is he also a good friend of mine, the potential to reach a whole new client base through his connections has my stomach fluttering in anticipation.

I make sure my ballerina bun is still intact, zip up my Tiffany blue shift dress, and slip on my flats before heading out the door to meet him. I make my way outside and hail a cab. Luxe, the upscale French bistro on the Magnificent Mile I'm heading to, is close enough to where we live that I could hop on the red line and walk the rest of the way, but I don't want to risk being late for this meeting.

The cab eventually pulls up to Luxe so I exit, but as I turn to pay the driver a long, suited arm reaches in and hands the driver a wad of bills, effectively preventing me from paying.

"Thanks, chap. Have a good day," a cultured, British voice says.

I step back onto the curb and turn to the man who paid my fare. "Thanks, Ollie. It's good to see you again," I smile at him.

"Likewise, love. Give me a hug. It's been forever."

He holds out his arms, and I step into his strong embrace. He pulls back just slightly and looks me in the eyes, concern clear in his gaze. "You okay? Cade told me about what happened with that todger back in Tennessee."

My eyes start to water slightly at the reference to Lawson, but I shake my head and smile wider. "Nothing I can't handle, but thank you for checking." I lean into his hug for a few more seconds before stepping back. "Let's head in."

We walk into Luxe and Ollie keeps his hand on my lower back. I can't help but compare his platonic touch with how I felt whenever Lawson did this. Why is it he's the only one who makes my body and my heart act out of sorts? The hostess eyes Ollie with interest and leads us to a quaint table for two out on the patio.

I glance at Ollie and take in his tall frame as we sit down. Like Lawson and Cade, he's incredibly good-looking but in a reserved, buttoned-up way. Although he's British, he looks like he came straight from a beach somewhere in California with his golden, tousled hair and bright, blue eyes. He looks like a gorgeous hybrid of all the best parts of Paul Walker (may he rest in peace) and Charlie Hunnam. The combination of his looks and accent bring to mind one word: drool-worthy. He's sexy and definitely rocks the suit he's wearing but, like with Cade, I've never felt that extra spark that I've only managed to feel with Lawson.

"So what'll you be having, love? And I'm telling you now, you're not paying, so don't give me any of that tosh about going dutch," Ollie tells me, his voice smoother than the softest silk. I may not be attracted to him in that way but I could listen to the man talk all day.

"Well, now that you've made that statement I'm definitely not getting the salad," I laugh, and he joins in. "If you want to share a cheese plate with me, we can do that," I say as I look over the menu. "Then I'll probably get the steak frites. What about you?" I ask as I rest the menu on the table.

No sooner do I set the menu down than a waiter appears to take our order. Talk about speedy service.

"Hello, Mr. Taylor. Nice to see you again, and welcome to your lovely guest," the waiter gestures toward me. "What can I get for you both today?" I smile at the personalized service. I'm used to this happening when I go out with Cade, but it never fails to impress me.

"Hello, Weston. Thank you. I always look forward to dining here, as does Ms. Layne," he nods his head at me. "We'll start off with *l'assiette de fromages*," he says, ordering our cheese plate with a perfect French accent. "For her entrée, Ms. Layne will have the steak frites. How would you like that cooked, love?"

The waiter turns his gaze on me, his pen at the ready. "Medium rare, please."

After scribbling down my order, Weston turns back to Ollie. "And for myself, I'll have the beef bourguignon. As far as drinks, I'd just like a water, please. I need to head back to work after this. What would you like, Mac?"

"Water with lemon, please."

"Fantastic," Weston says. "The waters will be right out, and your food will be out shortly. Thank you, sir."

We both smile as he walks away. Within seconds, we both have water and our cheese plate follows shortly after.

We take our time enjoying the cheese, jams, and bread before Ollie asks me about my plans for my business.

I explain to him my situation earlier in the year and my plan for when I move back to Starwood. He listens attentively and nods when he hears something he likes. He has an astute business mind, and I'm thankful that he lets me pick his brain for new ideas. Our conversation slows when our entrées arrive, but we continue to chat between bites.

I spear a fry with my fork as I wrap up my business talk. "Thank you for all the advice, Ollie. Between you and Cade, I don't see how I can fail," I laugh. "Please think of me if you have any clients who may need a new designer or rebranding, but only if you want to," I say quickly. "Please don't feel obligated to just because we're friends. I want to earn someone's business because of my talent, not because of who I know."

Ollie smiles and unbuttons his suit jacket so he can lean back and cross his legs. "Oh Mac, I've already taken that liberty. And to ease your mind, I never recommend someone if I don't think they have talent. My name and business is on the line, and I'm being completely honest when I say I'd endorse you even if we weren't friends."

His words warm me from the inside, and I give him a wide smile. "Thank you, Ollie. That really means a lot."

He gestures with a wave of one hand. "Don't mention it. It's my pleasure. I've already had a few express interest, so once you have your new business established let me know and I'll give them your contact information."

Excitement wells in my chest, and I feel my eyes water again at his kind gesture. This is really happening. "You're the best. Thank you, Ollie. I don't know how I can ever repay you. This seriously means the world to me."

"All I ask for in payment is one thing," he says, his tone serious.

I lean forward, eager to hear what he wants. "Name it."

He leans forward as well so our faces are close together over the center of the table. "I need you to send me some of that apple butter and jam. I was at Cade's and tried it, and I need more. My morning toast will never be the same without it."

I laugh hysterically. I feel validated that they love the butter and jellies so much that they're asking for them here. Maybe one day I can start shipping them if business is booming at the orchard. "You have yourself a deal."

We sit here, laughing and smiling goofily at each other, when a throat clearing to our right draws our attention. I turn and my jaw drops at what I see before me. Am I dreaming?

29

Lawson

I stare up at the huge, modern skyscraper before me. I can't believe this behemoth of a building belongs to someone I know. I enter through the revolving doors of Carson Taylor Enterprises in downtown Chicago, and make my way to the center of the room to what looks like a welcome desk. I stand in line and approach the steel-haired receptionist when she waves me over.

"Hello, welcome to Carson Taylor Enterprises. How may I help you?" she asks briskly.

"Hello," I peer at her name badge, "Susan. I'd like to meet with Cade Carson, please."

"Your name, please." She has her fingers poised and ready to go above the keyboard.

"Lawson Westbrook, ma'am."

Her eyebrow lifts slightly, but she types in my name at a rapid pace before turning back to me.

"Do you have an appointment?"

"No, I was hoping I could step in if he was free."

Susan looks at me as if I've grown a second head. "My apologies Mr. Westbrook but no one, and I mean *no one*, sees Mr. Carson or Mr. Taylor without an appointment."

I resist the urge to roll my eyes. "Okay, may I schedule an appointment please?" She nods her head and I add on, "Could we please make it for the earliest time available?"

She nods again and picks up the phone. "I just need to dial his personal assistant. One moment, please." She relays my appointment request to the person on the other line and bobs her head a few times before moving the mouthpiece away from her lips. "Certainly. The earliest I have available is in January. Does a specific day work for you?" she asks as she looks at me expectantly.

"January is the earliest available appointment?" I ask, shocked. It's September, for fuck's sake. I don't envy the man if he's booked out that far in advance.

"Mr. Carson is a very busy man."

I run my hand over the back of my neck in frustration. This is a lot more inconvenient than I anticipated. I'm trying to go over my options when a voice behind me speaks.

"Lawson, is that you?"

I turn around and I see Cade, thank God. He looks surprised and weary to see me standing in the lobby of his building.

"Yeah, you got a sec? I was hoping to talk to you if you have a free moment."

He looks at me for a moment before nodding. "Sure, follow me."

I turn to look back at Susan. "I won't be needing that appointment, thank you." I smile broadly at her and want to laugh at her surprised expression.

I follow Cade into a private elevator and we stand next to one another in silence, the air starting to get heavy with tension. We travel all the way to the top floor, and Cade removes his key card before exiting. We walk onto what looks like the executive level and head to the right, past the desk where his assistant sits, and into a huge office with floor-to-ceiling windows.

I whistle as I take in the modern decor and breathtaking views of Lake Michigan. "Nice digs, man."

Cade makes his way over to his desk and takes a seat as he gestures for me to do the same across from him. Here, in his element, he looks every inch the successful business-man. From what Mac told me before and from what I had observed, I knew he was well-off. But seeing him now, looking like a king of the concrete jungle that is Chicago, I realize how different our worlds are.

"Thank you. Now, why are you here?"

Okay, he really doesn't want to beat around the bush. I can respect that. I take in a deep breath and decide to be upfront as well. "I want to see Mac."

"Why?"

"I want to apologize, and I don't know where she lives or else I'd be there. I feel an apology is always best given in person and didn't want to risk having her ignore my calls. I figured I'd have the best chance of getting to her by visiting you."

He watches me as I speak, his expression neutral and not indicative of any emotion. He sizes me up before he responds to my statement. "For the record, she still lives with me." His words cause the jealousy I felt before to rise back up momentarily. My expression must give away how I'm feeling because he smirks. "As far as an apology, you definitely owe her one, but you better be doing a hell of a lot more than that."

"I...I'm not sure what you mean," I falter.

"Oh, I think you do. And if you don't know what I mean, then get the fuck out of my office and stay away from Mac." He moves to stand and I hold out a hand to stop him.

"I know I fucked up," I start. The words are hard to say but I force them out. "Nothing happened with Della. I made a stupid mistake because I couldn't deal with how I feel about Mac. It was juvenile, but I thought her catching wind of me on a date with someone else would cause the cleanest break since she is moving back."

Cade looks at me and his brow furrows slightly at my last words. He doesn't say anything though, just continues to look at me, so I continue.

"After the charity auction, I drank way too much beer and my sister practically ripped me a new one when she stopped by my apartment. She basically told me Mac left and at that thought...that I caused her to leave early...it gutted me, man. Mac told me she loved me, and I couldn't handle it but I realized that, if I'm being honest with myself, I..I love her, too."

"I already know this. You and Mac both wear your hearts on your sleeve, whether you realize it or not. I'm glad you pulled your head out of your ass and are finally able to admit it. What I want to know is what do you intend to do about it?" He leans over his desk and gives me an intense stare as he waits for my answer.

"I'm not sure," I say. "I won't lie to you. I plan on telling her how I feel and that I made a mistake, but I don't know what's next. I need to try and make things right though, and I can't do that if I don't know where she is."

Cade doesn't look particularly satisfied with my answer, but he reclines in his chair again and watches me for a few moments as he thinks.

"You better not fuck this up," he warns as he checks his

watch. "But if you want to see her, she's actually at a restaurant down the road called Luxe. If you head over now, you may be able to catch her."

I launch out of the chair and reach a hand out to him for a shake. His hand grips mine and he stands so his eyes are level with mine. With a firm squeeze he says, "You fuck this up, Lawson, and you'll have to answer to me personally. I don't like seeing my best friend sad. She deserves better."

"Don't I know it," I squeeze his hand in return. "Thank you, Cade."

He nods and I turn, exit his office, and leave the building as quickly as I can. I pull up Luxe on my phone's map search and see that it's half a mile away. I smile and walk, my strides eating up as much distance as possible. Before long, I see the restaurant's sign and see that it looks like a little bistro. My heart beats faster at the thought of seeing Mac again and making things right. I walk to the entrance and feel my skin break out in goosebumps at the sense of awareness I get. She's definitely here.

I walk to the hostess and tell her I'm meeting someone here and she lets me through. I navigate through the restaurant and soon enough, I think I see her on the outdoor patio. Her hair is done up in an elegant bun, which showcases her graceful neck, and she's in an eye-catching blue dress. My breath seizes in my throat and I hasten my steps. I make it outside and stop in my tracks. I didn't see from inside but now I can see that she has company. Male company. *Another damn suit*, I think. He's blonde and attractive and they're laughing over something. My heart stops for a second as I catch the smile on Mac's face. They're looking at each other as if they're the only people who exist. Am I too late? I step closer and clear my throat.

They both turn to look at me at the same time, but my

attention is solely on Mac. Her smile dies when she catches sight of me and shock colors her features. God, she's fucking beautiful. We look at each other, and I feel complete again just by being in her presence.

Her lips quiver before her sweet voice whispers my name. "Lawson? How? Why are you here?"

She's looking at me as if she can't believe I'm standing in front of her.

"I came to talk to you," is all I can manage to get out.

The silence stretches between us for a few more seconds before the man she's with stands up and approaches me. He's about my height and carries himself with an air of authority.

"Hello, I'm Oliver Taylor. And you are?" His British accent is crisp and formal.

He holds out his hand, so I give him a firm handshake in greeting. "Lawson Westbrook. Nice to meet you, Oliver." Something niggles at my brain before I realize what it is. "Are you the Taylor in Carson Taylor Enterprises?"

"Guilty," he smirks. "And would you happen to be Lawson Westbrook of Starwood, Tennessee?"

"Guilty," I admit with chagrin.

Oliver's expression clouds over as he steps closer to me and lowers his voice so only I can hear. "I'll give you two a moment, but if you hurt her please know that I'll be paying you a visit, as will Cade. No one hurts our girl and gets away with it."

"I know. Cade already expressed a similar sentiment. I'm here to try and make things right." I glance over his shoulder to Mac, who is watching with a confused expression on her face.

"Good ol' Cade. I can always count on him." He nods his head in approval before he steps back and raises his voice.

"Mac, love," he says cheerily, all hints of the threatening protectiveness he just displayed gone. "I forgot I need to give someone a ring about a business matter. I'll be back soon."

He walks away so I move closer to Mac.

"May I?" I gesture to the newly vacated seat across from her.

Mac simply nods and continues to look at me like she might be dreaming. "Why are you here?" she asks.

"I need to explain a few things."

"Lawson, you don't have to. You said it perfectly when you ended things—" she begins before I cut her off.

"Please, just let me get this off my chest."

She looks at me and doesn't say anything, so I continue. Holy shit, it's one thing to admit it to myself and tell Cade, but I've never been more nervous than I am in this moment.

"I don't know how many times I've said it and thought it, but I fucked up, Mac. I don't know how to handle everything you make me feel. It's not an excuse and it definitely doesn't excuse how I treated you, but it's the truth." My thoughts are running rampant, and I'm having trouble stringing together the apology I want to give. "I also want to let you know nothing happened with Della. After I dropped you off, she called me and I figured it was a good way to help her since her date was sick and also push you away. I'm sorry. I just couldn't deal with how I feel about you."

"And how is that, Lawson?" Her words are monotone and her face devoid of emotion.

"I think I love you, Mac." My words come out in a whisper.

I'm not sure what I expect from Mac, happiness maybe, but the last thing I expect is anger. "You *think* you love me? Fuck you, Lawson. Fuck. You. You came all the way here from Starwood to apologize? To apologize for being a dick because you can't deal with how I make you feel?" she says as she puts her fingers in the shape of quotes. "And you'd risk having people gossip about your love life by going on a date with someone else? What the hell is wrong with me that it'd be so bad to be seen with me or even talk to me about what's going on in that fucked up brain of yours? You don't make fucking sense! Let me set things straight for you. Your love," again with the quotes, "doesn't really convince me that you care if you have to fucking whisper it. We aren't even in our fucking hometown, and you still can't say it out loud. What the hell did you expect to happen when you came here, huh?"

"I was hoping you'd forgive me," I mutter.

"That's it? And what else, Lawson?"

"I don't know, I didn't think that far ahead." Oh God, this is not going the way I hoped or expected it would.

"You didn't think that far ahead," she repeats, her voice heavy with cynicism.

I try and salvage this moment as much as I can. "I didn't mean anything I said at the charity auction that night. You're mine and I'm yours, Mac. We're a perfect match. Besides, I feel terrible that you moved back here because of me."

"Oh God, Lawson," she scoffs. "Get over yourself! You're so fucking focused on yourself or on how people will get in your business that you don't even consider anyone else. You can't even fully take ownership of your actions because you're blaming your feelings on me. First, I didn't move back because of you. I came back to pack my things because I'm moving back permanently." She must register the shock on my face because she continues. "Yeah, you big jerk, I'm moving back. If you'd acted like an adult and talked to me, you would've known this. It was the news I wanted to share with you. And second, I am not yours and you are most certainly not mine. I don't want you, Lawson."

My stomach sinks at her words, and I don't even know where to go from here. This whole grand plan I had has completely backfired. The color is high in her cheeks, and her voice rises in volume with her next words. "In case you haven't noticed, we are *not* a perfect match. I may love you and you may "think" you love me, but that's not enough for me. Your words aren't enough for me. I need someone who isn't afraid to act on their words, someone who's going to stand by me and not be afraid to admit how they feel, whether it's in front of me or other people. I'm sorry to say but that person isn't you."

Her last words come out low and empty-sounding, her voice filled with sadness. I need to make this right, but I don't know how.

"Mac..." I start.

"Please leave, Lawson," she says. "I'm done." Her eyes are watering, and all I want to do is hold her.

I reach out to touch her arm, but a hand reaches out to stop mine.

"The lady asked you to leave, chap. I suggest you do so now before I forcibly remove you myself." Oliver is standing over me and is holding my arm.

I look between him and Mac and feel defeat wash over me. I try to look at her with everything I feel displayed in my eyes since I can't fucking say it properly. I get up and pull my hand back from Oliver's grasp.

"Smart choice," he observes.

I glare at him and turn back to Mac, my gaze softening as I look at her. "I'll make this right, Mac. I swear it."

She looks at me sadly, and I look on helplessly. I give her one last glance filled with longing before I turn on my heel and walk out of the restaurant. I need to go back home and figure out how to fix this. I obviously botched it with my words.

I mentally berate myself the entire flight home, but as I land an idea comes to mind. I may have messed it up with words but I've always been a man of action. Maybe I need to stick with what I know. I might fail again but I know, at the end of the day, I need to try again because she's worth it. Mac's worth everything, *is* everything to me. I know that now and I'm not going to give up until she knows, without a doubt, that I mean it.

30

Shady Layne Orchard—One Week Later

I'm officially back in Starwood, and I feel content in the fact I've made the right decision for me, my happiness, and my future. It feels amazing. Today's the debut of the barn's renovation and its official grand reopening. I'm inside the barn putting the final touches on the decorations when Langley waltzes in.

"Hey sugar, I've got the baked apple goodies. Where do you want them?"

"Over on that table," I point to the table where Lawson and I had our angry sex. Oh God, there I go again thinking about him. I need to stop this.

I look to Langley and see her head over to the table, but she's not holding anything. "Um, Langley?"

"Yes?"

"Where are the goodies?"

"I had to enlist some help," she smirks.

Just as the words escape her lips, I hear a groan at the door. Laughter bubbles past my lips when I see my brother and some of his friends carrying in stacks and large armfuls of baked goods. Langley sure has a way with the opposite sex.

"Damn girl, how much sugar you put in these things? I don't understand how you can bake something so light and fluffy and yet they weigh like a ton of bricks," Smith gripes.

"You need to work out some more, Smith," Langley teases. "I promise they're not that heavy. If you could please bring them here, I'd be happy to help take some of that burden away from you."

"You're lucky you're the prettiest girl I've ever seen, Langley," he laughs as he and his friends head to the table.

We all have a good laugh at his words and help finish the display of goodies that visitors can take home with them for attending our reopening.

I take a final look around at everything and feel my heart swell with so much pride. My dream has come together, and I can't wait to share it with everyone, especially my parents. I haven't allowed them to set foot in this place, so they'll be just as surprised as everyone else.

"Alright y'all, we have five minutes till opening. Thank you again for all of your help in setting things up and for making sure today goes off without a hitch." My throat clogs up a bit because I'm feeling so happy and, if I'm honest, bittersweet because this dream wouldn't have been possible without Lawson's help.

I force my thoughts away from him for the umpteenth time today and use the remaining minutes I have left to do one final check of everything. By the time I'm done, it's time to open up. My nerves kick in as I place my hands on the door and slide it open, the squeak that used to sound now silenced by a generous helping of grease. As I fully open the door, I release the breath I didn't realize I had been holding.

My fear is no one or just a handful of people would show up but, judging by the number of people already waiting, that fear is unwarranted.

I give the group before me an extra bright smile and welcome them. "Thank you all for coming to the grand reopening of Shady Layne's cider barn," I start. "As some of you may know, my family used to make cider every year and would sell it here and at the farmers' market. Unfortunately, business had slowed down a bit since my parents aren't as active as they used to be and a nasty storm made it so that my family couldn't use the barn anymore. What some of you may also know is I came home this summer to find myself. I was living in Chicago and was feeling like something was missing from my life. When I came home, I realized just what that was."

I pause to take another breath in an effort to keep the happy tears at bay. "I missed being near family and missed having a sense of purpose in life. Just like this barn, I needed a refresh and this project, which is so near and dear to my heart, helped me reconnect with my roots, my family, and the family business. I've officially moved back to town," I pause when the people waiting burst into applause, "and I've decided to make this barn more about cider and my life more about the things that matter. Thank you for coming. I hope y'all stay awhile and enjoy yourselves. Come on in now," I step to the side and wave them in with a grin.

What looks like half the town's population filters in past me, and I can hear their exclamations of wonder and excitement as they take in everything the barn has to offer. Warm fuzzies dance in my stomach at the barn's successful opening, and I want to dance when I hear people comment on the new logos and labels.

"Oh, these are so pretty," someone says.

"So professional," another says.

"I'm so glad they're open again. I love supporting local businesses," another person states.

"Oh my God, it's so beautiful," a voice I recognize says.

I swivel around and spot my parents as they look around, mouths open wide in surprise and awe.

"Do y'all like it?" I ask uncertainly.

"Like it? No baby, we love it!" my mother exclaims.

"We're so proud of you," my father says as he pulls me into a tight hug.

"Thank you," I reply, my eyes watering with joy. I pull away and gesture toward our surroundings with my arms. "The cider is up and running, the butters and jellies are on display, and I partnered with Langley to periodically sell some baked goods here with our apples. It's all pretty low maintenance, so you won't need to do any major upkeep and, now that I'm back, I can help with everything more."

"Thank you Mac, so much, for giving this back to us. You put the heart and customer hub back in our business." My father smiles at me, and I smile in return at his warm words.

"There are two things missing," my mother points out.

I'm surprised by her words, and out of instinct immediately look around to try and see if there was anything I forgot to do. I scan the room for a few moments before looking back at her in confusion.

"What's missin', Mama?"

"Well, I don't see your best friend, and I don't see a certain gentleman who worked on that roof of ours."

My heart sinks at the reference to Lawson. "That certain gentleman is not someone I talk to anymore, Mama. And," I tack on quickly, "Cade wasn't able to make it because of a family obligation of his own, but he made a point to send his support this morning."

"That's nice of him," my mother muses. "As far as the other man, I don't think he got the memo."

"What memo, Mama?"

"The memo that y'all aren't talking anymore."

I'm confused and stare at my mother, who is smiling at me knowingly.

"Turn around, baby."

I turn slowly and feel my world come to a halt when I see Lawson standing in the entryway to the barn. I inwardly curse my traitorous heart at the way it jumps in excitement and beats faster. It's only been a week since I've seen him, but he looks like he's missed out on sleep and spent more time in the gym. His scruff has grown in a little more and highlights the leanness of his features, and the muscles in his arms, which are being shown to perfection in his white shirt, look larger and more pronounced. The way he's looking at me steals my breath, and I have to remind myself to not get my hopes up. As much as it hurts and as much as I'd like to continue looking at him, I start to turn back around.

Before I can turn fully, I hear Lawson's raspy voice shout out to the group in the barn. "Everyone, if I could have your attention please."

The room almost immediately falls silent, which is impressive considering there are tons of people in here. Everyone is looking at Lawson with rapt attention, and when I fix my gaze on him again I see he hasn't looked away from me. Oh my God, what is happening?

"Thank you. I'm sure all of you know me, but if you don't, my name is Lawson Westbrook. I was born and raised in this town, I own a construction company, and I helped repair the roof of this barn. I'm sure you could all agree that while having a fixed roof is great, what's even more impressive is all the hard work put in by Mac Layne."

The room applauds at Lawson's charming speech. As soon as the sound dies down Lawson continues. "I've known Mac for years because I'm best friends with her brother, Smith. While I never paid her any attention when she was a teenager because, come on, I was a stupid kid," the room laughs, "I sure as hell paid a lot of attention to her when she came back at the beginning of summer."

My heart starts to beat wildly the longer Lawson speaks. I feel some eyes turn in my direction, and I feel my cheeks redden in embarrassment.

"Since the day she showed up again, my world has been turned upside down. I tried really hard to convince her to date me, and one day she finally gave in. But, like the ass I am, I told her I didn't want anything serious. I wanted to keep things strictly casual and even took her out on dates in other towns so people wouldn't talk about us...about me."

As Lawson speaks he takes slow steps toward me, and with each step that brings him closer, I have to fight the strong urge to launch myself in his arms or run.

"Before long, I was feeling things for this incredible woman I've never felt for anyone else. Except, like the obtuse man I can be, I ignored these feelings and tried to push her away. I'm here to tell every one of you here, and I hope you tell everyone you know, that I love MacIntosh Layne so, so much."

A low murmur runs around the room, the low buzzing not enough to drown out the pounding of my heart. The only other noise I can truly register is the thump of Lawson's footsteps as he closes the distance and comes to stand in front of me. Now that he's closer, I can see the dark circles under his eyes but, more astonishingly, I can see his feelings shining from his eyes like beacons.

"I know I messed up, and this entire summer I've tried to keep you at arm's length when I should've known I'd fail at that because you're here," he places his hand over his chest right above his heart. "Right here, Mac." His words and voice are full of emotion and his husky voice, thick with feeling, is making tears spring up in my eyes.

I stare at him and forget that the room's full of people until a voice in the room shouts, "Kiss her!" Laughter ripples across the room and Lawson's lips lift up on one side in a crooked smile.

"That's a great idea," he says. "I was never very good with words."

And with those words, before I can even think about stopping him or pulling him closer by the fabric of his shirt, Lawson pulls me to him and lays his lips on mine gently. His mouth moves slowly against mine, coaxing me to respond, and I shudder when his tongue gently licks at the seam of my own lips. One of his strong arms is wrapped around my back while the other reaches up, his hand caressing my jaw before cradling the back of my head. The kiss is slow and sweet before gradually picking up in intensity and passion. It feels as if Lawson's telling me, with every swipe of his mouth, what I mean to him. We've kissed countless times but never like this, not like he's burrowing himself deeper into my heart and past the walls I put up to protect myself.

He eventually pulls away but leans so his forehead is pressed against mine as we catch our breaths. His eyes capture mine and as our gazes lock, he reaches down to grab one of my hands and brings it up to place it over his heart. "I'm so sorry. I lied to myself and to you. I told you before I was unfailingly honest, but I was too afraid to handle the most honest feelings I've ever felt. I messed up, and I promise you I won't ever, ever do it again. But this," his voice cracks on the words as he presses my hand tighter against his chest so I can feel the intense beating underneath, "this doesn't lie. I meant every word when I said only you do this to me. I'm not afraid anymore. I've realized that it's scarier to face a world without you in it than to face how I feel. I'm not willing to risk losing you because I'm too stubborn to admit that I love you. I love you, Mac, no doubt about it. My heart is yours, and it always will be. Please don't tell me I'm too late," he ends on a hoarse plea.

I don't even realize I'm crying until he swipes the wetness from my cheeks. He doesn't say anything but looks at me earnestly, his heart shining through his eyes. My throat has clogged with emotion, so I reach for the hand that just wiped away my tears and place it over my heart. The cadence of my heartbeat matches his own, and I feel a watery smile start to form on my face as I see hope replace the remorse in Lawson's eyes.

"You're not too late," I whisper. "I never stopped loving you, Lawson."

"Thank God," he mutters before placing a quick, happy kiss on my lips again. "I'll never take you for granted again, Mac. I promise," he says fiercely.

I smile up at him, happiness lighting me up from the inside. "I didn't think you'd take my words to heart," I manage to joke.

As soon as the words leave my lips, Lawson picks me up and spins me in a circle, relieved laughter leaving both of our chests.

When he sets me back down on my feet he says, "They were what I needed to hear. *You're* my heart. I love you, Mac. So much."

"I love you too, Lawson. So much," I repeat back to him.

We're drawn out of our cocoon of happiness by the abrupt sound of applause. We bashfully look around the barn and see nothing but smiles and a few tears of joy. I blush at having had everyone witness this but am more pleased that what we have is no longer a secret. I was so upset with him before but I've got to give it to him, he's definitely redeemed himself.

We stand with our arms wrapped around each other as the reopening recommences, and we once again get lost in our own little bubble. I smile at the success of the barn and the sense of pride I feel is only trumped by the love emanating off of Lawson.

"It's about damn time," Langley says as she makes her way over to us, a huge grin on her face. "I was worried that I'd have to disown you, but you came through, Lawson." We both laugh at her words before she turns to me. "I'm happy it worked out, Mac. If y'all wanna go celebrate, I can handle the rest of this. I'm sure everyone is wonderin' why y'all are still here."

Before either of us can respond Smith walks over, confusion and brotherly outrage highlighting his features. "What's goin' on here? Mac, are you and Lawson a...thing? Why am I just findin' out about this now?"

Smith looks more shocked than hurt at not being in the loop. "It's a long story, Smith," I sigh.

"One I promise to fill you in on," Langley quickly adds on. She walks up to my brother, loops her arm through his, and starts leading him away. "These two lovebirds have a lot to catch up on, so let's leave them to it. You can talk to them later. Y'all have fun now," she throws back over her shoulder.

I blush at the mischievous twinkle in her eyes and

Lawson bursts out in loud laughter. "That's a great idea, Langley. Good lookin' out. Thank you. And Smith, don't you worry. I'll come 'round for a talk later." His words seem to appease my brother because he nods and turns to focus his attention on Langley as they walk to the other side of the barn.

Then, to the room, Lawson shouts, "We'll catch y'all later. I have to go show this gorgeous woman how grateful I am that I'm the lucky bastard she chose to love. Enjoy the barn, and we hope to see y'all soon!"

Lawson lifts me easily and throws me over his shoulder to the raucous cheering of the assembled crowd. I laugh as I cover my face with my hands and slap his tight butt as he leads me outside, places me gently in his truck, and drives me to his place. And it's there, in the privacy of his bedroom, where he shows me repeatedly how much he's missed me and how much he loves me. Even when I think I can't possibly continue, he proves me wrong and showers me with more pleasure and love. We fall asleep wrapped in each other's arms, our hands over each other's heart beats, and I know this is where I'm meant to be.

EPILOGUE

Two Months Later

LAWSON

I never thought I'd be happier than the day I showed up at the barn and Mac told me she still loved me, but each day I'm proven wrong. I've never felt such happiness and am constantly floored by how freeing it is to have our relationship out in the open. I make it a point to shower her with as much affection as she can tolerate out in public, and even though she tells me it isn't necessary, I can't hold myself back. I feel so lucky to have her and need to show the world that she's mine and that I'm hers. Another thing that continues to surprise me is my insatiable hunger for her. With each passing day we spend together and the stronger my love for her grows, the better the sex between us is. I'm one lucky bastard, that's for sure.

Mac is happier as well, both in our relationship and in everything else. Her design business is booming, and since she's her own boss she uses her extra time to help her parents out at the orchard. Soon enough, she'll have enough saved to move out on her own, and I know she is on cloud nine since everything worked out.

The grin that seems to have taken up permanent residence on my face grows as I glance over at the beautiful woman seated in the passenger seat of my truck. She's wearing a white, oversized sweater that makes me want to never stop hugging her, and her long legs are encased in dark jeans and knee-high boots. Her long hair rests in a braid over one shoulder, and her lovely eyes are covered up by the blindfold I put on her when she hopped in my truck. Excitement and nerves war with one another as I look at her and think about how she'll react to my surprise.

"How much longer, Lawson?"

God, I'll never get tired of hearing this woman say my name.

"Just a few more minutes, darlin'. We're almost there. If you're extra patient, I'll make sure to reward you later," I promise, my wicked intent clear in my voice.

"You better," she grumbles.

I laugh at her words. Ever since I picked her up from the orchard and blindfolded her, she's been fidgeting in her seat, anxious and curious to know what I have in store. We're almost at our destination and, in an effort to gain my composure, I slow down just a bit as we drive over what used to be loose rock and is now a smooth road.

After a few more minutes I put my truck in park, turn off the ignition, and lean back in my seat as I look at the woman next to me.

"We're here, darlin'," I say gently.

Her excitement is palpable, and she brings her hands up

to the blindfold shielding her gaze. "Can I take this off, please?"

"You can take somethin' else off later," I say, "but that needs to stay on for just another minute. Sit tight, please."

She nods her assent, and I hop out of the truck, remove the cooler I tucked out of view behind her seat, and open up the passenger door. I run my hands up her thighs and breathe in her sweet scent as grab her by the hand and guide her out of the truck.

"Almost time," I whisper. "Just a few steps this way," I say as I close the door and walk her a few paces.

Once I get her in place, I jog back to place the cooler next to her feet and move so I'm standing behind her. I wrap my arms around her waist and lean down so my lips brush against her ear when I speak.

"Okay, it's time." I reach up and remove the blindfold as I rub the silky strands of her hair.

"Oh, Lawson, it's stunning," she gasps.

I smile with pride as I take in the view as if I were her and seeing it for the first time. Before us is the new build I was working on months ago and, while she's technically seen it before, she hasn't seen it complete. The large house is now painted white, as is the wraparound porch, and the dark gray roof matches the shutters perfectly. The house looks welcoming and pristine, and the double front doors are painted vibrant, cherry red. Fresh flowers in the same bright hue hang from hanging flower pots and give more pops of color.

"I was hoping we could recreate our first date but, instead of eating outside, we can eat inside."

"I'm game," she murmurs before tilting her head to look back at me. "Are we allowed to do that though? The house looks done, so is the owner okay with that?"

Her concern tugs at my heart, so I give her an extra squeeze before answering. "I checked with the owner and it's okay. Besides, I'm the builder so it's only right I get to show it off and share it with someone. Let's go in."

I lean down to grab the cooler and lead her by the hand into the house. It's still empty, but the newly installed hardwood floors gleam under the sunlight filtering through the open blinds and the smell of fresh paint hangs lightly in the air. We step into the kitchen, and Mac gasps in awe at the huge space.

"I just fell in love," she says.

I laugh as I watch her run her fingers over the white quartz countertops and over the stainless steel faucet at the sink. "I fall in love with you every day."

"Well, aren't you sweet," she smiles at me as she continues to walk around. "I happen to do the same when it comes to you. Now feed me, please. I'm starving."

I laugh as I start to unpack the food from the cooler and point to the big blanket I set on the floor where a dining table would normally go. "Yes, ma'am. I hope you're okay with a picnic."

"I'm okay with anything."

I kneel down on the blanket and call her over. "I'm ready for you, darlin'."

"I love hearing those words," she teases as she makes her way over to me.

When she's in front of me I grab her hands as if to help her sit down, but I hold her in place while I stay on my knees before her. "Then I hope you'll love these next words, too."

She stills, and her face is painted with confusion but she doesn't say anything.

"Mac, I have something to tell you. The owner of the house doesn't know we're here."

"Oh my God, Lawson! We're breaking and entering?" She looks around in fear, as if she expects the cops to filter in at any moment.

"Of course not," I laugh. "The owner is you, if you'll have it. And of course me, I'm the owner, too."

"I...I don't understand."

"Darlin', this house has always been mine. The land, too. When we came here months ago for our first date, I should have known you were the woman for me. I hadn't shared it with anyone before but it felt so right—feels so right—having you here with me." Her eyes water slightly at my words. "You've given me everything I didn't know I wanted or needed, and I want to do the same for you." I reach into my pocket and pull out the little black box I've been carrying around for weeks now. My nerves are at an all-time high, but my heart jumps in joy as she catches her breath and gifts me with a heart-stopping smile.

"MacIntosh Layne," I say with my heart in my throat, "I've known you for most of my life and, for a while, I was so blind. That's not the case anymore. I love you more than anyone and anything. You make me so indescribably happy, and not a day goes by that I don't wonder how the hell I ended up so blessed to have you in my life, especially when I fucked up so colossally. I won't lie, I'll probably fuck up again, so please be patient with me. I can promise you though, with every piece of my heart, that I'll never lie to you or myself again. I'll never take you for granted, and I'll continue to prove my love in front of you and everyone else for the rest of my life." I can feel my own eyes start to tear slightly with the emotion coursing through me. "You'll always have my heart," I say as I place my hand over the appendage that beats solely for her. "I want nothing more than to be your husband, plant some roots, and start our forever and a family in this house, and I don't want to wait another day. Will you please do me the honor of being my wife?"

"Yes, yes, yes!" Mac launches herself at me and topples me over onto the blanket. She's sprawled out on top of me, her braid swinging by both our faces, and her smile is brighter than the sun. "I'd be honored to be your wife, Lawson Westbrook," she says as she tenderly kisses the area on my chest above my heart and then my lips.

We kiss for endless moments before I remember one little detail. I pull back and move us so we're both sitting, her draped across my lap, as I slide the ring I designed on her finger.

"It's perfect," Mac sighs.

Pride and relief flood through me at her words. "You're perfect," I say as I kiss her forehead.

"I know," she jokes.

We laugh easily and end up making love on the blanket before we tour the house together. We make plans to christen every room, and I tell her that her father offered to give us first pick of any of the furniture he's made that hasn't already found a home. This makes her tear up and she launches herself at me, which results in us breaking in the kitchen island.

As we clean up and leave, Mac snuggles into my side and hugs me tightly. "Thank you for making me the happiest of women."

My heart squeezes at her words. "Thank you for making me the happiest of men."

"And to think," she muses as she smiles up at me, "it all started with some sin and cider."

I lean down to give this woman who is so precious to me a sweet kiss that soon turns possessive. The road may not have been smooth at first but I wouldn't have it any other way. After all, there's nothing sweeter than knowing that what we have is permanent. She's mine and I'm hers, forever.

ACKNOWLEDGMENTS

Holy wow, I did it. At the moment, I'm a sleep-deprived cocktail of equal parts terrified and elated, with a shot of insanity and a garnish of pride. In short, I'm really hoping I don't forget to thank anyone.

If you've made it this far, thank you. I'm finally following my dreams and my heart is filled with so much joy (and anxiety) at the thought of sharing my words with the world. This book is a part of me and I'm happy to share it with you. All I hope is that you enjoyed reading it as much as I enjoyed writing it.

Liv Moore, thank you so much for being there when this book was just an idea. If we hadn't met at Madcap and become writing buddies, I'm not sure where I'd be in my writing journey. I am so happy to call you one of my besties and am grateful for all of the feedback, motivation, and support you've given me.

Krystal Still and Rachelle Velasquez, y'all are my A-team. Thank you, thank you, thank you for being my alpha readers and for pushing me to send you my chapters, even when I was struggling. You both are a huge reason why I had a fire lit under my butt to write. I'm so glad I have you two as best friends and to ping ideas off of, and I'm so excited that you're both excited about what's to come!

To my #MadcapCrew, you all rock! I can't even express how grateful I am that we all met in November. It's so wonderful to see how we are all progressing with our writing careers, and I want you all to know I'm here to support you as much as I can, in any way I can! Special thanks to the Madcap coordinators and to our inspirational instructors Laurelin Paige, Sierra Simone, and Whitney G. for dropping some serious knowledge and giving me the final push I needed to start this crazy journey. And, of course, thank you to the attendees I've bonded with who have helped support me: Liv Moore, Haylee Thorne, Barbara Blue, Katie Fox, and Jadyn Lucas. I love and appreciate you all so very much and I hope we're lifelong friends.

To all the bloggers who supported me and pimped me out like crazy, thank you. Whatever you did, whether it was review my book, share a post, like a post, what have you, I'll be eternally grateful. You all are so vital to spreading the word for indie authors and deserve as much appreciation as humanly possible.

To my Facebook family, thank you for taking me under your wing and guiding me through this crazy time in my life. I've bombarded you all with a ton of questions and have asked for a lot of help, and every single person who has assisted me has been beyond patient and gracious. If we've interacted at all, then please know you're being thanked right now.

To my ARC team, you have no idea how much your positive words quench my soul. Thank you for believing in me and for being so excited to read my words. I'm humbled each and every time I interact with one of you.

To my family, if you've read this far I hope I didn't scar any of you. Seriously, I hope you're okay, but don't say I didn't warn you ahead of time because I did. Thank you for supporting me in this dream and for providing words of motivation and support. I love you all so much!

To Scott and my pups, thank you for putting up with me while I holed myself away in my writing cave for endless hours. I know it can get old on your end, what with me being a hermit, but thank you for your incredible amount of patience and support while I chase this crazy dream of mine. I seriously could not have done this without you. I love you all.

To my readers, from the bottom of my heart I'd like to thank you all for taking a chance on an unknown author. I hope you'll continue to read my work. I would be so grateful if you would consider leaving a review, whether good or bad, because I love to hear from you all and will read each and every one left. If you'd like to stalk me, my details are on the next page.

Dear God, thank you for blessing me with the persistence to chase my dream and the words to put down on paper.

And last, but certainly not least, I'd like to thank myself for sticking to it and not giving up, even when things felt crazy and uncertain. Keep chasing the dream!

COMING SOON: SIN AND SUGAR

A SWEET SINNER'S RECIPE FOR LOVE

Ingredients:

- 1 tatted alpha male in a suit
- 1 sassy Southern baker
- 1 luxurious Chicago penthouse
- 2 cups of sugar
- An extra helping (or two) of sin
- Enough attraction and sexual tension to decimate an entire city block

Directions:

- In luxurious Chicago penthouse, combine alpha male and Southern baker. Leave unattended.
- Generously mix in attraction and sexual tension.
- Stir gently, and add sugar.
- Let tension rise.
- Pour on some sin, and let bake.
- Remove from penthouse.

- Sprinkle on more sin and sugar.
- Enjoy each mouthwatering bite. Best served hot. Multiple servings encouraged.

SIN AND SUGAR

Prologue

"Ms. Westbrook, I have your mail," our butler says as he enters the kitchen. "There's a rather official looking envelope here for you."

I look up from the dough I'm kneading because his words have peaked my interest.

"Thank you, Clive," I tell him. "I'm all covered in flour. Could you do me a favor please and open up that envelope, sugar?"

The older gentleman still blushes whenever I call him sugar, but he obliges with a nod of his head. I watch as he opens the envelope and unfolds the letter inside. I expect him to start reading but am surprised when he scans through the letter silently, a smile breaking out across his weathered face.

"What is it?" I ask.

"Ms. Westbrook, I think this is something you'll want to read for yourself. Here," he rounds the island and comes to stand next to me. "I'll hold it for you."

I smile my thanks and glance at the piece of paper he's holding, my heartbeat skyrocketing when I see the logo in the top right corner of the page. Oh my word, it's from Farine. I anxiously squeeze the dough in my hands as my lips part to read the words that can make or break my plans.

"Dear Ms. Langley Westbrook," I start, "We are very pleased to offer you a position as an intern this spring at Farine, one of Chicago's most renowned French bakeries and pastry shops. You have been selected from numerous applicants for this prestigious opportunity, and we look forward to having you join us. Please refer to the following confirmation for the specifics of your internship..." My words trail off as my eyes widen. "I got in?"

"That's what it sounds like, Ms. Westbrook. Congratulations!"

My heart is pounding. I can't believe this is happening. "Oh my God, Clive. Oh my God! Do you know what this means?"

"That we are all correct when we tell you you're incredibly talented?" Clive says with a smile.

I blush a little at the praise but shake my head. "It means I'm going to Chicago!"

Coming Fall 2017

ABOUT THE AUTHOR

Kimberly Reese is a contemporary romance author, and Sin and Cider is her debut novel. She grew up in a military family and currently resides in Illinois. When she isn't writing she enjoys reading, traveling, and spending time with family.

Connect with Kimberly
https://authorkreese.wixsite.com/home
authorkreese@gmail.com

Made in the USA
Lexington, KY
04 October 2017